LADYFISH

Visit us at www.boldstrokesbooks.com

LADYFISH

by
Andrea Bramhall

2012

This Trade Paperback Original Is Published By
Bold Strokes Books, Inc.
P.O. Box 249
Valley Falls, NY 12185

First Edition: October 2012

Credits
Editors: Victoria Oldham and Cindy Cresap
Production Design: Susan Ramundo
Cover Design By Sheri (graphicartist2020@hotmail.com)

Acknowledgments

Thank you to everyone at Bold Strokes Books. Radclyffe, Vic, Cindy—you guys rock! Without you, *Ladyfish* wouldn't be the book it is.

Louise, I know you end up getting stuck walking the dogs while I'm hunched over my laptop. Sorry, but you demanded I keep you in the manner to which you feel you should be accustomed. I'm trying! Merlin and Jazz—thank you for looking after your other mother.

Gran, read this copy with the black lines in it, and this copy only!

Dad—For everything. Thanks.

Dedication

Louise,
Nunc scio, quid sit amor

From Virgil, *Eclogues VIII*

PROLOGUE

This has got to be the most boring job in the whole of fucking London!" Mike tossed the clipboard onto the table and leaned back in his chair, propping his dirty work boots onto the table. "She never does anything!"

"Get your fucking feet off the table." Jack smacked his feet and picked up the clipboard. "I don't care how boring this is. If the boss wants us to watch her, we watch her. Do you understand me?"

"For fuck's sake! I'm here, aren't I?" Mike dropped his feet back to the floor, running his hand through his shaggy, greasy blond hair.

"It could be worse, Mike."

"And how do you figure that?"

"We could be watching that fucking faggot friend of hers."

Mike snorted. "You got a point there." He rubbed his hands over his grime-smeared jeans as he leaned forward to stare closer at the screens. "She certainly is easier on the eye." He laughed a little harder as his hand edged closer to his crotch.

"Knock it off, you fucking pervert." Jack flipped through the pages on the clipboard.

September twentieth.

0900 subject arrives at bio lab

0935 subject went to bathroom

1200 subject went to cafeteria for lunch

1232 subject returned to her desk

1730 subject leaves for the day.

"Do we still have the shadow on her computer to track what she's working on?" Jack asked.

Mike reached for a file at the far end of the counter and passed it to him.

Jack slid the information from the file and looked through the pages. "Looks like she's still working on that E. coli bacteria."

"Has the old man got her working on the toxin like the American guy? I didn't think she was involved in all that?"

"I don't know, and I find it's usually best to not ask questions with Sterling. What's she doing now?"

Mike peered through the binoculars before answering. "Packing her bags. Looks like she's getting ready for that holiday he organized for them." He let the binoculars fall to his lap. "I still don't get that. Why the fuck does he want her with that puff?"

"It's none of your business." Jack stuffed the pages back into the folder and stared out at the historic buildings along the prestigious Camden Town Terrace. A man jogged down the street with his pug trotting along beside him. Porsches, Mercedes, and Audis were parked in driveways, and people went on with their lives, oblivious.

"Yeah, yeah. I know. Do as you're told and don't ask questions. So are you heading to Florida to watch her?"

"That sounded like a question, Mike."

"He's got us watching them both twenty-four seven while they're at home and work. Now he sends them to Miami and doesn't want them watched. It just doesn't make any sense to me."

"He has plenty of people out there without having to send us to keep an eye on the little princess and her queen." Jack narrowed his eyes and watched Mike closely. "Besides, it's not like we don't have important things to take care of. He's always ten steps ahead of everyone else."

Mike rolled his eyes. "So what time do they fly?"

"They're on the seven p.m. flight tomorrow."

"And how long are they away for?"

"Undetermined at the moment. Sterling thinks a month should be fine."

"Is he still concerned about MI6 sniffing around?"

Jack snorted. "Not really. They haven't got anything on him."

"What are they looking for?"

Jack's hands paused, the pages stilled between his fingers. He looked at Mike.

Mike swallowed audibly.

"These sound an awful lot like questions, Mike. You sure are getting nosey now, aren't ya?"

Mike shook his head quickly. "No, no questions, Jack. Really. I'm just real bad at phrasing my statements." He straightened in front of the screens and grabbed the clipboard. He didn't move as Jack stood and moved about the room. Sweat slid down his forehead. He didn't turn his head as the floorboards creaked beneath Jack's feet. Jack moved around the dingy flat examining the light fittings, lamps, telephone sockets, behind the monitors, binoculars, radios. He silently screwed the silencer onto the barrel of his Glock.

"Stand up."

Mike shook as he stood, scraping the chair across the bare floorboards.

"Take your shirt off."

Mike's hands trembled as he reached for the hem of the stained T-shirt.

"Jack, there's really no need to do this."

"Shut the fuck up," Jack said, his voice low and menacing. "Take your shirt off."

Mike lifted his sweat-soaked shirt over his head, dropping it to the floor with trembling hands.

"Turn around."

Mike turned slowly to display the microphone taped against his skin.

Jack ripped it from his chest and used the butt of his gun to smash it to pieces.

"Where are the other devices?"

"Jack, please." The butt of the gun slammed into his mouth and he fell to the ground. He spat the stringy red saliva onto the floor and tried to stand again.

"Where are the other devices?"

"I don't know."

"Cameras?"

He shook his head.

"You sure?"

"Yes." The bullet ripped through Mike's skull. He was dead before he hit the ground.

Jack flipped open his mobile phone and clicked a button.

"Sir, it's Jack. Yes, sir, I'm sorry to disturb you. I think we may have a problem."

CHAPTER ONE

O z woke to the gentle caress of fingernails gliding down the naked skin of her back, teasing their way beneath the sheet and skimming across her hip until she caught them and stilled their advance.

"What time is it?" Her voice was husky with sleep and her eyes still refused to open.

"A little after seven." The soft whisper sent shivers down her neck until the words penetrated her brain and she sat bolt upright in bed.

"Shit." She jumped out of bed and ran for the bathroom, stubbing her toe on the doorframe as she did so. "Ow, shit."

"Oz, what's wrong?"

"I gotta be on the dive boat in thirty minutes," she said, her mouth foaming with toothpaste as she rushed through her morning routine.

"You mean you're leaving?"

"Shelley, you know I gotta work. I've got beginners out on the reef today."

"But it's my last day here, Oz. I thought you'd want to spend it with me."

Oz threw water on her face and dragged her fingers through her hair. Aiming for endearingly tousled and arriving at slightly damp bed head, she grabbed a towel and stalked from the bathroom in search of her clothes. She managed to find her shorts, tank top, and sandals in the living room. Her panties were nowhere to be found, so she dragged her shorts up her legs without anything under them. Shelley slid her arms around Oz's waist as she attempted to lure her back to bed.

"I gotta go, babe. Have a great flight home." She kissed her quickly on the check as she escaped the octopus-like arms and headed out the door. She didn't bother to look back, her mind already on the day ahead, the tourist's bed already forgotten.

Fortunately, the hotel was only ten minutes from the dive center and all her gear was already there. She ran the short distance and hit the front steps of the dive center as the cell phone in her pocket began to ring. She ignored it and pushed open the door.

"What the hell time do you call this?" Rudy stared at her, his hazel eyes flashing angrily under his ball cap. His jaw was heavy on the stubble, his skin a dark tan. He was pushing forty, but a desk hadn't done a great deal of harm to the muscled physique he had developed when they were both in the navy together, and the white tank top showed off his strong arms and pecs. She didn't look at his legs. She never did. Seeing his prosthetic leg brought back far too many memories for her. "I hope she was worth it. You can pick up the new zero from the airport. Flight gets in at eleven. I'll get you the details later."

"Aw, man, Rudy. You've got to be kidding?" She picked up the storage box full of her gear. "I'm like, five minutes late. You've got me on the early boat again tomorrow, and you know damn well picking someone up from Miami at that time means it's gonna be after one before I get to bed. Why can't you send Clem or Mac?" She headed down to the boat moored on the jetty knowing it was no use arguing with Rudy. She knew she would be the main trainer for the new zero to hero, the course that took candidates with no diving experience whatsoever and made them dive instructors in just six months.

"You're more than twenty minutes late and you damn well know it. Besides, you've only got to go to Key West airport. She's on an internal transfer. Now, get your ass on the boat and stop arguing with me. You're already giving me a headache and it ain't even eight o'clock yet." He moved past her to untie the boat from the dock.

She passed her box over to the boat hand and jumped nimbly onto the deck, grinning at Carlos as he stowed her gear at the aft of the boat for her.

"Jesus, Oz, you've only been here five minutes and he's chewing his shorts already."

"Rudy's always chewing his shorts. It's his main source of fiber."

Carlos laughed as he hurried over to grab other boxes of gear as they were passed over by other deck hands. Oz checked to make sure nothing was missing before they pulled out, then looked at all the divers on the boat, knowing she needed to go and chat with them, put nerves at ease, answer questions, build up the excitement. *I'm getting way too old for this shit.* She strapped on her smile and picked up her dive briefing file.

"Hey, everyone, if you'll all gather around, I'll go over today's dive site." She waited while they all huddled around and stared at her avidly. She flipped open her folder and pointed to a picture of the site.

"Hi, everyone. For those of you who don't know me, I'm Oz, and I'll be your dive guide and instructor for the day. Today we're diving The Elbow. It's situated between twelve to thirty-five feet, which is four to eleven meters, making this a real easy dive. There are some amazing coral formations and tons of sea life to see. There's also an amazing Civil War shipwreck. It sank in eighteen sixty-six and was a seven hundred and fifty-two ton steamer. Now it's home to some of the most amazing elkhorn coral I've ever seen. There are some scattered remains of a couple other wrecks about too. They aren't in as good a shape, but we're guessing they were a tug and a barge." She pointed to her map as she spoke, indicating points of interest and depths. "When we get in, we'll descend and hold at around eight meters for most of the dive. This way it's easier to keep our fins off the reef and the ocean floor. The more sand we kick up, the less we'll be able to see, so it makes things nicer if we do it that way. We're going to circle around the reef, and once we get back, we'll ascend as a group."

She tapped two fingers against her lips. "If I do this, I want to know how much air you have left in your tank. I need you to check your gauge and let me know." She held her hands up and made a T shape. "This sign means one hundred bar." She made a fist. "And this means fifty bar." She held up one finger. "Each digit is telling me ten bars. You all have two hundred to two hundred and twenty bar to start with, so that should be pretty easy to gauge. When you tell me a number, always tell me the lower option. So if you have one hundred and fifty-five bar, you tell me one fifty. Not one sixty. Are we all clear?" She waited for a round of okays. "If I point at you and do this, I'm asking the question, are you okay? If everything is okay, repeat the signal back to me. If not, indicate that you want to go up by pointing your thumb up toward the surface. Should this happen, we all go up as a group. We resolve whatever the problem is, and then decide on the course of action from there." She met the eyes of all six people around her. "Does anyone have any questions?" They all shook their heads, and she didn't notice anyone looking particularly anxious. "Okay, let's get into our wet suits."

She walked over to the storage boxes tucked under the benches around the back of the dive boat. She retrieved her own and pulled out her wet suit. She reached for the button of her shorts to strip down to her swimsuit before remembering that she hadn't had the chance to change before getting on the boat. She ducked into the small, cramped head and quickly slipped into the black and gray neoprene skin before hitting the deck again.

"Yo, Oz, you better get the gang together. We're about ten minutes out."

"How's the current?"

"Minimal. Hardly any chop on the surface. Should be totally calm down there today. You wanna do a quick check?"

"Thanks, Mac. I don't think I need to jump in today to know the water's perfect." She stared at the surface of the water before turning back to the passengers. "Everyone get ready. It's a great day for diving."

CHAPTER TWO

F inn waited until the aisle was clear before getting up to grab her rucksack and camera case from the overhead bin. The Nikon D7000 inside was her pride and joy.

"I got it, Finn." She smiled at her best friend Pete as he retrieved her bags and handed them to her before grabbing his own and slinging the strap over his shoulder. He slid a navy blue baseball cap over his curly blond hair and pushed on dark, wraparound sunglasses. "Are we ready to show Florida a thing or two?"

Without waiting for a response, he sauntered toward the exit, smiling broadly into the sun as it kissed the carpeted floor of the cabin. Finn pushed her long hair out of her eyes, tucking it behind her ears as she pulled her own sunglasses out of her pocket and slid them into place. Pete was already on the tarmac and heading for a building with a large banner saying "Welcome to the Conch Republic" hanging from it when she reached the door, and she nearly tripped as she bounded down the steps, well aware she was the last person off the plane.

"Come on, Daniela Finsbury-Sterling! I can't wait for you forever." Pete laughed as she practically had to run to keep up with him.

Finn landed a punch on his well-muscled arm.

"Ow. I think the bugs are biting me already," he said, playfully swatting non-existent bugs from his arm.

"Watch it, or I'll really have to hurt you." Her British accent caused a few sidelong glances as they entered the terminal building.

"Nah, you'd be lost without me."

"Please." She hitched her bag further onto her shoulder and eased her hair out from under the strap. "Who's picking us up anyway? Didn't the dive school say that someone would meet us?"

He fished a page from his pocket and passed it over to her. "We are meeting one Olivia Zuckerman. This says she'll be the main contact for you through the course and your main dive instructor if you decide you really want to go through with this."

"What do you mean 'if'?"

He held up his hands to stave off the onslaught. "What I mean is if you decide you like being under the water. You haven't been diving before, and for all you know, you could hate it when you get down there."

"And if I do?"

"Then I'll be here with you as long as you want me to be. I can find plenty of onshore attractions to keep me entertained while you play with the fishies!"

"What about my dad?"

"I told you. I don't want the job. I would rather be penniless and happy than sell my soul to Satan himself." He turned and grinned sheepishly at her. "No offense."

"None taken. I feel pretty similarly about him myself."

"Besides, I have a good education. A top class degree in IT will get me a job just about anywhere. In fact, I already have an offer on the table. This guy Pritchard has offered me a chance to join a team he's putting together. Tracing bad guys on the old computer, baby. I may have to work my way up and not get the easy ride I would have in the office with your father. But what can I say? I like to sleep at night, and your dad's offer comes with far too many strings attached." He watched her as she walked along beside him. "I won't be staying in a closet because your dad is homophobic and wants to see us producing heirs to his fortune."

"Peter, I don't want you to make any rash decisions that could affect your future. When my dad finds out I'm not going back home, you know it's going to get ugly. And if he knows you're helping me, he could make you miserable."

"Finn, I don't care. The more you worry about his reaction toward me, the more it makes me worry about you. I love you like you were my own sister, and I hate what that man has done, could do, and dares to think about doing to you. Treating you like you're just something else he owns." Pete stopped and held up his hands. "I'm sorry. Let's forget all about the old fart and figure out how to have the most fun possible. We're in Florida, baby. Let's go find this Olivia Zuckerman and then find somewhere to party! Maybe she can give us a few hints about good places to go."

"Hi."

Finn almost crashed into Pete's back as he stopped.

"I didn't mean to listen in, but I'm Olivia."

Finn found herself staring at the hand held out in greeting, suddenly and uncharacteristically tongue-tied.

"Zuckerman. You said you were looking for me."

"Hi, I'm Pete Green, nice to meet you, Miss Zuckerman."

"Oz. Everyone calls me Oz."

"It's nice to meet you, Oz." He shook her hand before pointing to Finn. "The mute one is Daniela."

Finn met Oz's curious stare for a moment before looking away. She realized she must look like a child wearing her mother's clothes. Black utility shorts, at least three sizes too big, hung from her hips, cinched in place by an army-style webbing belt. A loose purple cotton shirt wrapped around her torso and snagged awkwardly on the rucksack hanging from her shoulder. Her long hair was pushed back from her face by a pair of sunglasses acting as a headband. She looked around them, focusing on anything, everything, but Oz. She didn't want to see the disparaging look in her instructor's eyes before she'd even had a chance to get to know her.

"Hi, Daniela." Oz held her hand out to her.

"Hi." She shook Oz's hand tentatively, barely making contact at all. Finally, Finn's eyes settled on her. "Most people call me Finn." She gave Oz a small smile, relieved when she couldn't discern anything judgmental in the smile she got in return.

"Finn it is then. Shall we get out of here?" Oz didn't wait for a response but led them out of the airport and toward the car park where she had left the SUV. "I understand you're staying at the Ocean Key Resort? Is that right?"

"Yeah, Finn's dad booked it for us so we thought we'd make use of it," Pete said. "I figure I'll hang out in the spa while Finn's busy working and studying for the diving qualifications."

"Where in England are you guys from?"

"London born and bred me, but Finn's from more northern climes. Aren't you, honey?"

Finn nodded as she watched the world pass by outside the window. "Manchester. I was the ripe old age of five when we moved to London."

"Did you have any problems getting visas for the time that you'll both be here? It can take a little while to get all the dives in for your certificates."

"Well, I'm only here on holiday, and Finn's mum was American so she has an American passport."

Oz's eyebrows rose and she glanced at Finn through the rearview mirror. "Really? Where was your mom from?"

"Sarasota Springs, Florida. She moved to England when she married my dad."

"So do you come to Florida with your mom a lot?"

"No. This is my first time here." Finn shifted in her seat, uncomfortable with all the questions the woman was asking. She didn't even know her, for God's sake. And her family was the last thing she wanted to discuss with a stranger.

"Well, it's a beautiful place, and if you're going to be here for a while, it's probably a good time to visit." Finn met Oz's eyes in the rearview mirror and smiled, giving a slight shrug before looking back out the window.

Oz glanced at Pete. "So you're not diving?"

"Nah! I'm strictly holidaying here before returning to my life in London."

"And what do you do with your life in London that could possibly compare with life under the water?"

"A gentleman doesn't kiss and tell." His chocolate brown eyes were twinkling with mischief as he spoke in an exaggerated whisper.

"I absolutely understand that, but you don't seem quite the gentleman to me." Oz winked at Pete, and Finn started giggling from the backseat.

"She's got your number already, pal."

Oz glanced again through the rearview mirror and smiled at Finn. Finn's stomach did a little leap and she took a deep breath to settle herself. A woman's smile was nothing more than that. A smile.

"I worked for Finn's dad doing IT stuff."

"Worked?"

"Yeah." He pushed his fingers through his hair. "Definitely worked. He will *soooo* not want me back when he realizes that Finn isn't going back home. He'll think I kidnapped her. It's really the other way around. Don't let that innocent face fool you." He threw a smile back at Finn. "She's stubborn as hell. She has a foul mouth when drunk. And if you're really lucky, she'll show you her tattoo!" He grinned when Olivia's eyebrows shot up. "Yeah, I know. She looks so sweet and innocent—like butter wouldn't melt in her mouth!"

"Pete! Shut up!"

"See? Ow." He rubbed his shoulder after Finn punched him from the backseat. "Did I mention that she has a tendency toward violence too?"

"I'll do my best not to get on the wrong side of her. I bruise easy."

"Hey, don't you start too." Finn felt the tension in her shoulders ease with the easy flow of conversation. She nearly sighed in relief.

"We're almost there. I'm out on the early boat tomorrow with a bunch of tourists, so it's probably best if we meet up in the afternoon to go over the game plan and do the paperwork. Is that okay?" Oz asked as she navigated her way through traffic.

"Sure. What time's best for you?" Finn swallowed the sudden lump of fear in her throat. She wanted to do this. She knew she could do this. Nothing anyone else said mattered, and Oz could teach her what she needed to know in order to stand on her own. She met Oz's questioning glance in the mirror, noticing her shrug slightly before she continued speaking. Finn had clearly missed whatever Oz had been saying, but Oz didn't seem terribly fazed. Tension knotted her shoulders once again.

"I should be back at the dock around three and have the boat cleared in thirty minutes. If you come to the dive center at four, I should be about done and I can introduce you to everyone."

"Sounds good. Is there anything I need to be reading in the meantime? Anything I can do or get?"

"Not really. We'll sort everything out when we meet tomorrow. I'm sure you'll be a little jet-lagged, so it's probably best to get plenty of rest and just chill for the day. The pool at the Ocean Key is supposed to be absolutely gorgeous." She pulled up outside the hotel entrance and walked around the car to open the boot as the bellhop arrived with a trolley. "If you ask the concierge, they'll arrange a ride for you tomorrow. We're not too far from the dive center, but it's probably easiest to use the shuttle the hotel operates." She closed the boot and turned back to them. "Pete, it was a pleasure to meet you and I'm sure I'll see more than enough of you." She held out her hand and sputtered when he pulled her into a fierce hug.

"You make sure you look after her. She's special." Pete threw an arm around Finn and hugged her close before mussing her hair. "Short people like her make me feel really tall!"

"Hey! You lanky piece of piss!"

"I told you she had a foul mouth."

Oz shook her head. "Finn, I'll see you tomorrow. Four o'clock."

Finn looked her straight in the eye, determined to let Oz know she was ready and not in the least afraid. Even if it wasn't completely true. "I can't wait."

CHAPTER THREE

William Sterling stared out his penthouse office window across the London skyline, but, as always, he didn't see it. His focus was purely internal. He rested his hands on the slight paunch of his stomach, the pale blue shirt pulled taut across the flabby flesh. His fingers moved in time with each thought as it flittered across his mind before being dismissed. The telephone rang and snapped him from his reverie.

"Yes?"

"Mr. Sterling, Dr. Ethan Lyell is on line one." He didn't respond as he punched the button.

"Dr. Lyell. You have good news for me I trust."

"Sir, I've created Balor. Your daughter's work was impeccable. Without her, it wouldn't have been possible."

"Balor?"

"Yes, sir. I felt it appropriate—"

"From Celtic mythology?"

"Yes. Myth describes him as a cyclops able to paralyze and kill with a single glance."

"Is that what you think of your creation, Doctor?"

"It is—"

"No matter. I trust now you'll have some results for me on how effective the bacteria are?"

"Yes, sir. How would you like the results?"

"E-mail them to me."

"Of course."

"When I get the results, I'll let you know what to do next."

"Of course."

"And, Doctor…"

"Sir?"

"I want a projection on how long it will take to synthesize a quantity of this stuff."

"How large a quantity?"

"Fifty-five gallon drums. Twenty of them." He could hear the scientist swallow on the other end of the line.

"Sir, I don't have the equipment here to—"

"Then you had better get it, hadn't you, Ethan? Marissa is counting on you."

"Please, Mr. Sterling. Please don't hurt my wife. I'm doing everything you want me to do. Please. Please let me see her. Talk to her. So I know she's okay—"

Sterling slammed the phone back into its cradle.

"Pathetic." He spun around in his chair and stared at the London skyline. The dingy gray clouds marred the view as he contemplated the upcoming deal. A harmless tummy bug would turn into a lethal killing machine. He mentally counted the millions of pounds riding on the back of the deal. He was already picturing his bank balance reflecting the transfer of funds.

He smiled as he recollected one of his minions bringing the discovery to his attention. The discovery made by his own daughter. The ability to incorporate toxins inside bacteria so that they reproduced and infected the host; it was absolutely priceless. *And she thought I'd only want to market the discovery to treat illnesses. So naïve. If I hadn't had her DNA tested, I wouldn't believe she was mine. Shame really. She has the brains to make my little empire even bigger.*

He turned back to his desk and picked up the telephone. *She's got the brains, but not the aptitude.* He punched a number on the phone and waited for his secretary to answer.

"Yes, Mr. Sterling?"

"Susan, I need you in here a moment." He hung up the phone and watched as she stepped inside.

"What do you need, Mr. Sterling?"

He turned his chair to the side and unzipped his pants. "Take care of this, Susan."

She clearly swallowed her revulsion and turned to close the door. "Leave it."

She froze. She paled and he smiled. She knew too much. Too many of his secrets were stored in that pretty little head. If she weren't so good with her mouth, he would have dealt with her long ago. He waited, her hand on the doorknob obviously shaking.

"Is there a problem, Susan?"

She slowly turned around and crossed the room before dropping to her knees.

It wasn't desire for her that made him hard. It was knowing that she hated doing this. It was knowing that she despised him. It was knowing that she despised working for him. But still she got down on her knees and took him in her mouth. No, it wasn't desire. It was power. He closed his eyes and reveled in it.

CHAPTER FOUR

A t two on the dot, Finn pulled her newly purchased 1967 green ragtop Mustang into the parking lot at the back of the dive center and walked down to the dock. She could see that the boats were all still out and she smiled, glad she would be there to help with the chores common to her new profession. She found a perch on a low wall and leaned back against the trunk of a palm tree, her mind wandering as she stared out across the ocean. The waves broke gently against the dock and the jetties; the sun, hardly above its zenith, moved away behind her, casting long shadows as it marched onward.

Slowly, dots on the horizon grew into the boats heading home for the day. Closing her eyes, she imagined herself on the deck of the boat, the feel of the wind in her hair, the sea spray on her face, and the sun warming her skin. She craved the freedom she knew she would find there. She could feel the shackles that had held her in London falling away. She hadn't even noticed as the boat finally pulled up alongside the dock and the deck hand jumped off, taking the mooring line with him and bending it around the cleats, before catching the second line and making the boat secure. A gangplank bridged the gap and people with sun-reddened cheeks and windswept hair scurried off as fast as they could, none of them wanting to hang around and feel pressured into helping unload the equipment.

She hopped off the wall and made her way the last few feet to the boat. Catching the eye of a well-built man wearing his wet suit pulled down to his waist heading away from the boat, she smiled at him.

"Hi, is Oz on this boat?"

"Yeah, but she's probably gonna be pissed that you turned up here. She's working and she don't really like it when you girls show up like this. It's probably best if you just head off home and call her later." He put an arm around her shoulders to turn her away from the boat. "She did give you her number didn't she?"

Finn's eyebrows drew into a frown. "Yes, she gave me her number. I know she's working. That's why I'm here. I'm a bit early, but I thought—"

"Hey, Mac, go and get the cart or we're gonna be here all day." Finn turned to see Oz at the top of the gangplank starting to pass boxes along to a man on the dock receiving them. She gave a quick wave when she saw them talking. "Hey, Finn, you're early. Is everything okay?"

Finn ducked under the man's arm and headed the last few feet to the boat as he shrugged and headed away from them. "Yeah, everything's fine. I was just a bit bored hanging around the hotel waiting, so I thought I'd come over and take a look around. Is that okay?"

"Sure." Oz reached for another box stuffed with lead weights, masks, snorkels, BCDs, regulators, and fins, before tossing it across to the man on the dock.

"Since I'm here, can I help with anything?"

Oz's head snapped up. "You want to help?"

Finn shrugged. "Yeah. Is that not all right?"

"It's more than all right. It's just unusual. This is the end most people try to duck out on." Another box hit the dock. "When Mac gets here with the cart you can help stack the boxes so that we can get it all back to the dive center to wash it off before we store it all. Is that okay?"

Finn nodded as she turned to look in the direction Mac had gone. She began straightening the items in some of the boxes so that they would sit better atop each other without damaging any of the delicate and expensive equipment in them. By the time Mac returned, she had all the boxes ready to stack and began lifting them onto the wheeled cart.

"Finn, make sure you leave enough room for all the tanks to go on there too."

"Will do." Finn liked the burning in her shoulders as she stacked the equipment neatly onto the cart. Her muscles would ache the next day, but she didn't care. Right now, the sun was shining, the birds singing, and the air was heavy with the salt of the ocean. It felt good to be active.

"So, Oz, you going to introduce us to the magic worker bee over there, or shall we just call her your mystery friend?" Mac whispered under his breath loud enough for everyone to hear, his shaved head glistening in the sunlight, his wet suit unzipped and rolled down to his waist leaving his broad chest and abs clearly visible.

"No mystery, guys. That is Daniela Finsbury-Sterling, our new zero to hero candidate."

"That's the chick you had to pick up at the airport last night?"

"Yup." She grabbed some more gear and tossed it onto the dock.

"And then you drove her to her hotel?"

"Yup."

"And then you worked the old Oz magic?"

"Knock it off, Clem. We aren't all animals like you."

"Very true, Oz, my friend, very true, but there are even fewer like you."

Finn felt her cheeks flush as she tried to ignore the conversation. She kept stacking boxes, moving things around, and keeping busy. She tried not to think about Oz playing the field, though she couldn't figure out why the thought disappointed her. She glanced at Oz, surprised to see her looking uncomfortable.

"I wasn't talking about myself." She didn't hang around for him to answer but jumped onto the dock and jogged over to Finn. "You ready to roll this thing home?"

"Yep." Finn headed around to the back of the cart and got ready to push, trying to put as much distance between her and Oz as possible.

"If this thing starts rolling backward, we're gonna be scooping you up off the dock. Always head for the side and use the rail there." Oz pointed to the far side of the cart. "Don't want to squish anyone who helps unload a boat when they don't have to."

"Thanks. I'll bear that in mind." She grabbed hold of the rail and started to haul when Oz counted to three.

"So why did you really head here so early?"

"I was bored. Pete was chatting up some bartender at the cocktail bar, and I felt like I was about to become a third wheel, so I thought I'd give my new car a run out and look around. I can't stay in the hotel for the rest of the time I'm going to be here, so I thought I should get to know the area." She smiled over at Oz as she tried to catch her breath. "That was the plan anyway. The next thing I knew, I was sitting on the wall watching the ocean and I thought I might as well give you a hand."

"Sorry, back up a bit. Did you say you bought a car?"

"Yeah."

"Why?"

"Well, I'll need it to get around. I don't imagine I'll be able to get a place close enough to the dive center to be able to walk here every day with any gear I might have to haul with me, and while I don't mind working hard, doing so just for the sake of it seems stupid."

"So what kind of car did you get? A junker to run around in?"

"Erm, no, not really." For a moment, Finn felt silly for buying such a nice car when she'd be spending most of her time in the water. But just as quickly, she let the feeling go. She wanted something nice, something she could enjoy without anyone to condemn her.

Oz steered the cart to the back of the shop and they pulled it to a stop.

"We need to get all the equipment rinsed off so the salt water doesn't do too much damage. The easiest way is to dunk it all in these tubs." Oz pointed to the two giant vats filled with water. "We use the one on the left for the first clean then the second one as a final rinse. Just throw all the wet suits and BCDs in first. The salt takes a little while to leach out of the fabric." She grabbed an armful of wet neoprene before hauling it over the edge of the tub and watching as Finn followed her example. "So?"

"So?"

"The car?"

"Why? Do you have a thing for cars?"

"Yes. Now tell me."

Finn jerked her head over her shoulder. "It's the moss green one under the tree."

"The dark green one with the top down?" Oz grinned. "The dark green one with the top down that is probably one of the sexiest cars ever made?"

"You really do like cars, don't you?"

Oz wasn't listening anymore. She practically skipped across the asphalt to the car.

"A nineteen sixty-seven moss green Ford Mustang. Leather bench seats. Twenty-one spoke wheels." She ran her hand from the headlights down to the windshield. "This isn't a car."

"No?"

"No."

"Then I should take it back. I specifically needed a car."

Oz looked at her like she'd gone mad. "This is so much better than a car."

"Really? And why is that?"

"This is an orgasm on wheels!" Oz was grinning from ear to ear. "I would love a car like this." Oz's enthusiasm was infectious and Finn laughed as Oz ran her hands across the leather seat, the hood, and delicately across the chrome along the top of the windshield. She loved the jubilant reaction and felt like she was watching a child open her favorite Christmas present. Finn reached into her pocket and pulled out a set of keys. She tossed them to Oz, who caught them easily.

"Go on, then."

"Huh?"

"Take her for a ride. I'll finish unloading the cart and I'll see you back here when you're done." She was already heading back to the cart when Oz caught hold of her arm and stopped her.

"You'd let me just take off in your new car?"

"Sure," Finn said, still smiling. The smile faded quickly as she saw the pleasure in Oz's eyes replaced by anger. She felt the fingers gripping her arm tighten and grabbed Oz's hand to pry it off.

"You don't even know me. I could just take off and never come back. Why would you do that? Do you really have so much money that it doesn't matter if someone just disappears with your car?"

"I thought you'd enjoy taking the car for a ride. I thought I could help you out with the work that needs to be done. It's not like I don't know where to find you. That is why I offered it to you. I'm sorry I offended you." She finally yanked her arm out of Oz's grip. "I'll try to make sure I don't do it again." She stalked back to the tubs and heaped the rest of the equipment into the clean water.

"Finn?"

Finn continued pushing the equipment in and out of the dirty water, trying not to let Oz see the tears threatening to spill. She had wanted to do something nice, and Oz had thrown it in her face. She wouldn't make the same mistake twice.

"Finn, I'm really sorry. I didn't mean to upset you. That car is probably my dream car. I guess it upset me that you could part with it so easily."

"I can take care of myself, Oz. I'm not a child." She pulled another mask out of the tank and shook off the excess water. "I'm here to get away from someone who was smothering me. I don't need a replacement, and I don't need someone telling me what to do with my life."

"Sure. I'm sorry. Please, can we start over? You've been fantastic, helping with the work, offering me a ride in your fabulous car. I've been a jackass."

Finn snorted her agreement at the frank assessment and felt the tension leaving her shoulders.

"Please let me make it up to you?"

"And how do you plan to do that? Point out the water so I don't get wet?" Finn glanced up from the water and grinned to take the sting out of her words.

Oz pushed her hand through her hair and the salt coating it made it stick out at odd angles. "Yep, I totally deserve that, but I have something else in mind. Let me take you out to dinner. Show you some of the sights. Maybe a drink after? You are over twenty-one, right?"

Finn splashed some of the water at her. "Of course I am. You were doing well till then. Don't blow it."

"Hey, it's a compliment."

"Yeah, right."

"Seriously. Most women would have loved that comment."

Finn sighed and punched at the material in the water. "I'm sure. The only problem is that I know I look about twelve. Even with ID, sometimes I can't get served. So yes, in twenty years I'll be very grateful for my youthful looks. Right now, I'd love to be taken for a grown-up."

Finn watched as Oz stood back and looked at her, taking in the forest green T-shirt, at least three sizes too large and the baggy black cargo shorts. Finn found herself hoping Oz liked what she saw, but she doubted it. A messy ponytail kept her hair off her face, and her sunglasses hid her eyes, which she considered her best feature.

"Can I make a small suggestion?" Oz asked, her head tilted slightly as she continued to look Finn up and down.

"And what would that be?"

"Maybe, if you do want people to see you as a grown-up, and I'm not saying that you should, but you know, if you do, and don't be offended or anything, but maybe you should…"

"Not dress in clothes that are too big and look like I'm wearing my mother's, father's, and older brother's all at the same time?"

Oz blew out a relieved breath. "Yeah. That's it."

"I'm in disguise."

Oz laughed. "Disguise?"

"Yup."

"Like Superman and Clark Kent type disguise?"

"I think more like Supergirl and whoever the chick was without the blue tights."

"Really? And what are you disguised as?"

Finn shook her head. "It's not what I'm disguised as, but what I'm trying not to be."

"And what is it that you're trying not to be?"

"My father's daughter."

"And looking like a little girl playing dress-up helps?"

"At the moment. My new disguise is going to be as a diving instructor. Working woman of the world, able to make a living for myself, and not dependent on anyone." Finn looked away, trying to figure out how to move the conversation away from her family issues.

"What other changes does this disguise include?"

"Well, let me see. New place to live, new car, new career. Everything, really."

"What about Pete?"

"What about him?" Finn frowned as she began rinsing the snorkels.

"Does he have a place as your boyfriend in this new disguise you're making?"

"My boyfriend?"

Oz nodded.

"Pete?"

"Yeah, Pete. The guy from the airport last night."

Finn burst out laughing, enjoying the look of confusion on Oz's face.

"What's so funny?"

"Pete isn't…" She was laughing again before she could finish her sentence. "Oh God, that's funny. Pete isn't my boyfriend. Never has been, never will be." She stretched tight back muscles, noting the way Oz's eyes strayed briefly to the tight material pulled across her breasts. "Trust me, I'm *soooo* not his type, even if he were mine. Did you miss the part earlier where I told you that he was chatting up the bartender at the hotel? Male bartender."

"I guess I did." Oz was smiling again. "Sorry."

"No need to be sorry. I haven't laughed like that in ages. Pete and I have been friends for as long as I can remember." She turned back to the water vats. "My father has decided that he'd like us to get married. We both object to this. Strenuously. Pete will most likely lose the job he has at my dad's company when he gets back to the UK for helping me get away."

"That doesn't sound like a good thing. What about you?"

"What about me?"

"Well, if your dad will do that to your friend for helping you, what will he do to you?"

"Well, if I'm lucky, he'll disown me."

"And if you're not?"

"He'll try to get me back home and make life very difficult if I don't, for me and anyone else around me."

"Sounds like a nice guy."

"He's great." Finn smiled sadly at Oz. "But let's not talk about him anymore."

Oz grinned and grabbed an armful of equipment. "So, tonight. Dinner?"

Once again, Finn felt the tension start to recede. It seemed Oz knew how to defuse a situation. Which made sense, since she couldn't have tense, panicked people diving with her. Suddenly, dinner with her sounded like the best thing in the world. "Sounds good. I'll go back to the hotel to change and let Pete know I'm heading out for the evening. Where should I meet you?"

"Well, I can pick you up from the hotel?"

"You could, but then you'd have your car and you wouldn't get to drive the, and I quote 'orgasm on wheels,' would you?"

Oz's eyes lit up. "This is very true. What do you have in mind, Linda?"

"Who's Linda?"

Oz smiled at Finn's confusion. "Supergirl, without the tights. Linda Lee. Superman's much more gorgeous cousin."

"Right, got it. How about if I pick you up?"

"Really?"

Finn looked at her quizzically. "Yeah, really. Never had a girl pick you up before?"

Oz thought for a moment. "As a matter of fact, I haven't."

Finn burst out laughing again. "Sorry. I don't believe you."

"It's true. Honest." She leaned forward conspiratorially. "To tell you the truth, it's always been the other way around."

Finn's laughter stopped and a slow smile slid across her face. "Now that I can believe."

"So don't tell anyone. I have a reputation to protect."

"Your secret is safe with me."

CHAPTER FIVE

John Pritchard pushed his hands through the little hair he had left and puffed out his cheeks before addressing the team before him.

"Listen up, people. Mike Shepherd was found floating in the canal at Camden Locks with a bullet through the head. The location is less than two hundred yards from Sterling's daughter's home. We know his cover was blown on Friday night when his wire went out. We know he was with Jack Kant at the time, and we know he was watching Sterling's daughter. Now we know he's dead. Without him, we have diddley fucking squat." The MI6 chief waved the pages he held in his hand at them. "These pages"—he tossed them across the desk—"are all we have to show for six months' worth of digging on this bastard." He looked at each face in turn. "William Sterling is laughing at us."

"Sir—"

"I don't want to hear it. Peter Green has agreed to come on board. He's in Florida with Sterling's daughter at the moment, but he's not due back for nearly three weeks. I want to know as soon as he lands. Do you hear me?" He looked pointedly at the men and women crowding the conference table.

"Sir, do we know if Green is involved in the money laundering?"

Pritchard pointed at the scattered pages. "Does it look like it? His network has proven nearly impossible for our people to crack, and we have yet to gather direct information."

"So he could be playing both sides of the fence here?"

"It's possible, but having spoken to him, I don't think so. He seems to be up front. We asked him to come in and work with us to get information on Sterling. If he's as good with computers as he's supposed to be, we might actually get some evidence on this bastard before his bank balance is bigger than the national debt."

There were murmurs of agreement around the table.

"I want eyes on Green once he lands. He's the key to cracking this wide open and I want him in here. Safe. Are we all clear?" A murmur spread around the room. "See to it."

"Sir, do we have anything more regarding the rumors about the bio labs?" another agent asked.

"No. We've got rumors that he's got scientists building biological weapons and more rumors that he's selling them. Hell, I've even heard rumors that his daughter is the one building them, which makes no sense since we know Sterling is having his lackeys tail her. But there's nothing concrete. Green may be able to shed more light on this side of Sterling's operation too. We'll have to wait and see."

"Sir, I may have a lead."

"What is it, Bates?"

"It's not definite, but I have a contact who's been working as protection for Masood Mehalik. He's under the impression that there's a big deal in the works. He doesn't know details yet. But he's prepared to give them to me when he does."

"Finally, some good news. This guy got a name?"

"Hakim Qadri."

"Is he sure this deal is tied to Sterling?"

"He said he overheard a phone conversation between the two of them, discussing a quantity of product. The only things Mehalik deals in are drugs and weapons."

"Well, we've got nothing to suggest Sterling's branching into drugs. Will he wear a wire?"

"I'll ask."

"Then get me everything you can find on this Mehalik guy."

CHAPTER SIX

"Pete, you here?" Finn closed the door behind her as she slipped quietly into their suite. Getting no reply, she began flicking through the hangers to locate an outfit for dinner. She pulled out the only clothes she had that weren't too large and draped them on the outside of the wardrobe door to let the creases drop out of them. She headed for the shower and emerged twenty minutes later, pink from the hot water and humming gently to herself.

"What ya up to, sweetie pie?"

"Shit, Pete! You scared the living crap out of me." Finn grabbed the doorframe and tried to steady herself. Her father had taught her that bad things happened when you allowed someone to sneak up on you.

"Sorry." He fell backward on the bed. "Have you had a good day?"

She towel dried her hair with one hand, keeping the towel around her chest tight with the other. "Yep. I got my new car, went down to the dive center, and I'm picking Oz up in about an hour to go out for dinner. Will you be okay on your own for the night?"

"Actually, I was gonna ask you the same thing. I have a date for the night."

"You dog!"

"Yeah, I know. I'm hitting the shower. You all done in there?"

"Yup. I'll probably be gone before you get out, so I'll see you tomorrow. Pop down to the dive center if you're getting bored, and I'm sure someone will be able to suggest something for you to do."

"I'll be fine. Probably sleep all day. Have fun, sweetie." He sauntered off to the bathroom.

Fifteen minutes later, she pulled up the zip on her jeans and tucked in the tail of her black tailored shirt with three-quarter length sleeves, checking herself in the mirror. She smiled, pleased with what she saw, and honest enough with herself to acknowledge that she wanted Oz to like it too. The memory of Oz's eyes traveling the length of her body earlier made her blush. She shook her head and reminded herself that this was just a friendly dinner between two colleagues, not a date, and she had nothing to be nervous about. That didn't seem to stop her hands from shaking though. She checked her makeup and ran the brush through her hair one last time before taking a deep breath and heading for the door, grabbing her car keys and wallet as she did so, and repeating over and over in her head that it wasn't a date. She wouldn't pin hopes on anything in her new life until her old life had been erased.

Oz's breath caught in her throat as she watched Finn climb out of the sexy car and walk slowly toward her, her hips swaying as she moved. Oz realized it was the first time she'd actually seen Finn the woman, rather than just the girl in baggy clothes. She was stunning. And she was definitely all woman, not the girl looking to get out from under her daddy's thumb like Oz had thought. Instead, Finn arrived in clothes that fit her trim, sexy body, and there could be no denying she was one of the sexiest women Oz had gone to dinner with in a long time. She swallowed against an unexpected tide of nerves.

"Sorry, I know I'm early, but I worked up a bit of an appetite hauling tanks earlier. Why are you looking at me like I grew another head? What's wrong? Do I have lipstick on my teeth?" Finn pulled off her shades and started to use the reflective surface to check her teeth.

Oz smiled, enjoying the sound of Finn's accent. "Is this another disguise?"

"Excuse me?"

"You look great. Clothes that fit and everything." The blush dancing across Finn's cheeks added to her appeal. The fitted black shirt was tucked neatly into jeans that fit like a second skin, and her dark auburn hair hung down her back like burnished copper. The fading daylight turned her eyes to polished jade and her high cheekbones were a light pink from the day spent in the sun.

"Yeah, Pete bought me these ages ago, but I never wear them. He actually packed them in his case and hung them in my wardrobe when we got here. It's his way of dragging me into the world of modern fashion. It's taken me three years to get into these. All part of the new disguise."

"I see. Well, it looks great on you. I think I'll be beating them off with a stick." She noticed Finn's frown. "What? What's wrong?"

"I think you have a tendency to exaggerate. I'm sure you'll have no need to worry about that at all."

"Are you kidding?" Oz looked into Finn's eyes and saw with absolute certainty that Finn had no idea how beautiful she was. Oz took a chance and blatantly let her eyes roam over Finn's trim figure, noting how her full breasts tugged slightly at the buttons with each movement, a teasing testament to how easy it would be to pop the shirt open and view its hidden jewels. "You will definitely have admirers wherever we go tonight. Men will ask if you're with me. If you say no, they won't leave you alone. If you say yes, and they're brave, they might ask how open you are to new experiences. With or without me. Women will ask you the same thing and probably respond in the same way."

"Oz, people don't see me like that. They look at me like I'm a little kid and ask for my ID before I even get to the bar."

"Dressed like you were today? Sure. Dressed like this? You still look young, but you definitely don't look like a little girl. You look like a lovely, beautiful, sexy young woman. Who could, and should, have her choice of company." Oz watched as Finn searched for something to say. She took pity on her and decided the situation had gotten far too intense. "But I might just be saying that so I can drive your car."

Finn burst out laughing and clearly relaxed. "Show me this mansion of yours and then you can take me out to dinner like you promised."

Oz fiddled with her keys, uncomfortable. "I wasn't really expecting visitors. This place is a mess." She shrugged, looking more than a little sheepish. "Would you mind if we just went straight to the restaurant?"

"Of course not." Finn smiled. "Have you lived here long?"

"About four years. I'm still doing some work on it though. I'm remodeling the kitchen at the moment. I've hung most of the cabinets, but it's a mess in there."

"How very butch of you."

"I'm not butch."

Finn crossed her arms over her chest and gave her a look of disbelief.

"Well, not that butch, not really."

"It's your disguise, right? You're really a lipstick lesbian and hiding it well?"

"Not that well, obviously! Anyway, who told you that I'm a lesbian? Lipstick or otherwise?"

"Well, a guy on the dock thought I was your latest fling and that you wouldn't be pleased that I had turned up where you were working. And there's the fact that you usually do the picking up when you go out to dinner. And you thought Pete was my boyfriend. Actually, thinking about it, that's probably a point against the lesbian thing. Where is your gaydar?"

"Hey, I knew Pete was gay. I just didn't know if you knew."

"Of course, so why did you think he was my boyfriend?"

"I guess I was fishing for information."

"About me?"

"No, I wanted to ask Pete to marry me. Duh! Of course about you."

"You mean you can't tell?" Finn stopped and faced Oz when they got to the car and Oz felt that familiar heat between her own legs. Damn, Finn was gorgeous.

"I mean, I thought maybe. But really?"

"Will it make you feel better if I tell you I was winding you up?"

"I assume that means teasing me. Were you?"

Finn gave her a Mona Lisa smile. "I'll let you decide for yourself. So where are you taking me for dinner?"

"Do you like seafood?"

"Yup."

"Good. We're heading to Turtle Kraal's. They do the most amazing conch fritters and seafood platters."

"Sounds great." Finn held the keys out for Oz. "You can drive, Jeeves."

"You sure?"

"Totally. You probably love this car more than I do, so yeah, I want you to drive. If you still want to?"

"I love to drive."

"Somehow that doesn't surprise me."

The restaurant was packed and Finn's eyes wandered constantly while Oz studied the menu and the waiter brought their drinks.

"Have you decided what you would like, ladies?" They both ordered seafood platters, and an awkward silence developed when the waiter walked away.

"This place is lovely. I can't believe it's so busy though. It's only a Monday night."

"It's always like this. If you come on a Saturday night the chances of getting a table aren't great."

Conversation stalled again and Finn played with her napkin. Maybe accepting Oz's dinner invitation wasn't a good idea after all. Although, she couldn't have asked for a better looking dinner companion. Oz's forget-me-not blue eyes watched the room from under heavy blond bangs, constantly scanning everything around them. She sat with her back to the wall, her strong shoulders nicely filling the white cotton shirt she wore, and its high collar accentuated her high cheekbones. She turned her glass between her fingers before taking a sip, making Finn wonder if Oz was nervous too. Finn smiled as she realized that the thought of making Oz nervous calmed her a little.

"So how did you end up as a dive instructor?" Finn knew that the best way to get people talking was to get them to talk about themselves. It was something she had learned at the many parties her father had forced her to attend. She watched as Oz seemed to consider the question.

"Long story really."

"I'm in no rush."

"Well, my family is all in the navy. My dad, uncle, cousins. Except AJ, he's in the coast guard. My dad jokes that our love of water started with the Vikings we came from." She smiled as she sipped her drink. "I went into the navy straight out of college and was a navy diver for ten years."

Oz sipped her drink and Finn watched a shadow skitter across her face, darkening her eyes as she remembered something. Then she put her glass back on the table and shrugged, seemingly shrugging off the memory.

"When I left the service, I didn't think I'd want to dive again. My cousins talked me into going on vacation with them to Egypt and we went to the Red Sea. They badgered me to go diving with them, and eventually, I gave in and we all went for a joy dive. They picked the wreck of the Thistlegorm, a cargo vessel that sank during World War II. It was carrying supplies and stuff across the Red Sea to the troops fighting in Africa."

The waiter arrived with their starters and they stopped speaking for a moment. When he left, Oz didn't seem like she was going to keep talking. But Finn wanted to hear the rest, to know about the woman she would be under the waves with.

"You were telling me about the Thistlegorm."

"Oh, yeah. Well, I kind of set it as a test to see if I still actually enjoyed diving, and it was just the navy rules that bugged me, or if I was genuinely sick of it all. So I signed up for this dive. I'd dived more times than I can count by then, so gearing up was like going through the motions. Same with the descent, then it was like I was looking underwater for the first time. I'd dropped down to about eighty-five feet, and straight in front of me, just sitting on the sea bed, was a steam engine. It had been on the deck of the ship when it sank and had landed twenty or so feet from the wreck. I was just staring at it, letting myself drift on the current, when this manta ray comes out of the blue, floats above the engine, and just keeps going past me. Manta rays glide so effortlessly it looks like they're flying through the water. It felt magical or something." She ate slowly as she spoke and Finn could see the memories passing through Oz's eyes.

"Anyway, I finally got past the engine and on to the wreck. There are tanks sitting on the deck, practically welded on now with all the coral over the years. In the hold, there are cars, trucks, motorcycles. There's even one room full of rain boots. This whole room is full of nothing but boots and a moray eel hiding inside one of them. The juxtaposition of it all, of man and nature coming together to create something so beautiful and bountiful from the death and destruction of the Second World War made me look again. At what I had done in the navy, and it wasn't—isn't—the sea that was the problem. It was me. I went into the navy to find order. And I found it. But what I really wanted was peace. And that's what I found under the water. Not the navy's water though.

The water as it is. It's raw and beautiful, lethal but calming. The ocean just exactly as it is."

"Wow. That's amazing." Finn wondered if she would ever have the kind of passion Oz had for the water. For anything or anyone. Her focus had been on getting away from her father and everything that entailed. Now that she could look beyond that, she suddenly felt as though she were facing an abyss. She shivered slightly.

They ate in silence for a few minutes, the emotion behind Oz's words enough to fill the silence comfortably and keep them both occupied with their own thoughts.

"So have you ever been diving before?" Oz said suddenly, putting her fork down and looking at Finn intently.

"Nope."

"But you've already booked and paid for the whole course. What if you don't like diving? What if you can't equalize your ears? You'll have wasted all that money and time. Yours and mine."

Finn finished the last bite of her food and crossed her cutlery on the plate, contemplating her answer.

"Oz, I'm not wasting anything. This is what I want to do. I know I haven't been diving before, but I know I'll get the hang of the ear thing. I've done a lot of swimming. A hell of a lot, and I know I can dive deep in the pool and equalize, which isn't entirely the same I know, but close enough that I know if I take it steady, I'll learn whatever I need to learn to get the hang of it. As far as not liking diving goes, I really can't see that happening. I've spent more hours visiting aquariums than I can count. I loved walking through the tunnels where the water and animals were all above me. I loved the feeling that I was down there with them. I'd stand there watching the sharks and the rays, turtles, so many varieties of fish, and the amazing array of colors." Finn smiled at Oz, glad to see she looked interested instead of bored. Or worse, judgmental.

"I wanted to be there, wrapped up in the peace of the water like they were. I want it even more now. Why the water calls to me like it does?" She shrugged. "I honestly don't know. Maybe it's because I know my dad can't swim so he would never follow me there. Maybe it's the quiet. That peace you found down there? Maybe that's what I'm craving too. All I know is that when I close my eyes, I can picture all the things I see in the aquariums right there with me. But I'm floating along in the water. It's something I've always dreamed of doing."

ANDREA BRAMHALL

"Can I get you ladies anything else?" the waiter said after setting down their meals.

"No, thank you." Oz picked at her food, frowning as she did so.

"You think I'm nuts, don't you?" Finn sighed, ignoring the meal in front of her.

"Yup."

"Thanks."

"No problem. It's a kind of nuts that I think I understand, though."

"You do?"

"Sure. I think that's why I ended up in the navy in the first place. It felt like it was in my blood. My Uncle Charlie calls it saltwater in our veins."

"I have trouble picturing you in the navy."

"Really?"

"Yeah. Do you have any proof?" Finn relaxed, glad they were moving on. It seemed like their conversations kept getting serious, and she wanted to see the lighter side of Oz. And she certainly didn't want the conversation to turn to her family.

"Not on me, but I do at home."

"Really? Like what, your uniform?"

"No, they make you give that back when you leave, but I probably have a picture of me in uniform." Oz laughed and then leaned forward. "You really are gay, aren't you?"

"Are you asking me or telling me?"

"Asking, I guess."

"Then I refuse to answer. I told you earlier you have to work it out for yourself." Finn cracked a crab claw and peeled out the meat.

"How old are you?"

"It's on all the forms I filled out."

"I know, but I don't look at those things really. They feel like such an invasion of privacy."

"You're slightly odd. You know that right, Oz?"

"Yeah, yeah. Spill it."

"I'm twenty-eight."

"Really? Wow. You look so much younger, as you know. But talking to you, you seem so much older. I thought you might actually be closer to my age."

"Which is?"

• 44 •

"Thirty-six."

"*Sooo* old, how can you stand it? Pete will be thirty this year, and he's dreading it. He'll be glad you're older than he is."

"So how did you two become friends?"

"Pete kind of took me under his wing. As I said, I've known him for as long as I can remember. He's a couple of years older than me, and I guess he's like my big brother. He always looked out for me when I was a kid."

"How did you meet?"

Oz speared a piece of seafood from her plate and Finn was mesmerized by the way her full lips opened and sucked it in smoothly. She focused on her own plate, and the question. "He was hanging around with some of the boys whose parents worked for my dad. I was about five at the time. My dad had just moved me to London and I didn't know anyone. I had no friends, no family except my dad, and I kept watching the staff kids playing in the grounds from my window every day. I watched them for hours. I snuck out of the house one day and followed them around for the whole day, but they kept trying to lose me. They all disappeared at one point into the woods. I'm sure you can picture it, dark scary woods. Whiny little girl, crying about being left behind. Big butch Uncle Pete."

"Are you kidding?"

Finn shook her head. "Nope, he was only eight and in denial. Anyway, big butch Uncle Pete comes charging to the little girl's rescue. Tells her it will all be okay, that he'll look after her. I loved him there and then and I've stuck to him like glue ever since. He was like my babysitter, best friend, and big brother all rolled into one."

"Does your dad know he's gay?"

"You've met him; everyone knows he's gay."

"But he still wants the two of you to marry?"

"Yup." She knew where Oz was going with her questions. They were questions she'd asked herself many times before. She still wasn't sure she knew the answers to them, or the true reasons behind her father's intractable desire to see them wed.

"Why?"

Finn shrugged, debating how much she wanted to share with someone she didn't know. "Well, Pete is brilliant with computers and programming and all that stuff. My dad wants to groom him to take over the IT and communications aspects of his business. For some reason, he seems to think that getting Pete and I married will, I don't know, cement his plan for world domination or something. Like the old-fashioned kings marrying out their daughters for allegiances, power, and money."

"But that makes absolutely no sense. Pete is gay. Forcing him to marry you surely wouldn't make him inclined to stay with the company."

"Obviously, but my father thinks the whole world will bend to his world view. Pete will no longer be gay if he marries me and we make lots of grandchildren—preferably boys—to take over my dad's company when the time comes. One would be a jumped up little Hitler just like my dad and one would turn out a genius just like Pete. Company and Daddy live happily ever after. The gay thing is an issue that will go away if Pete just lives a heterosexual lifestyle."

"And you?"

"What about me?"

"What does Daddy dearest think will happen to you in all this?"

"Oh…well, in between churning out at least one little Hitler and one little Einstein, I will also be expected to become a female Hitler and learn to run the company just like my dad does. If I don't show the aptitude for that, I just get the pleasure of running the bio labs."

"Bio labs?"

"Yeah, my dad's company has two. One in the States and the one I've been working at in London."

"So Pete's good with computers so he gets IT and communications. You get the bio labs. Why?"

"I studied microbiology and medical science at university. I was working on the DNA sequence of the E. coli bacteria so that I could incorporate another sequence into the structure. The idea is that I could then create a treatment protocol for a variety of diseases by using the E. coli as a host."

"I had that once. Food poisoning, right?"

"Well, one of the strains is food poisoning. E. coli has many different serotypes, some of which can cause stomach upsets, but most are actually harmless. It's a very common bacterium in the human gut so it makes the perfect host to treat illnesses of the gut. Intestinal cancers are the most obvious, but it could be used to treat other things too by being absorbed through the intestinal wall and into the blood."

She stopped at the expression on Oz's face. "Sorry, I know it's really boring, but it could be a really big step forward for medical treatments. I get carried away talking about it."

"You're a genius."

Finn laughed. "No, I'm not. I was just trying an experiment that hasn't worked, and I won't get to finish. I'm a grunt, I guess."

"I doubt that." Oz sipped the final drops of wine from her glass. "So that's why your dad thinks you'll churn out Einsteins and run two bio labs, on either side of the Atlantic." She topped up her glass and held the bottle up in question to Finn. When she nodded, Oz poured the remaining liquid into her glass. "Finn, I totally see why you want to escape into the ocean. Does your dad really think this is going to happen?"

"Indeed he does."

"So this trip?"

"My dad's gift to us. To encourage the creation of little Hitlers, with an engagement ring expected on our return."

"He really is going to be in for a shock isn't he? What does your dad actually do?"

"Ever heard of Sterling Enterprises?"

"Sure. International company, fingers in lots of pies. Software development, property development, oil and gas, telecoms, that Sterling Enterprises?"

"You missed biomedical science development, alternative energies, diamond trading, a bank, and several other pretty large sectors, but yeah. That's the one."

"That's your dad?"

Oz looked suitably impressed, and it made Finn feel even worse. Whenever someone found out who she was and where she came from, she had to wonder what their angle was when it came to being her friend.

"Shit. I mean—Shit!" Oz sat back in her chair, clearly dumbstruck. "Wow."

Finn took a long drink, hoping the burgeoning friendship wouldn't flounder now that Oz knew her background, and wondering why the fear that it would caused her stomach to tighten uncomfortably. Keeping people at a distance wasn't something new to her. But she had wanted her new life to be different.

"So the longer you looked like a little girl, the longer you got before your dad tried to put his plan into action."

"It seemed like a good idea at the time. But he started seeing beyond the disguise because I had the knowledge he wanted. So I took his suggestion for a trip and went along with his ideas. Pete was told to go on the holiday or lose his job. I was told to go on the holiday or lose my inheritance. Neither of us is bothered about the prospect of losing either, but we do know that it's the end of the road, so we decided to go on the holiday to get away from him and give me some time to get started on my new life."

"You're very crafty aren't you?"

"Are you asking me or telling me?"

Oz laughed. "This one I'm definitely telling you."

"In that case, yes, I am."

"Does he know where you are?"

"Of course." Finn frowned.

"So you aren't actually trying to hide or run away from him."

"I'm trying to break away from him. There's a difference." Finn clenched her napkin in her lap. She didn't want to be perceived as a coward, as someone who ran and hid when things got tough.

"Do you think he'll let you go?"

Finn shook her head sadly. "No, I don't think he'll let me go. He's not used to being told no. He won't let go because it will hurt his ego. Not because he actually cares what I want to do, where I want to do it, or even who I want to do it with." She wiped her napkin across her lips before tossing it onto her plate. "He'll just be angry I haven't followed his plan."

"What will he do?"

Finn sipped her drink and shrugged slightly again. "Hard to tell, but he'll probably close my bank accounts. The ones he knows about anyway. He'll cancel my credit cards."

"Isn't that illegal?"

"He owns the bank. Legal or illegal, it doesn't matter. I don't think I'll be able to go back to England, as I won't have anywhere to live. He owns the house I was living in, so no doubt he'll change the locks. Any way he can make life difficult for me, he will. It would be damn near impossible to get another job in my field, and if I did, he'd try to get me fired. Things should be a little easier with the distance and the fact that I am technically an American citizen, thanks to my mum, but he has enough business contacts and deals out here that it could still be difficult. Hence, the change in career paths. I can't honestly think of any way he can influence a dive school. Another bio lab, however, is a totally different story."

"Do you have enough money?"

"I have other accounts in different banks. My mother died when I was four and left me a sizable trust fund. I get an allowance annually from it that has just been gathering interest, and the trust becomes accessible either when I marry or turn thirty. I had it all transferred to an account my dad knows nothing about before we left the UK. And I've made some good investments with the money I've earned from working at the bio labs. I'll be fine. I want to try to be frugal with it, as I don't know how long I'll have to live off it before I can get work as a dive instructor, but I'll be fine."

"I know I don't know you very well, and you don't know me, but if I can, I'd really like to help."

"Why?" Finn fought to keep the sharp note of suspicion from her voice, but knew she failed. She watched Oz reach slowly for her glass and take a long drink, her eyes darting around the room. Whatever conflict she was fighting was etched in the frown furrowing her brow. Finn held her breath as she waited for the answer that would either fan the flame of the fledgling trust growing between them, or douse it entirely.

"In all honesty, I don't know." She put down her wine glass. "You seem like a really nice person and I know that sounds lame, but I think you might need help. If I can do anything, or even just if you need to talk." She shook her head again and looked down at the tablecloth. "You said Pete has to go back to England at some point. I don't like the idea of you being here all alone." She shrugged again. "Like I said, I really don't know. I'd just like to help if I can."

"People don't offer to help me for no reason." Finn sipped her wine and twirled the liquid around in the glass. "They want to get closer to my father. They want to get closer to the money they think I have from him. They want me to put in a good word to him about a company, or a deal, or so many other things." She put the glass back on the table and rested her elbows on the tablecloth. "People don't just want to help me." She stared deep into Oz's eyes, trying to see anything that would give her a reason not to trust her. She needed to find something, someone, she could hold on to. Pete had been her only friend, and it wouldn't be long before he went back to England and she was truly alone. She took a deep breath and exhaled slowly before she continued. "Please don't be offended, but I don't understand why you would. I have nothing to offer anyone, except maybe a hell of a lot of trouble." She felt tears at the corners of her eyes. "Not to mention we've known each other for a day. You don't know me. So I have to ask, why?"

"I like you."

One of Finn's eyebrows arched and she flushed.

"No, not like that. I mean I do like you, but that's not what I meant. Jesus, I can't even speak." Oz ran her hand over her face and Finn laughed.

"Finn, you are a beautiful woman, but what I was trying to say, very badly, is that I like you as a person. You didn't have to come to the dock today. But you did. You didn't have to help unload the boat. But you did. You didn't have to help me rinse all the gear. But you did. You were nice to me even after I was an asshole about your car. You've been really sweet and funny and open, and I like you. I have excellent instincts about people, and my instincts tell me that you're the type of person I'd like to have around. I want to be your friend. And I like to help my friends if I can. So that's why I want to help you. If you need it, of course."

Finn gently placed her hand over Oz's, liking the feel of the soft, warm skin under her own. Time would tell if Oz meant what she said, but for now, over a seafood dinner at the beginning of her new life, she was willing to allow for the possibility.

CHAPTER SEVEN

O z waved as Finn roared the car engine and pulled away from the curb before she closed the door behind her. *What the hell is going on with me?* She replayed the evening in her mind: the way Finn moved, the way she looked with that tight top on, the vulnerability in her eyes when she talked about her father. *I like you and I want to help my friends! For fuck's sake, I've never said anything like that before.*

She grabbed the phone and hit speed dial. It was the fourth ring before a sleep roughened voice answered.

"Hey, Rudy, are you near your computer?"

"Hey, Oz. Nope, but I can be. What do you need?"

"I left the file you gave me on Finn in the office and I needed to check through some stuff tonight before I start working with her in the morning. Can you e-mail me the stuff you have, please?"

"Sure thing. Everything okay?"

"Yeah. No problem. Just want to know what I've got on my hands; that's all." She clicked her laptop on and waited for it to boot up.

"It's not like you to ask questions like this, Oz. You let me know if there's a problem, you hear me? I've got your back. Just like always."

"I know, Rudy. Now let me go and look at this stuff. See you in the morning."

"Later, Ladyfish."

She hung up, logged into her mail program and deleted half a dozen spam mails before opening the message from Rudy. The files were attached. Medical questionnaire. General background. Application for the instructor internship. Interest in accommodation. Swim test results: 26.21 for the fifty meter swim. Oz grunted, surprised. The world record was only just under twenty-four seconds. She clicked open her Internet browser and started a search of Sterling Enterprises. Something felt slightly wrong about it, as though she were snooping. But Finn had offered the information, and if she was going to be able to help at all, she needed plenty of background.

She dialed a number she knew by heart and waited.

"Yeah."

"Billy, it's Oz."

"That's Dad, Daddy, Pops, or Father to you, Ladyfish. You hear me?"

"Yes, sir." Oz grinned as she pictured her dad sprawled across the sofa, phone in one hand, beer in the other, her mom curled up next to him, her head resting on his chest, reading a book.

"That one wasn't on the list either." His strong southern accent got stronger as she teased him.

"Yeah, yeah, Pops."

"So, to what do I owe the honor? This is an unexpected pleasure, little Ladyfish. It's been a long time with nothing but silence. How ya been?"

"Good. I need some information and I know you still have contacts."

"He's your uncle for God's sake, Olivia. You could call him yourself you know."

"He might be my uncle, but he's a busy man. Commanding the base and stuff. It just seems like you should be the one to call him."

"He's still your uncle and he'd still take your call. And you damn well know that."

"Yeah, I know, but I've already called you now, so will you ask him for me or what?" She heard him huffing and puffing down the line.

"Tell me what you need."

"Thanks, Dad. Sterling Enterprises. I need everything you can find out about the CEO. William—"

"William Sterling. Rich bastard and twice as nasty. Not to be crossed. The main company owns several subsidiaries working on weapons development and military software here in the States. Do you need the full breakdown?"

"Yeah. Like you were putting together an op for Junior."

"Why?"

"A friend of mine might have some problems with him."

"Him personally or with him in business?"

"Personally."

"Shit, Olivia, what are you getting into? This guy is a major player. How the fuck are you involved in this?"

"I told you, a friend of mine—"

"Are you screwing his wife or something?"

"Thank you very much, Dad. No, I'm not screwing his wife. I'm friends, *just friends*, with his daughter."

"So you've bedded his daughter and now he's after you, is that it?"

"Dad, I haven't slept with her. She's a student at the dive school. I met her yesterday; we had a meeting and dinner tonight. End of story. I didn't sleep with her. She dropped me off ten minutes before I called you."

"So why are you expecting trouble if you didn't sleep with her?"

"I'm not. She is. Look, Dad, I like her, she's a really nice girl, and she's trying to get out from under this asshole. I want to be friends with her and I just want to get some kind of idea what to expect and see if there's anything I can do to help her."

"Is she ugly or something?"

Oz felt herself bristling. She knew her reputation. Hell, she'd reveled in it before now, but the possibility her own dad thought she would only help someone in return for sex hurt. "Dad, am I so horrible that you really don't believe I would do anything for someone else unless sex was involved?"

Her dad paused, obviously hearing the sadness in her voice. "No, baby girl, you're not. But even you've got to admit this isn't what you usually do, is it?"

"No, I guess not."

"Are you okay there, baby girl? Do you want me to come over and chat for a while?"

"Thanks, Pops, but I'm fine. I just want to know what I'm getting into."

"I'll call Charlie and see what he can find out."

"Thanks, Dad."

"So is she?"

"Is she what?"

"Is she ugly?"

"No, she isn't ugly. She's beautiful. Inside and out."

"You know what, girlie? Information or not, I don't think you have a clue what you're getting yourself into. Night, darlin'."

CHAPTER EIGHT

William stared at the screen, absorbing every scrap of information he had received about his daughter. Every detail of her research had been forwarded to him, and despite his reservations over her lack of ambition, he had to marvel at her intellect. He felt a tiny flicker of parental pride before he pushed it aside, replacing it with the much more familiar numbness that usually settled in the pit of his stomach. There was no room for sentimentality in his world. After all, he could hire other people to do the work she had done, and take it where he wanted it to go. Develop her work in the directions she wouldn't take it. His disappointment was just another emotion he didn't need and couldn't afford. He'd found power and money were excellent substitutes for affection. He closed the file and checked his e-mails, swearing under his breath as he reached for the phone.

"Susan, get Lyell on the phone."

"Yes, sir." He waited until the phone rang. He cleared his throat, tugged his shirt, and smoothed his hands down the front of it before he answered.

"Mr. Sterling, how can I—"

"I am still waiting for the projections on making the quantity of Balor I want."

"Sir, I'm still trying to locate a supplier who can get me the equipment quickly. It's a specialized piece of machinery, and the estimates on delivery and installation time are running into months at the moment."

"Give me a name."

"I'm sorry, sir, I don't understand?"

"E-mail me the details of the supplier and the equipment you need. I will see that this matter is expedited."

"Sir—"

"I expect that information within the next five minutes, or Marissa will not be thanking you." He paused and listened to the heavy breathing on the other end of the phone. "Are we clear, Dr. Lyell?"

"Yes, sir."

Sterling replaced the handset and called Susan again. "Get Jack in here, now."

"Yes, sir."

He was pouring himself a coffee as the well-dressed young man stepped into the room. He held up the pot and poured a second cup when Jack nodded.

"Jack, we have a situation." His e-mail program signaled the arrival of new mail. He rounded the desk and printed off the information. "This gentleman needs some persuasion to give us his best efforts. He seems to think I have the time to wait months for a piece of equipment. I expect it to be delivered and installed in Lyell's lab by the end of the month."

"Are there any restrictions, sir?"

Sterling sipped his coffee. "What do you have in mind?"

"Sir, it depends on the circumstances."

"I want you to do what's necessary."

"Do what we've done with Lyell." Jack sipped his coffee, looking thoughtful.

Sterling liked the cold steel in Jack's eyes. He was no-nonsense and did what he was told when he was told to do it. "And if there's only a wife?"

"I'll encourage her to be my guest for a while. If there are children too, he may be more cooperative if we make our purpose clear with the wife and keep the children as our guests."

"And if neither is an option?" Sterling asked, not because he really cared, but because he wanted to make sure all the options were covered.

"Money. I'll either pay him a sizable bonus for his efforts or find a skeleton in his closet to use as leverage."

"Why go to the family first?"

"It's the fastest option and the most reliable. Fear keeps them from thinking straight, especially if a child is involved." Jack rinsed his coffee cup, dried it, and set it in its precise place on the table.

"Very good. Keep me informed."

Jack recognized the dismissal and left the room, the page firmly in hand.

CHAPTER NINE

O z sat at one of the tables outside the dive school, sipping her coffee as she leafed through Finn's file again. She had a small stack of papers in front of her weighted down with her saucer to keep them from blowing away, ready for Finn to fill out when she arrived. One was an application for a house share. *Mrs. Richmond is only three doors down, and she's mentioned looking for a tenant. That'll be perfect for Finn. And she'll be close to me. Close enough to see every day, if I wanted to.*

Mrs. Richmond had been a longstanding friend of the family. Her husband was the commander of the naval base before he retired, and both her father and uncle had served under his command. They had all become good friends, and now Oz considered Mrs. Richmond a member of her family.

"Good morning." Finn dropped into the chair opposite her and smiled broadly. "What's with the frown?"

Oz felt her tension dissipate at the sound of Finn's voice. A smile twitched at the corners of her mouth. *God, that accent's cute on her.* "I was just thinking about something." She moved the saucer out of the way and pushed the stack of papers over to Finn. When Finn had them in her hand, Oz rummaged around for a pen and tossed it over the table. "Are you ready to get started?"

"Sure." Finn began filling out the forms. "Thank you for last night. I had a really good time, and I'm sorry if I talked your ear off." Finn glanced up and Oz's heart stuttered slightly at the warmth in her eyes.

Oz waved her hand. "Not a problem. When I first met you at the airport, I thought you were going to be really quiet, which would make working on this course with you really difficult. I'm glad I was wrong."

"Does that happen often?"

"What?"

"You being wrong?"

Oz laughed. "More often than I'll ever admit to."

"This one looks like a tenancy application." Finn indicated the page on top. "Do you know somewhere I might be able to rent?"

"It's possible. It's a house share, but there's only one other person in the house. It's a big house though, with plenty of space for two people. There are four bedrooms as well as the living areas."

"It sounds great. Where is it?"

"It's the other side of Key West. It's still a drive from here so your car won't be obsolete or anything, but it's pretty close."

"What's the rent?"

"I need to double-check with the owner, but last time I spoke to her about it she said two hundred a month."

"What?" Finn's eyes opened wide.

"Is that too much? Maybe I can get her down a bit. How about one fifty?"

"Are you kidding me? When I was looking online before I came here, everything seemed closer to five or six hundred a month. What's wrong with this place? Does it have rats or something? Is it falling down? Or is it a crack house?"

Oz stopped laughing long enough to answer. "No, it's a nice house, in a nice neighborhood. The owner said that she doesn't really need the money, but she would really like the company." *Which is exactly why I was thinking about inviting her to my house first. Why the hell is that? I'm going to be working with her every day. Do I really want to spend my off time with her too?* She looked at Finn as she mulled the thought over. *Yeah. I really do. Shit.*

"Oh. That still seems really cheap. What are the extras? Phone, utilities, and stuff?"

"Nothing, two hundred a month, everything included but your food. There's Internet and everything already installed. You get your own groceries."

"It sounds too good to be true. Is she an old lady or something?"

"Compared to you, I guess you could say that." Oz grabbed her coffee cup and took a sip to hide her smile. Mrs. Richmond was preparing for her seventieth birthday party. Everyone and their dog had received invites just last week to the party she was planning.

"Well, if she'll have me for two hundred a month, I don't really care if she smells like wee and lavender."

"What?" Oz almost choked on her coffee, barely managing to get her hand to her mouth and stop it from spewing across the table.

"Maybe old people smell different here, but I always find they smell a bit like stale wee with a strong hint of lavender or rose water to cover it up." Finn laughed along with Oz.

"Stop or I'm gonna smell like wee."

"Can you take me to meet her later? See if she likes me? I'll let you drive the Mustang again."

"No problem. I'm sure if you let your landlady drive the Mustang she'll definitely let you stay. Maybe even for free!"

"Wow, it really is more than a car."

"Yup, I told you that. Now get back to those forms or we'll never get out of here and on to the fun stuff."

"Aye, aye, Captain."

"It's admiral, actually," said a male voice.

They both looked up as a tall, uniformed sailor stopped next to the table. He twirled his cap in hand, a broad grin on his face as he watched Oz jump up from the table.

"Uncle Charlie. What are you doing here?" Oz wrapped her arms around the big man. He slung an arm around Oz's shoulders easily as he towered over her by at least five inches. His broad chest and shoulders were obviously solid muscle and his blond buzz cut accentuated the open features of his face. There was no question about a family resemblance, and Oz suddenly wondered what Finn saw when she looked at her.

"Well, I got a call from your dad last night and I thought I'd pop down and see you." He offered his hand to Finn. "I'm Admiral Charles Zuckerman. I have the honor of looking after the base over at Key West, and of being uncle to Ladyfish here."

"Daniela Finsbury-Sterling. It's a pleasure to meet you, sir."

They shook hands before he turned back to Oz. "You got a few minutes for your old uncle?"

"Sure. I'll be right back, Finn."

"Don't worry. I've got more paperwork to fill out. It was nice to meet you, Admiral."

"And you." He followed Oz as they headed into the dive shop and into a small office in the back.

"So that's who all this is for, eh?"

"She's a friend. She's doing some training here, and she'll be here a while. Her dad wants other things for her, and she doesn't expect he'll be very happy when she says no to him. She's expecting trouble, and if I can, I want to help her. There's nothing sinister going on."

"I didn't say there was darlin'. But I've dealt with William Sterling myself, and that man is colder than a witch's tit and twice as nasty."

"Wonderful imagery, thanks, Uncle Charlie."

"You know exactly what I mean. What is she expected to do?"

"Marry her gay best friend Pete and make lots of babies."

"Is he up for it?"

"Pardon the pun, hey? No, he isn't"

"Is it just him she's against marrying?"

"No. She doesn't want the life he has planned out for her in any way that I can see. She's happy enough to give it all up right now and walk away."

"Is she strong enough to do that?"

"I don't know. She says she is, but I don't know her well enough to be sure yet."

"She looks mighty young. I can see exactly why you feel protective of her."

"Yeah, but she's not as young as she looks."

"I know. It's all in here." He handed her a large manila envelope. "There's very little about her in here. It's like she doesn't exist in a lot of ways. Almost like he doesn't know she exists. Maybe he'll just let it go."

"I don't think so. From what she's told me, his pride won't let him if nothing else."

"That's what I thought too. Do you think he'll try to hurt her? Physically, I mean."

"Not sure. Mentally? Definitely. Financially? Absolutely. I'm not sure he'll go so far as to hurt her physically." Oz glanced back at Finn, noticing the way the sun fell across her hair and highlighted the different shades in it.

"Do you know about her mother?"

"She told me her mother died when she was a child."

"Did she tell you the circumstances?"

"No."

"Very suspicious circumstances. Never found a body." He pointed to the envelope she was holding. "The report is in there. Along with some newspaper clippings and a police report I managed to get hold of. A lot of it she may not even know, so you may want to be careful about what you say to her. Oz, this guy is a real piece of work. And I mean that in the worst way. He's got a lot of legitimate businesses, but there are more rumors of underground illegal stuff than I can shake a stick at. I had to go through some serious channels to get some of that stuff for you. And there was more than one government agency calling my office this morning when I did, asking why I was snooping around."

"CIA?"

"Throw in Interpol, MI6, and the NSA."

"Wow, full house. I'm gonna really hate this bastard, aren't I, Uncle Charlie?"

"Yes, baby. You really are." He handed her a card with a number penned on the back while she fought back her own revulsion. "That's my sat phone number. Any time, Oz. You need anything. And I mean anything. You call me on that number. You understand?"

"Yes, sir." She threw her arms around him again. "Thank you, Uncle Charlie."

"You still have a weapon?"

"Yes, sir, I have a few."

"You keep 'em ready, you hear?"

"Yes, sir. Can I get you a cup of coffee?"

"Thanks, but no. I gotta get back to the base. It's Thanksgiving next month. Why don't you invite her over?"

It's only the second of October, Uncle Charlie!"

"That makes Thanksgiving next month. She's still going to be here, isn't she?"

"Yeah."

"Where is she staying?"

"She's at the Ocean Key Resort at the moment, but she'll be moving pretty soon. I was thinking about Mrs. Richmond—"

"Old lady Richmond?"

"Yup."

"You spoken to her yet?"

"No, I was going to give her a call in a little while."

"Tell her we'll all be at her pool party on Sunday."

"Sure."

"I think that's a good idea, having her with Mrs. R. She's got more guns than I do!"

Oz chuckled, knowing it was probably true. "It will make her harder to trace and easier to protect. She's only a few doors down from me then, and Mrs. Richmond is always looking out those curtains at what's going on."

"You've been spending a lot of time with her?"

"Only met her two days ago, but I took her out to dinner last night."

"Dinner? Like a date?"

"No, like an apology." Oz chuckled. "I was an asshole to her yesterday and invited her to dinner to say sorry."

"Right."

"I don't know what it is, Uncle Charlie, but whenever I'm around her, I just want to protect her, and I fly off the deep end with it." Oz ran a hand through her hair and sighed. "I say things without thinking, and then I try and find something to say to her just to stop her from looking sad or being mad at me. Or better yet, to make her smile. Or laugh. She has this wonderful laugh. It's like music or something."

"Right."

"Anyway. Thanks for the info, and the help."

"No problem, Ladyfish." He gave her a tight hug and gave her a long, searching look before kissing her forehead and striding off, flipping open his cell phone as he walked away.

Oz watched him go and contemplated her next move. She didn't want to scare Finn off by letting her know she was digging into her family life. But she also felt like Finn had a right to know Oz was snooping. She looked at Finn, still signing paperwork, the sun making her skin glow. Her stomach flipped and she pressed a hand to it. *Shit.*

CHAPTER TEN

Finn was still working her way through the forms when Oz took her seat again. She shuffled the manila envelope to the bottom of the stack and started looking over the information in front of her, though she didn't really see any of it, absorbed as she was with the turn her life had taken.

"Oz?"

"Hmm?"

"Is everything okay?"

"What?"

"With your uncle? Is everything okay?"

"Oh, yeah, it's fine. I asked him to get some information for me, and we haven't seen each other for a while, so he decided to pop down and see me." She turned back to her papers.

"Oz? What's a ladyfish?"

"It's a fish."

Finn snorted. "I guessed that much. Why did your uncle call you ladyfish?"

"It's just a stupid nickname. It's renowned to be a particularly difficult fish to catch, has a tendency to take the bait from the hook, and when it is caught, it's supposed to be more difficult to land than a barracuda or a shark."

"Ah, okay. I can see that, I guess. So, Ladyfish. No long-term girlfriend?"

Oz stared at her before slowly shaking her head.

"Ever?"

"Never." Oz looked back down at the papers in front of her and didn't notice Finn move until she felt a hand resting gently on her shoulder.

"It'll be a lucky girl who finally finds the right bait, Ladyfish." She squeezed her shoulder gently and then made her way toward the bathroom. Oz sighed as she watched Finn saunter away from her. *Shit, shit, shit.*

She couldn't drag her eyes away from the sight of the loose-fitting black board shorts and forest green tank top that hung loosely on Finn's small frame. Her long auburn hair hung down her back, almost to her waist, the sun catching highlights of red and gold. A gentle smile curved her lips, but it was her laughing eyes that made Oz shiver. She had eyes that shone like emeralds in the sun, and Oz wondered what they would look like in a moment of passion. She was so caught up in her own thoughts that she didn't notice Finn come back.

"I finished with those papers you gave me, so what's next?"

"Swim test."

"I did one back in the UK. They said they sent the results to you with the other paperwork."

"I think there may have been a mistake with the times so we have to repeat the tests. Sorry."

"What did they put down?"

"Twenty-six point two one."

"For the fifty? That's about right."

"Are you kidding me?"

"No. I told you I swam when I was younger."

"Not in the Olympics, you didn't."

"Not quite. I couldn't break twenty-six seconds. I needed a few more inches in height, really. Don't say it." She wagged a finger in Oz's direction.

"I wouldn't dream of it," she said as she smothered her laughter.

"So do we still need to do the swim test again? I really want to start getting into this, and I know there's a lot to learn."

"I'll let it go. Here." She pushed a book in front of Finn. "This is what you need to start studying. We'll go over it tomorrow with the rest of the class, but if you can prepare ahead with the material you can also be looking at the presentation for teaching styles and techniques too. That will help you later on when you have to teach the course you're going to attend tomorrow."

"Okay. Is there somewhere I should go out of the way or am I okay to hang out here?"

"You can hang out here or there's a training room empty today, so feel free. If you want to go back to the hotel, that's cool too. We can always meet later so I can show you the house if you like?"

"No, I'll hang around here."

"We also need to get your equipment. Wet suit, dry suit, your buoyancy control device or BCD, fins, mask, et cetera. I would recommend a dive computer too, but you don't have to do this all at once. For now, you can borrow stuff from the dive center and then buy when you have the money." Oz looked away, suddenly aware that she might be intruding on Finn's personal space and unsure why she felt the need to take control. She let all her other students and divers make their own purchases.

"Oz, I have the money I need for the equipment. I take it everything I need I can get here?"

"Yeah. And I'll make sure you get a good deal. I have some time before I have to be out on the boats, so I'll take you through, if you want?" Oz knew she was burying herself deeper every minute she spent with Finn, but she wanted to spend time with her, even if she didn't want to know why.

They made their way through the store, picking up the various items Finn would need. Oz walked behind her and held a jacket open for her to put her arms through. She lifted it onto Finn's shoulders and turned her to begin fastening the straps and buckles, tightening each as she went, trying to ignore the swell of Finn's breasts under her hands and the subtle scent of Finn's sun-warmed skin. "How does it feel?"

"Like wearing a rucksack for a hike."

Oz smiled. "Wait till you feel it with a full tank attached. It looks pretty good. There are different colors, so if you wanted a pink one, it could be arranged."

"Pink? Do I look like a pink girl to you?"

"Maybe green, then? It would bring out your eyes." Heat rushed to Oz's cheeks as she realized she had actually spoken the words out loud. "I mean—you know. It would look good on you."

Finn was smiling at her again. "Thank you." She unbuckled the BCD and slid it from her shoulders. "You're cute when you blush. So what's next?"

Grateful Finn didn't continue to tease her, Oz ran with it.

"Wet suit. There are loads of different makes and models out there. Shorties, two-piece sets that have a jacket you can leave off. Different thicknesses. Men's, women's, unisex. Even children's if we need to." Oz ruffled through a rack of wet suits. "Do you have a preference?"

"I leave myself in your expert hands, Oz."

So many possible double entendres ran through Oz's head she felt dizzy, but she managed to stifle them. "Okay, so I like SCUBAPRO suits. They have a really good shape for ladies. Generous in the right places without allowing too much space for extra water. Are you looking for a thick wet suit?"

"What difference does it make?"

"Well, the thicker the wet suit, the more buoyant it makes you in the water. It means you have to carry a little more weight to descend."

They worked out what would work best for Finn based on her body weight and height, with only a bit of teasing about the small size of the wet suit they decided on. Oz did her best to keep her hands to herself, but couldn't seem to resist pressing the various options against Finn's body to feel the soft curves beneath the neoprene. She headed into the dressing room with the best option to make sure it fit.

Oz continued picking out the required items. Boots, fins, regulator, gloves, and a snorkel. She pulled several masks from the shelves and put them together with the pile for Finn to try on.

"Any chance you can zip me up?"

"Sure." Oz turned to her and felt her breath catch in her throat as Finn stepped out of the changing room in the wet suit, turning as she did so. *Jesus.* She eased the zipper up while Finn held her hair out of the way.

"Thanks. So does it fit right?" Finn did a catwalk style turn.

"Definitely." Oz's mouth went dry. *Focus, Zuckerman. Jesus, you're acting like a teenage boy!* She turned away and rambled, desperately trying to get her body under control. "I pulled out some other stuff here for you. The fins I recommend are boot fins. That way, if you're walking into the water or anything, you have the boots to protect your feet and you don't have to walk in barefoot. I've been using the Mares ocean fins for the last couple of years. I like 'em. Plus they have lots of colors. It makes it harder for people to pick yours up by accident, and you can coordinate with your wet suit." *That's better, Zuckerman. Keep it professional.*

"So what else do I need now?"

"Mask and computer. I pulled these masks out because I think they may work, but we'll have to try them on you for fit. What you need to do is fit it to your face and pull your breath in. If you can make the seal, then the mask fits. If it falls off easily, then it will leak." She handed one to Finn. "Go ahead. Give it a try."

Finn placed the tempered glass mask over her eyes and nose and sucked her breath in. She let her hands down from her face and raised her head only to have the mask slip before she was standing straight.

"The technique was right. It's the fit that isn't. Here, try this on." They went through the process with six masks before Oz walked back to the shelves.

"I think my face is shaped wrong."

"There's nothing wrong with your face." *Believe me, there is absolutely nothing wrong with your face. It's perfect.* "Give this one a try." Finn repeated the process only to find that this time the mask stayed attached to her face however much she shook her head around.

"Perfect fit. So what's different about this one?"

Oz inclined her head toward the shelf where she had retrieved the mask. "It's from the children's section." Her laughter brought a look of outrage to Finn's face. "I'm sorry, but it's true. Look."

Finn laughed and shrugged. "Oh well, at least I didn't have to get a children's wet suit."

Oz grinned and turned away. Finn's body in the tight wet suit was anything but childlike. It was all woman, and Oz wanted to run her hands over every seam of the wet suit. "I think that's everything," she said, looking at the mound of gear on the counter. Do you want me to get that zipper for you?"

Finn quickly turned around and pulled her hair out of the way. "Please. Is there anything else I need?"

Oz's mouth went even dryer as she unzipped the wet suit to reveal the long expanse of bare skin beneath. Smooth, pale skin begging to be kissed. "I'll grab them while you get changed."

"Okay, thank you, Oz." She disappeared into the changing room again while Oz grabbed the rest of the small gear: a flashlight, a weight belt and weights, some pouches and lanyards, and a mesh bag. By the time Finn returned and plopped the wet suit on the counter, Oz had packed most of the equipment in the bag and started folding the wet suit to add to the stock of goodies.

"Wow. I think there's more in there than I brought with me from England."

"Good. That'll make moving to the house much easier."

"I haven't even met the owner yet. She might not like me."

"I'm sure it's just a formality. When would you want to move? Would you do it right away or wait until Pete goes back to England?"

"Pete really wants to get back as soon as he can so he can start the job he has in the works before my dad knows and makes things more difficult for him. He said he'd stay until I found somewhere to live, and then stay a couple of weeks while I get settled. So I guess the sooner I move the better it will be for him too. So if she'll have me, I guess I'll move as soon as she wants."

"Well, that's good because I'm pretty sure Mrs. Richmond said she's looking for it to start right away. Sounds like the perfect setup for everyone. Will you miss him?"

"Pete? Yeah. Like I said, he's been my best friend for pretty much as long as I can remember. He's been the most constant and stable part of my life. A part of me wishes I could just marry him and be happy. But neither of us would be, so we have to let things change and be happy for what we had." Finn handed her credit card to Oz. "I don't want to think about all that today. I'm sure I bored you with it more than enough last night. Tell me more about how this is all going to work."

"The training?" Oz let the change of topic go as she held a pen out for Finn to sign her credit card slip before ringing it through the register. The last thing she wanted to do was make Finn uncomfortable. "Would you like some coffee? I'll go over it for you while we have a drink, then I can leave you to your studying."

"Sure."

Oz got them drinks and when they were both seated, she explained the program. "The first few qualifications you have to get are fairly straightforward. The open water and advanced open water we should have you through within two weeks. Then we spend the next week getting in a few dives because you have to have twenty logged dives plus your first aid course to take the rescue diver course. The first aid certificate you have is absolutely fine, so it's just about getting the number of dives in. Have you had a look at the specialty dives list yet?"

"Briefly."

"Anything stand out to you?"

"Photography. I was going to ask you about underwater cameras and housings."

"I'll get Juanita to come talk to you about that. She's the photographer that goes down with the tourists and sells them pictures afterward. She's definitely better to advise you, as long as you aren't planning on trying for the same gig. Is photography a hobby already?"

"Yeah, I spent a lot of time walking when I wasn't at the pool, anything to keep out of my father's way. Taking pictures gave me a good excuse. Then I found I was actually quite good. Pete would come with me sometimes. I made him go camping one time. He actually asked where to plug in his hairdryer."

"You're joking, right?"

"Nope."

"Oh my God, what a girl!"

"I know."

"So you're good?"

Finn shrugged noncommittally.

"Understood. You're brilliant. It'll be good if you take to that. We don't have a diver on staff who specializes in the underwater photography that isn't just for the tourists. If you do, and you decide to stay, that could work really well for the dive center." Oz liked the thought of Finn diving with them all the time, taking pictures, that wet suit hugging her as she swam in front of Oz. She pulled the seam of her shorts away from her suddenly oversensitive crotch. She went on to tell Finn about the certificates they would be working on, watching Finn closely to make sure she understood.

"All clear?"

"Yes, boss."

"And don't you forget it. Do you have any questions?"

"Just one."

"What's that?"

"Ever had anyone fail this course?"

"Nope. I have had a couple of people who quit. But not fail. This isn't for everyone. It sounds idyllic in many ways, and the experiences you can have, well, they can be magical. But this is also a job, and like any job, there are good days and bad days. There will be customers you can't stand and others you'll miss when they leave. There will be days when you feel like crap, but you've got a boatload of tourists and you have to dive anyway. When the reality of that sets in during the internship, not everyone likes it. And a few people quit."

"Thank you."

"For what?"

"For being honest with me. I won't quit on you. Now, if you'll excuse me, I've got some studying to do." She picked up her book and headed into the shop.

❖

It was four thirty when Oz popped into the training room. Finn had her chin on her fist as she scribbled notes and flipped pages. Oz's stomach flipped again and she ignored it.

"How's it going?"

Finn looked up, startled, and placed her hand dramatically against her chest. "You made me jump." She took a deep breath before she continued. "It's going fine actually. It seems fairly simple so far."

"Well, you are a brainiac scientist."

"Yeah, yeah. What time is it?" She leaned back in her chair and stretched, and her shirt pulled tight against perfect breasts. Oz looked away quickly, but not before her own body reacted.

"Four thirty. We better get going, if you want to check this place out. I happen to know that the room isn't furnished yet. It had been a study till a little while ago. Mrs. Richmond said she'll take care of that but has asked that you go pick out the furniture. If you want to move as soon as possible, then ordering the larger pieces is probably best done today. It's only Tuesday so it should be possible to get things delivered for Friday."

Finn scooped the books and papers together and stuffed them into her backpack. "What should I do about all that gear?"

"I can lock it in the office if you don't mind leaving it here overnight."

"That's fine. Will I get to play with it all soon?"

"The day after tomorrow. We'll be doing some pool skills and taking your first breath underwater the day after tomorrow. That's an experience you never forget."

Finn fished around the pockets of her shorts and tossed the car keys to Oz. "I like to look at the scenery. I can't do that while I'm driving somewhere new. Do you mind?"

"Do I mind?" Oz looked at her like she was crazy. "Do I mind driving that amazing car of yours so you can stare out the window? Nope, I don't mind at all."

They traveled in silence for a while before Finn started to recognize the streets they were traveling.

"Aren't we near your house?"

"Not too far."

Oz pulled into the driveway a few minutes later. An elderly woman was sitting on the porch swing and waved as they both climbed out of the car. "Hi, Mrs. Richmond."

"Hello there, Olivia."

Finn stifled her laughter as Oz rolled her eyes at the use of her first name. "Can I call you Olivia too?"

"No, you can't. Mrs. Richmond, this is Finn."

"Pleased to meet you, Finn. Olivia tells me you're looking for somewhere to live while you're learning to be a dive instructor. Is that right?"

"Yes, it is."

"Excellent. Well, why don't I show you around and we can get to know each other a little bit. See if you think you can put up with an old woman like me." Mrs. Richmond didn't wait for an answer as she pulled open the door and ushered them both inside. "I haven't had your response about my birthday party, Olivia. Shall I expect you to grace us with your presence?"

"I'm planning on it. Uncle Charlie said they'd all be coming too."

"Wonderful. I'll be seventy next week, dear." She clasped her arm around Finn's elbow as she showed them each room.

"Really?"

"Absolutely. You'll come to my party too, won't you, dear?"

"I'd love to."

Oz followed close behind her and whispered in her ear. "Does it smell like lavender and pee?"

Finn laughed softly and followed Mrs. Richmond about the house until they were sipping lemonade on the front porch, Mrs. Richmond happily ensconced in her swing.

"So what do you think, dear?"

"I think it's perfect, Mrs. Richmond."

"Call me Emmy. If you're going to live here, I can't be doing with hearing Mrs. Richmond over the breakfast table. So when do you want to move in?"

"Oz said we should order furniture today to get it here for the end of the week. If that's okay with you Mrs—Sorry. Emmy. If that's okay with you, Emmy?"

"That works perfectly for me. Olivia, you go and show this young lady where the best deals are. And then I'll settle up with you later."

"Sure, Mrs. R. Finn, are you ready?"

"Absolutely. Thanks, Emmy."

"Okay, let's go shopping. You'll need a bed and a chest of drawers, the desk and chair in the study are a bit dated—" Oz started to pull her toward the door and realized she was still holding Finn's hand. She dropped it like she'd been burned.

"Do you always ramble?" Finn teased her.

"No, mostly, I'm accused of being the silent and broody type."

"I find that hard to believe. You never seem to shut up around me."

"Maybe it's just you. Have you thought of that?"

"Yes, I have actually."

"And?"

"It is definitely you rambling, not me."

"Ha ha, very funny. Let's go shopping before I change my mind."

Oz ushered Finn back to the car and wondered just how much her life was going to change with someone like Finn being a part of it.

CHAPTER ELEVEN

John Pritchard smoothed his shirt over his stomach and waited. He watched the small monitor as Bates led the Arabic man into the small cell-like interview room, two other officers flanking him. He was tall, well built, and confident. Even in this situation, he looked calm, cool, controlled. Pritchard only hoped that it boded well for them all.

He took a final sip of his tea before walking to the interview room.

"Mr. Qadri, I'm John Pritchard." He dropped a file onto the table between them and sat down. "Mr. Bates tells me that you have some information that may be of interest to us."

"I want protection for my family." He slid a scrap of paper onto the table. "When I know they are safe, I will tell you everything I know about Balor."

"I can't possibly take your family into protective custody without knowing what you have to offer."

Qadri stood. "Then we are done, Mr. Pritchard." He took two steps toward the door.

"Wait. Tell me what it's regarding and I'll see what I can do."

"I am not here to play games, Mr. Pritchard. By speaking to you, I know that I am signing my own death warrant. I have no problem with that. The reason I am doing this is to make sure that my family is safe. Not just now, but in the future."

"Mr. Qadri, I need specifics."

"And I will give them to you. When my family is in your custody."

"What is your connection with Mehalik?"

"I am his personal bodyguard."

Pritchard picked up the scrap of paper, looked at it, and handed it to Bates. "If I do this, I'll want you to wear a wire."

Qadri shrugged. "Like I said, my death is already assured. I do not care. This madness must be stopped."

"Bates, get Mr. Qadri's family to one of our safe houses."

Qadri sat back down, and his shoulders sagged as the tension left him. "Thank you."

"Don't thank me yet, Mr. Qadri. I have a lot of conditions that go along with this."

"I would expect nothing else, Mr. Pritchard."

"Now tell me what you know."

"Masood is planning a war. A war unlike any other. He is buying a weapon from William Sterling that will destroy us all."

"You mentioned Balor. What is it?"

"Balor is a biological weapon that Sterling has had created. But I will not say anything more until I speak to my family in your safe house."

"Qadri, you have to tell us now."

He folded his arms across his chest and stared at Pritchard. "Not until I know my family is safe."

CHAPTER TWELVE

A nd where have you been? I was starting to think you'd run off and joined the circus or something." Pete clambered to his feet as Finn opened the door.

"I've been shopping."

Pete looked her up and down, spun her around, and shook his head. "I'm not buying. You have no bags with you, and I know you only go shopping when I drag you."

"I went shopping with Oz. I needed to organize some new furniture for the house I'm moving into next week."

"Next week! Wow. If I didn't know you better I'd think you wanted to get rid of me. Why did you go shopping with Oz? I would have gone with you." His mouth formed a perfect pout as he folded his arms over his chest and plopped onto her bed.

"I know, but she knows all the shops in the area, and she took me to see the house. It just made sense to go with her tonight. That way the furniture will be delivered later this week and ready so I can move in. It's only a few doors down from where she lives. So I guess we're going to be neighbors too." She sat on the edge of the bed and looked at him, her eyes firm but understanding. She called it her "humor the child" look.

"You went out to dinner with her last night."

"Yes."

"You're going to be working with her at the dive center all the time."

"No flies on you, hey, Sherlock?"

"And I'm going to be back home in a couple of weeks."

"Are you feeling a bit jealous?"

"Don't be stupid. I'm not jealous. You know she's gay, right?"

"What do you think I am? Six? Of course I know she's gay. And in case you missed it when I came out to you, so am I."

"I'm sorry, honey. I'm just worried about you. This whole trip seems really out of character for you. I know I've been trying to get you to be more spontaneous for years, but this just seems like everything all at once. Moving to the States. Changing jobs. Hell, you're even dressing differently. Looking fabulous by the way. It's just scaring me a little. That's all. I'm worried that you're taking everything too fast."

"And you think Oz is what part of that how, exactly?" She watched as he shrugged sheepishly.

"I don't know. I just don't want you to get hurt."

"Why on earth would you think Oz would hurt me? For God's sake, what makes you think she'd even be interested in someone like me? Pete, I'm twenty-eight years old and I have never had a girlfriend. I've never had sex. Do you really think I'm going to fall into bed just because tall, blond, and beautiful pays a little attention to me? Because she tries to be my friend?" Pete was hanging his head in shame. "Give me a little more credit than that."

"Finn, I'm really sorry. I shouldn't have said anything."

"I know you're worried about me. But you have to trust me, that I know what's right for me. What I want and what I don't want." She flopped onto the bed and lay next to him. "I think I can actually be friends with her. I don't exactly have an abundance of those. There's you and, let me think, oh yeah, you." She leaned her head against his shoulder and rubbed her hand across his stomach. "Be my friend, Pete." She looked him in the eyes, resting her chin on her hand. "Be happy that I have somewhere to live. Be happy that I've made a new friend." She felt the tears well in her eyes as she stared at him. "We don't exactly have long left before you'll have to go back and then, who knows when we'll get to see each other again."

He wrapped his arms around her, almost crushing her to his chest. "I'm going to miss you so much." He held her so long in silence she almost thought he had fallen asleep. "Maybe I am jealous of her. She's going to get to see you every day for the next, however long. And I get to say good-bye. Is there any way around this?"

"Can you stay in the States?"

He shook his head. "Not unless I get a job here, and that would probably be New York or Washington rather than Miami. Any chance you can go home?"

"Not unless you're willing to marry me."

"Okay, I'll do it."

"And give me babies." Finn felt the shudder run through him and chuckled as he spoke.

"Turkey baster?"

She stretched and kissed him sweetly on the lips. "I wish we could make it work, but we would both be miserable. I love you too much to do that to you."

He squeezed her tight again. "I know. But I'm really going to miss you."

Finn relaxed in his arms, enjoying the warmth and solidity he offered. She didn't want to think about losing it, or him.

"When do you move in?"

"The bed is getting delivered to Mrs. Richmond's on Thursday; she said I could take my stuff over this weekend."

"Okay, so this weekend we're moving you out of the hotel."

"Are you going to stay here?"

"Sure. The room's booked for another two weeks yet. I think I'll stick around and work on my tan."

"What about the job you were telling me about?"

"Oh, that. This guy John Pritchard wants me to work for a team he's leading. They're a multidisciplinary team tracing bad guys on computers. It should be a really interesting job for me."

"Are they some kind of private firm or something?"

"Yeah, something like that."

Finn watched him pick at his nails, a sure sign that he was hiding something, but she couldn't figure out what, and every time she asked him a question, he just got more and more evasive. She wasn't in the mood to dig around in his secrets, as her emotions were running far too high. "When are you supposed to start?"

"Well, he knows I'm on holiday for a few weeks. He told me to call him when I get back and we'll organize a start date."

"I'm going to miss you so much."

"I know, sweetie, me too."

"You're the only one who's ever been there for me."

"I still will be. Just at the end of a phone rather than in person."

"I know." She'd tried to remind herself of that very fact every day since they had come up with this plan, and it still wasn't working. Pete had been the only constant in a world where every person wanted something from her. He'd been her only friend, laughing with her during the good times, and holding her when she cried every year on the anniversary of her mother's death. He'd stood beside her through her father's angry, humiliating words, and cheered her up when the days and weeks of being ignored were too much for her to take. The tears began to fall again and sobs racked her body. He hugged her tighter and let her cry herself to sleep.

CHAPTER THIRTEEN

O z peeled open the envelope Charlie had given her and poured the contents onto her desk. The portfolio of businesses, properties, deals, and estimates about William Sterling's wealth brought very little in the way of surprises. She told herself that this was for Finn's own good and that in order to protect her, to help her, she needed to know what she was dealing with. Oz's own distaste at snooping was irrelevant.

She riffled through the paperwork, looking at Sterling's various enterprises. The bio labs that Finn had already told her about. The bank. IT and communications company that operated globally. Expanding quickly into China and Korea. Property development. Stocks. Shares. Sterling Enterprises was worth an estimated billion pounds.

She leafed through the pages and found a large photograph of a woman holding a young child. She smiled at the image of mother and child. The little girl had her finger on the tip of her mother's nose and was grinning widely. The second picture showed them both when Finn was a little older, maybe three or four years old. Her mother, Cassandra, sat on a swing with Finn on her lap, one arm clasped tightly about Finn's middle, the other holding on to the swing as they rode. Finn was giggling and clapping her hands, Cassandra grinning right along with her. The adoration so clear on each face that Oz felt her heart break for the tiny child and all she had lost.

She flipped through a few more pages and found the police report on the disappearance of Cassandra Finsbury. Her car had been found at the bottom of a cliff, after the tide had gone out. Her body was never found, and all indications were that her body was washed out to sea.

There were photographs of a car crumpled at the bottom of a cliff.

Oz whistled when she saw the concertinaed, twisted metal shell, convinced that anyone inside would not have survived the crash.

There was a photocopy of a suicide note.

A printed suicide note read, "I can't do it anymore."

Oz looked back at the pictures of Cassandra and Finn. *That doesn't fit. Where's the note to Finn?* Pages of the coroner's report were blank, his conclusion: suicide. She checked the date of the finding. Less than a month from the date of her disappearance. She flipped to the next page. It was the financial statement for the coroner, showing a large deposit shortly before the date the cause of death was set. Even so, the suicide ruling effectively stopped the investigation.

The witness statements from the staff at the house, however, told a story of a turbulent marriage and other women. Doctors' reports showed no previous evidence of mental illness. No treatment for depression. There was nothing to indicate a predilection toward suicide.

A cheating husband, combined with the payoff, looked ominous.

She looked through the rest of the pages. *How do you prove a murder with no body?* The money used to set up Sterling Enterprises had come from Cassandra. Her father was a leading defense attorney who had made himself a very wealthy man defending high profile people in very big cases, and had insisted on a prenuptial agreement when Cassandra had married Sterling. If she'd divorced him because of the adultery, she would have owned the company.

Oz tidied the papers into a neat pile and slid them back into the envelope. She rubbed her eyes, and knowing sleep wouldn't come easily, she decided a run might clear her head. The rhythmic pounding as her feet hit the asphalt helped to ease some of the anger welling inside her. She tried hard to banish the thoughts of William Sterling, but she couldn't shift the picture of Finn cradled in her mother's lap from her mind's eye. She pictured them on the swing, Finn's little legs trying to push them higher, her hands clapping with glee. She looked so happy and free, exactly how a little girl should. She tried to hold on to the fact that Finn had known happiness, and push away the thoughts of her growing up with the man who may have taken that from her. Her fingers twitched with the ache to pummel him. Her arms ached to wrap around Finn and wipe away the tears she must have cried, that she probably still cried when she was alone. The need to protect Finn grew stronger every day, and the more she saw of her, the more she learned about her, the more Oz wanted—needed—to know. She wondered how much Finn knew, or even suspected, and her heart ached all the more for the friend she was coming to care about far too much for her to ignore. In this way, Finn was far more dangerous to her than William Sterling ever would be.

CHAPTER FOURTEEN

Six nervous faces watched her as Oz demonstrated breathing through the regulator while they stood by the pool. She motioned for them to try themselves. Finn was pleased she was the first one to get the tank strapped to her back and the breathing piece in her mouth. The new wet suit and gear fit perfectly, and her scores in the classroom earlier had been perfect too. Oz had already seen her showing her buddy how to perform a proper buddy check on the side of the pool, and she was looking forward to showing Oz what she could do in the water as well. The rest of the group, four men and one other woman, were something of a mixed bag. One guy in particular, did very well in the classroom, but seemed to be all fingers and thumbs getting his gear together.

"Okay, everyone, put your masks on, then one by one you'll make a giant stride entry into the water. Everyone put two small puffs of air into your BCDs and get ready." She watched as each person did as she asked. "Nigel, you need to let some air out of your BCD. It's two small puffs. If your jacket is all puffed up like the Pillsbury Doughboy, you've got too much air in there and you're never going to be able to get under the water. Raise your second stage and let some of the air out." He stared at her blankly even as she held up the relevant pipe of her own. Finn tapped him on the shoulder and lifted up his second stage, wrapped her fingers around the button, and pressed. When he was completely empty, she pumped two small puffs into the jacket with his own fingers in place.

"Thanks, Finn. Okay, is everybody ready?"

Finn nodded and caught the rest of the class doing the same out of the corner of her eye.

"Remember, everyone, if you want to tell me you're good to go, that you are fine, or that everything is cool, I want the okay sign. So we'll try that one again. Is everybody ready?"

Finn signaled she was okay, and wished the butterflies in her stomach would settle down so she could enjoy the new experience.

"Okay, Steve, you're up first. Nice big stride and give me the okay when you're in and set." The group watched the man edge to the very lip of the pool before stretching his left leg out in front and almost hopping off the right into the water. "Not bad, Steve. But you don't need to jump into it. Literally just step off the side of the pool. Okay, next." One after the other, they entered the water until only Nigel and Finn were left. "Okay, Nigel, you're up. Nice big giant stride." He shuffled to the edge of pool and stood looking into the water, swinging his arms like he was trying to take off.

"Nigel, are you okay there?" Oz sounded concerned and was clearly getting ready to get out of the water. Finn gently touched his shoulder and smiled at him.

"Nigel, would you feel better if we did it together?"

He spat out his regulator. "Yes, please."

"You know you don't have to do this if you don't want to, right?"

"I want to do this. It was one of the things my wife always wanted us to do together."

"So does she already dive?"

"She died of cancer this summer. She made me promise to try and do this for her."

"Then this is really brave of you. I'm sure she's really proud of you. What I'm going to do is stand right next to you and hold your hand, okay?" When he didn't object, she took hold of his hand and smiled at him. "I need you to put your regulator back in, then use the other hand to hold your mask on just like Oz showed us before."

"Okay," he said as he put the mouthpiece back in.

"Once I've got my mouthpiece in, I'll swing our hands for the count. On three, we step in together. Let go of my hand as soon as we get in the water and let Oz know that you're doing fine. How does that sound to you, Nigel?" He gave her the okay sign straight away and placed his free hand over his mask. She quickly replaced her mouthpiece and her hand over her own mask. She looked him in the eye and nodded her head with the first swing of her hand; on the third swing, they both stepped perfectly into the water. He let go of her hand and gave the okay signal immediately. Finn did the same and tried to ignore the feeling of pride it gave her when Oz gave her a thumbs-up. Learning to dive was important, but lately, it felt even more important that Oz was happy with what she was doing.

Finn closed her eyes as they all began to descend at the deep end of the pool, fighting her natural urge to hold her breath and taking her first breath underwater. The taste of metal and rubber tainted each mouthful, but the sense of wonder as she opened her eyes and really processed where she was and what she was doing finally hit her. She wanted to laugh, but the regulator made it too awkward. She wanted to tell Oz what she was feeling, how amazing it felt. She located Oz and found her watching her, and Finn was sure she could see the smile in Oz's eyes too.

Finn concentrated as Oz started taking them through their drills. Clearing their masks. Removing the masks. Fin pivots. Maintaining the genie position. Getting used to the depth gauges and air gauges attached to the regulator and getting them all used to relaying information without words. Oz brought them all to the surface as she explained the emergency drill, signaling out of air, and accepting your buddy's octopus while making a controlled ascent to the surface they were going to go through at the deep end of the pool. Finn signaled Nigel to buddy with her, and they were the only pair to complete the drill perfectly the first time. So Oz made them do it again, just to check. Perfect the second time too. Finn swelled with pride. She could do this. And Oz could see she could do it.

By the end of the session, Finn was confident and competent in all the drills that Oz had shown her and asked her to do. Without warning, Oz swam to Finn and signaled low on air and asked for Finn's BCD and tank to swap and for Finn to return to the surface. Finn was startled but gave the okay signal. She mirrored Oz's movements, loosening and undoing her buckles and straps. Once she was holding the tank and BCD in her arms she moved closer to Oz and signaled for her regulator. They performed the swap quickly and seamlessly.

Her head broke the surface to a round of applause and Oz surfacing just behind her, grinning.

"Some of the guys still can't pull that off so smoothly. Well done." She turned around to face the rest of the students. "Well done, guys. You've all done really well. Tomorrow, we'll have another lesson in the classroom in the morning, then we'll be heading out into the ocean for our first open water dive. So if you all start heading out of the pool, Carlos and the other guys will give you a hand getting your kit off and show you how to clean it down for storage before you all go and get changed. Finn, Nigel, can I have a word with you both before you leave?" They both agreed before swimming to the steps and climbing out of the pool.

Finn stepped out of the changing room with her wet hair slicked back off her face to see Nigel talking to Oz and Clem. She took a seat by the pool to wait until Oz finished talking to Clem. Oz was still wearing her wet suit. The neoprene second skin hugged her backside as she walked around the edge of the pool, pointing to tanks and equipment that needed moving. Finn had never really thought of herself as a sexual person before, but all she wanted to do was run her hands across Oz's tight ass and feel the muscles ripple beneath her fingers.

"Finn, come and join us?" Finn was shocked out of her reverie and looked up to see Oz and Nigel both smiling at her. She could feel the heat rising over her face and hoped that no one else noticed, particularly Oz. "I was just checking that Nigel here felt okay about the session today. I was also going to keep you two as buddies tomorrow. I know earlier today I said that I like to switch pairs around, but I think you two worked really well together, so for the first dive tomorrow, I was going to keep you as a team. Nigel was pretty happy with that, but I wanted to make sure you were too." Finn could actually hear the pleading in Oz's voice. She knew none of the others in the group wanted to take the chance that his fears would overcome him again and that he would freeze in the open water.

"No problem. I think we made a pretty good team, Nigel. I'm sure your wife would be so proud of you."

"Thanks, Finn. I know I would've quit today if you hadn't helped me. You should think about being an instructor, you know." Oz bit back her laughter.

"I'll think about it. I've been wondering what career to go into."

"Well, I'll see you tomorrow, Finn." He was halfway to the door before he turned around. "Thanks again, Finn. Oh, night, Oz, see you tomorrow."

Oz was laughing as the door closed behind him.

"That's another one hopelessly in love with you, Supergirl."

"Don't be ridiculous."

"I'm not. It's all over his face. He's totally smitten. Ow, I told you I bruise easily. Don't whack me like that." She rubbed her shoulder gingerly. "Seriously, you did great today. Rudy reckons you're a natural, and Carlos is more in love with you."

"Will you stop, please, before I really have to hurt you?" Oz held up her hands in surrender and Finn laughed, liking the way Oz's eyes crinkled at the corners when she smiled. "So did I really do okay today?"

"You have to ask?"

Finn shrugged, uncomfortable with her own need for reassurance.

"You did great. You're a natural teacher and you have a great way with people. They trust you and have confidence in you. Nigel would have quit. I wouldn't have gotten him into the pool today because it never would have occurred to me to literally hold his hand. I would have expected him to panic when he hit the water and try to pull me down."

"If he did, I had a tank on my back and a regulator in my mouth. Half a dozen instructors were on hand to come to my rescue if I needed it, and there was no way you would let anything happen to me. Mrs. Richmond would never forgive you if you did. I was in good hands and I knew it. So was Nigel. He just doesn't realize yet that the good hands we were both in were yours, not mine. He did all right after that though."

Finn followed Oz to the seating area, trying not to stare at the gorgeous ass in front of her.

"Anyway, did you talk to Pete last night?" Oz asked.

"Yeah, he's going to help me move in to Mrs. Richmond's over the weekend, then stay at the hotel for another couple of weeks. My dad's already paid for it, so he might as well use it."

"Sounds like a good idea. Do you need any more help with the move?"

"Well, I don't have much stuff to move, but if you're any good with a screwdriver, I could certainly put you to good use. I hate putting together furniture."

"Just tell me when you want me."

Finn could feel her cheeks heating again and found it difficult to meet Oz's eyes. "Saturday morning. I told Emmy we'd get there about ten. Is that okay for you?"

"Absolutely. I can't wait."

CHAPTER FIFTEEN

William Sterling threw his tie over the chair and flipped open his cell phone.

"Yes?"

"Mr. Sterling. It's Jack."

"What can I do for you, Jack?"

"I'm just calling to let you know that the equipment has been attended to. It will be delivered on Monday. The installation, however, will take a week or so from that point. I've checked, and evidently, it's not possible to rush that part."

"Very good." Sterling smiled, pleased with his young apprentice's results. He showed promise and that he could be trusted with all aspects of the business.

"Sir, do you have any preference on how I resolve this situation?"

"How many people are there involved?"

"I have two children staying in the flat."

"How old?"

"Four and six."

"Have they seen your face?"

"No, sir."

"Take our dithering supplier out of the equation. I don't feel the need to permanently have the children taken care of. At that age, they'll be of no use to police or anyone else. Once the installation and production of the batch is completed, finish off our Mr. Machine and dump the children somewhere." While killing was necessary at times and enjoyable at others, there was no need to kill the supplier's children. They were just a means to an end. *Just like my own daughter. She brought me her research, and in trying to win my approval, she brought me the means to make the biggest deal of my life. How close are we to the end, Daniela?* He wondered if she would actually follow orders and marry the faggot, another test she had to pass to prove her worth to him. "Jack, I want an update on Daniela's whereabouts too."

"Yes, sir."

Sterling disconnected from Jack and dialed again. He walked to the drinks cabinet as he waited for the call to connect.

"Balor is almost ready for delivery."

"Excellent news, William. I wish for delivery in New York at the warehouse we have used before."

"Of course, Masood. Have you solidified your plans for distribution?"

"I have men working in the water purification plant. Do you have estimates of the efficacy of the bacteria yet?"

"Yes. The numbers are far higher than you wished for, Masood."

"That is excellent news, my friend."

"Are you ready to talk numbers?"

"Where do you wish to meet?"

"I'll send you the details." He disconnected the call, poured the brandy into his glass, and swallowed. His lips twisted into a smile as the liquid burned the back of his throat.

CHAPTER SIXTEEN

Finn tossed the last pair of shorts into her case before zipping it closed.

"Are you nearly ready?"

"Just about. Are you in a hurry to get rid of me?"

Pete assumed a look of mock innocence. "Me?"

"Yes."

"Okay, I do have a date tonight, but not till late. He's working till ten."

"The concierge?"

"Of course."

"Well, grab that suitcase then and we can go." She tossed her rucksack over her shoulder and followed Pete out the door and to the car. After loading the boot, Finn climbed into the driver's seat and waited for Pete to buckle up.

"So tell me more about this woman you're moving in with."

"I only have the bit of information Oz has given me, really. Her husband was the naval base commander until he retired ten years ago, and he passed away three years ago. From what I can gather, she's a nice old lady who's a bit lonely."

"And it was Oz who introduced you?"

"Yeah. She's an old family friend. It seems most of Oz's family are in the navy, and when her dad and uncle both served under Mrs. Richmond's husband, they all became pretty good friends."

"I still wish you'd have let me come with you when you went to see this place. What if she's some kind of axe murdering granny and you'll be found years from now under the floorboards?"

ANDREA BRAMHALL

"You do know how ridiculous you sound, don't you?"

"I do not!"

"Yes, you do. She's a perfectly nice old lady. She's having a birthday party tomorrow. Be nice or I won't invite you."

"Can I bring my concierge?"

"No! I don't even know her yet. I'm not unleashing you on her birthday party."

"Spoilsport."

She pulled into the drive outside Mrs. Richmond's house, and smiled as she waved from her porch swing. "Good morning. This is my friend Pete. I brought him along so we can use his muscles."

Pete stuck his hand out to Mrs. Richmond. "She didn't tell me I was slave labor though."

"Well, how about I promise to feed you in exchange for your hard work? A ton of boxes got delivered yesterday," Mrs. Richmond said.

"A ton? How much furniture did you order?" Pete asked.

"Not that much."

"Don't let her fool you. She went crazy in Walmart. I thought she'd never seen a store before." Oz crossed the lawn, grinning broadly. She had on black shorts and a black tank top, her hair covered with a black bandana, and she had a small black toolbox in her hand. She looked good, really good, and Finn found it difficult not to stare.

"I think you have a tendency to exaggerate." Finn returned the grin, unable to keep from staring down the long expanse of exposed leg as Oz climbed the steps to the porch.

"And you definitely have a tendency toward understatement. Hi, Pete, Mrs. R."

"Olivia, how many times do I have to tell you to call me Emmy?"

"At least a few more." She stooped over and kissed her cheek lightly. "Mr. Richmond would still tan my hide if he heard me calling you Emmy."

"Yes, well. All this standing around chitchatting isn't going to get that room sorted, is it? I've boxed up all of Malcolm's things, but the boxes need to be moved to the basement or to Goodwill." She led them off the porch and through the house. The room that had once been Malcolm's study had a half dozen boxes stacked in the middle of the room, neat black handwriting on each one. The shelves and walls were all bare, and the room felt a little cold and unlived in. Along another

• 90 •

wall were a dozen flat boxes that had shipping labels with bar codes on each end, and a queen-sized mattress.

"Well, the sooner we get started, the quicker you can get to your date, Pete."

Oz grabbed a box and grinned at him. "A date? Do tell."

"Not a lot to tell."

"It's the guy he abandoned me for the other day."

Pete and Finn both followed Oz lugging boxes of their own. "This is the waiter, right?"

Pete shook his head. "Concierge. With no tan lines."

"Oh, my. And where are you off to on your date?"

He dropped his box and started back for another. "Hopefully nowhere."

Finn and Oz laughed at his retreating back. They all worked steadily, and soon the room looked like a bedroom. They moved the existing desk under the window next to the bookshelves. The bed and chest of drawers were against the opposite wall. Finn was hanging the last of her clothes in the closet when Mrs. Richmond shouted at them all for lunch. After washing their hands, they found her setting plates of sandwiches on the table by the pool.

"Iced tea?" She waited for them all to sit before pouring glasses. "How are you all doing in there?"

"Just finished, Emmy." Finn took a long drink and watched Oz as she took a huge bite out of her sandwich before chasing mayonnaise off her lip with the tip of her tongue.

"That's wonderful." Emmy took her seat. "Now I haven't heard anything from that rabble of yours, Olivia. Are they coming tomorrow?"

Oz swallowed quickly, wiping her mouth with her napkin. "Yeah, I thought I told you, Uncle Charlie said they'd all be there."

"All of them?"

"Except Evan. He's still deployed in Afghanistan at the moment."

"Oh my. I think I might need to get more food for the barbecue."

"No, I'll tell my mom and Aunt Alex just to bring some stuff from their freezers. You know they will anyway."

Finn's curiosity was piqued. "Do you have a big family then?"

"I'm an only child, but Uncle Charlie has four boys."

Emmy snorted. "Two marines, a Navy SEAL, and a coast guard. They aren't boys. They are machines of mass destruction."

Pete's face lit up. "And they're all coming to this pool party tomorrow? Ow. What was that for?" He bent over and rubbed his shin where Finn had kicked him.

"You were drooling."

"I was not," Pete said.

Oz chuckled. "Yes, they'll be here. Except Evan."

"And is he a marine or a SEAL?"

"Evan is a marine and so is Will. Will's in the JAG corps though. Junior is the SEAL, and AJ is in the coast guard."

"And you were in the navy too?"

"Yes. I was a navy diver."

Finn watched as Oz's face switched from the animated, friendly countenance they had seen all morning, to the dark and shuttered visage that seemed so prevalent whenever Oz thought no one was watching her. Finn wondered what caused that look. What was the darkness that hid behind those beautiful eyes? How could someone so friendly remain so guarded at the same time? The contradictions in Oz were fascinating, and she wanted to unravel them, one by one. The scientist in her longed to uncover each little fact about her, but there was more to her curiosity and she knew it. She was fun and easy to talk to, she was kind and considerate, and she was hot.

An elbow to her ribs pulled her out of her reverie. "I'm sorry, what?" She saw Oz and Mrs. Richmond heading inside.

"Looks like I'm not the only one drooling."

"Get lost, Pete."

"Look, I get it; she's gorgeous and she seems really nice. I'm just looking out for you."

"I don't need a babysitter, Pete."

"Hey, I'm—"

Oz came back out and sat back down. "Everything okay?"

"Fine." Finn smiled and hoped her annoyance wasn't showing, but from the look of concern in Oz's eyes, she knew she was unsuccessful.

Pete excused himself to the toilet and Finn tried to relax again.

"Is something wrong?"

Finn opened her eyes and smiled a little. "Just Pete trying to wind me up. He's very good at it."

Oz grinned. "You don't seem too bad at it either."

"What? Winding myself up?"

"No, at holding up your end of the deal. Wait till you meet my cousins. They're constantly teasing everyone."

"And you're still close to them?"

"Yeah, mostly Junior and AJ. Will works in Washington a lot, and Evan's been on one deployment after another for the last five years. If he and Junior weren't identical twins, I'd have probably forgotten what he looks like."

"I doubt that. Something tells me you don't forget very much at all."

"Maybe." Oz shrugged noncommittally.

Finn saw the shadows flitter across Oz's face again and wished she knew what to avoid saying to keep Oz happy. Or better yet, she wanted to know how to erase those shadows when they came. She knew that every moment she spent with Oz only made her care more about her, but she knew Oz wouldn't be interested in her. Oz wanted fast women and plenty of them. She made no secret of it and no excuses for it. Finn told herself that being Oz's friend was a much more satisfying relationship to have with her. It certainly lasted longer and had much more meaning. *I can be friends. Friends is good. Like I told Pete, you can never have too many friends. Please let that be enough.*

CHAPTER SEVENTEEN

O z checked her reflection in the mirror and rubbed her fingers over the puckered scar on her belly that had long since healed. She could still feel the burning sting as the red-hot bullet ripped through her skin. The smell of seared flesh, cordite, and blood filled her nostrils again. Every move she made tore her flesh open a little more, and the pain threatened to render her unconscious.

Rudy was gripping his thigh, trying to stem the flow of blood. They needed to find cover and they needed to do it fast. She grabbed the back of his shirt and dragged him behind a bulkhead, spraying bullets behind her as she went. A simple repair mission on a cargo vessel turned deadly.

Enough! She shook her head viciously, trying to dislodge the memories and focus on the day ahead. She always enjoyed spending time with her family and Mrs. Richmond. She was inordinately fond of the meddling old woman. But that didn't account for her nerves today, or her impatience to get to Mrs. Richmond's and hang out for the day by the pool. It also didn't account for her indecision about whether to wear a one-piece swimsuit or a bikini. Finn was the reason for that, and she knew it.

She sighed before tossing a towel over her shoulder and heading for Mrs. Richmond's. Music filtered through the crisp summer air from the backyard, and she could already hear the party in full swing. Laughter and splashing water were accompanied by a small shriek as she assumed Finn had just been doused. She couldn't help but smile as she opened the gate and saw Junior shaking water out of his eyes while Finn was pointing at him, water dripping off her and Pete holding his sides as he laughed from his lounge chair.

"Junior!" Finn wiped her face and glared across the water at him.

"I see you've already met my wayward cousin."

Finn turned around and smiled through her dripping hair. "Yeah, he's a barrel of laughs."

"Hey, Ladyfish, you coming swimming?" Junior was dragging himself out of the pool and heading for the diving board.

"Yeah, in a while." She took Finn by the elbow and moved her away from the pool. "You might want to back up if you don't want to get wet again."

"I think it's too late to worry about that now, don't you?" She pointed down at her soaked shirt before she pulled her hair back into a ponytail. "He's a big kid."

"I know. Always has been. You wouldn't believe he was a SEAL, would you?"

"Well, maybe. He's got enough muscles."

"Don't tell him that; he'll get a big head."

"Too late." Neither of them had noticed Junior sneaking up on them until he grabbed Finn around the waist and jumped backward into the pool with her in his arms. Finn screamed until the water silenced her. By the time Oz reached the side of the pool, she was swimming for the side. Junior was floating on the water holding his crotch and turning red.

"It serves you right." Finn grabbed Oz's hand and allowed herself to be pulled out of the water.

"It was only a joke."

"Very funny."

Oz grabbed a towel. "You okay?"

"I'm fine. Not sure about him though. You didn't want to be an auntie did you?"

Oz laughed. "Not to worry. I've got three other cousins who can do the honors."

Finn pulled her shirt over her head and tugged off her shorts. Oz couldn't tear her eyes away. She'd seen Finn in all kinds of swimwear over the last week or so, but seeing her actually disrobe affected Oz in a way she hadn't expected. There was something more intimate about it, something more revealing than just seeing Finn appear in a bikini. She felt her cheeks flush, first in response to seeing Finn, then in embarrassment when Junior let out a long whistle. She wanted to drown him as Finn's cheeks turned bright red and she stared at the ground.

"I'm sorry about him."

"It's not your fault. Maybe I should go change."

"No, don't." She grabbed hold of Finn's arm. She didn't want her to leave, even for a few minutes. She just wanted to be near her and couldn't understand why she was so drawn to Finn. She had seen beautiful women before, in all manner of undress. Why did Finn affect her so much? Finn looked down at Oz's hand on her arm then met her eyes, her question clear. Oz let go of her arm and shrugged. She grappled for some kind of response. "He has to learn to behave like a human being some time."

"So I get to play guinea pig?"

"I was thinking more like a teacher."

Finn put a hand over her chest. "Oh my God, I'm so lucky."

"Sarcasm doesn't suit you."

"Sure it does." Pete came up next to her and wrapped an arm about Finn's waist. "It's the lowest form of wit, but wit nonetheless."

"Gee, thanks, sweetie."

Oz grinned. "Are you having a good time, Pete?"

"Oh, yes. Your cousins are certainly entertaining."

"Hey, Pete, are you coming in?" AJ shouted from the water.

"Excuse me, ladies." Pete took a run and executed a perfect cannonball, and Finn and Oz managed to jump back and avoid the spray.

"Boys." Finn shook her head before turning to look at Oz. "Are you okay?"

"Yeah. He didn't get me."

"That's not what I meant. You look a little…I don't know." She shrugged. "You don't seem yourself."

Oz blanched at the thought she was so easy to read. She forced a smile to her lips. "I'm just a little tired. I didn't sleep too well."

"I'm a good listener."

Oz debated telling her the truth. Talking to Finn didn't seem like a bad idea, and that bothered her almost as much as the memories had earlier. "I'll bear that in mind."

"Do you want a drink?"

Oz breathed a sigh of relief when Finn seemed willing to let it go. "Sure. I'll come with you."

"No, you stay here. I'll just be a minute." Oz watched Finn walk away, unable to take her eyes off her ass.

"She's certainly not ugly."

Oz grinned as her father wrapped his arm about her waist and her mother pulled her into a tight embrace.

"I never see you. Why haven't you been around?"

"Mom, I've been busy working."

"You've been doing more than just working, Olivia." Her mother pulled back and looked at her. "I can see it in your eyes, baby. You need to let those things go."

"Mom—"

"Don't Mom me. I know when you're hurting, Olivia. I can see it. It wasn't your fault. And you need to let go of it."

"I can't."

"Yes, you can."

Oz wanted to pull away from her mother and just walk away, to start running and not look back. She knew that none of them blamed her, but that only made it worse. The guilt she lived with day after day over the people she couldn't save and the lives she had taken, gnawed at her soul until all she wanted to do was keep on running.

She saw Finn coming back out of the house. She pulled away and accepted the drink Finn offered her. "Finn, this is my dad, Billy, and my mom, Ellie."

Finn held out her hand. "I'm very pleased to meet you both. Can I get you something to drink?"

"I'll get them." Her dad headed for the house.

"Olivia tells us you're here training to be a dive instructor."

"That's right."

"And do you like it?"

"I love it. Oz is a fantastic teacher. I'm very lucky to have her."

Oz couldn't stop herself from staring at Finn as she spoke, but she barely heard a word she said, she was so focused on the way her lips moved when she smiled. The soft rose color against the deepening tan and white teeth had her itching to lean forward and taste Finn's mouth with her own. The haphazard ponytail that she wanted to run her fingers through and the skin exposed by the skimpy bathing suit had her balling her fists at her sides to stop herself from reaching out and touching her.

She realized they were both looking at her, waiting for her response to something.

"I'm sorry, I must've spaced out. What were you saying?" Oz knew from the smile on her mother's face that she hadn't gotten away with her distraction and its true cause.

"Finn was saying how lucky she is to have you as her teacher." Her mother was grinning widely while Finn and Oz both shifted uncomfortably.

"I think I'll go and join Pete in the pool. It was lovely to meet you, Ellie."

They both watched as she disappeared beneath the water.

"She's lovely."

"Yes, she is."

"You like her?"

Oz nodded.

"You going to ask her out?"

"You know I don't date. Besides, I don't even know if she's gay."

"Oh, please. She looked at you the exact same way you were looking at her. And I thought you were going to eat her alive!"

"Mom!"

"What?"

"You can't say things like that to me."

"Why ever not?"

"Because you're my mom."

"Olivia, you are thirty-six years old and well past the blushing virgin, so don't even try and pull that with me."

Oz felt her cheeks flame as her mother shook her head and joined her Aunt Alex under the gazebo. Her mind was reeling playing over her mother's words. Was it true? Did Finn look at her like that? Was Finn attracted to her too? Did it matter? She knew Finn wasn't the kind of girl to fall into bed at the drop of a hat, but that was the only thing Oz knew how to do. She watched Finn playing in the pool with Pete, Junior, and AJ, laughing and smiling as they splashed and dunked each other, and she knew it mattered. The memories invaded again, and she knew she would never deserve a woman like Finn in her life. It was easier to believe there was no mutual attraction. No mutual attraction, no one gets hurt, no one gets disappointed. Especially her.

CHAPTER EIGHTEEN

William Sterling made his way across the hotel bar and sat in a dimly lit corner near the back. He ordered a whiskey and waited.

He quickly downed the drink and picked up the napkin under it, checking its message before he wiped his lips, then he balled it up and stuffed it in his pocket. He made his way to the lift, punched the button, and waited. He slid his hands into his trouser pockets and fiddled with the coins on the left hand side. Ordering them. Small to large. The smallest coins closest to his fingertips, then slowly, one by one, switching them round.

The pennies pressed against his palm. The angular profile of the fifty pence piece sat in the crease between his knuckles.

The lift arrived. He punched the button for the fifth floor. And waited, shifting the penny back to his fingertips, the fifty pence against his palm.

The doors slid open and he quickly walked to the room number written on the back of the napkin.

He knocked once and entered the room as the door was opened, spreading his arms before he was asked and waiting as the electronic wand was waved across his body.

"He is clean." The man-mountain moved away and a tall, thin Arabic man moved toward him, his arms spread wide.

"Thank you, Hakim. William. It is good to see you, my friend."

"Masood." They clasped wrists and wrapped each other in a stiff, one-armed embrace.

"Can I offer you a drink?"

"Thank you, Masood, but I will decline your generous offer. I have other matters I must attend this evening."

"Of course. Shall we?" He indicated the seats and they sat down.

"You have good news for me?"

"I do." Sterling opened his briefcase and pulled out a sheaf of papers. "My people have managed to create the toxic bacteria that we discussed. We have been calling it Balor, as you know. This information indicates its lethality and predictions for its effects in non fatal cases." He handed them to Masood, who looked at them briefly before passing them to another man.

"This is Dr. Shikhar. He will understand this information far better than I could possibly hope to."

"Of course." Sterling smiled.

"While we wait for him to verify the information, perhaps you would indulge me in some information."

"Of course."

"Tell me how this works?"

"Well, my scientist has managed to develop a technique to incorporate toxins into a relatively harmless bacterium."

"Can this be any toxin?"

"In theory, but we have been working with botulism as you requested."

"And what have your results shown?"

"As you know, using botulism as a weapon is limited, as the bacterium doesn't make the host contagious. By incorporating it into this harmless little stomach bug, I've managed to do just that."

"You have made botulism contagious?"

"Well, my scientists have."

"And it is effective?"

"Very."

"We are amongst friends here; please tell me a little more about this Balor bug you have developed."

"Our tests show that the numbers are extremely impressive. Infection rate in the non-vaccinated group is one hundred percent. Mortality rate in the untreated is over ninety percent, and those infected survivors are debilitated to the extent that constant care is required. Our estimate for contagion spread is dependent on the method and geographical location of initial dispersal, but even our most conservative estimates establish global distribution within a month."

"This is excellent news, my friend. Now tell me, William, how is your family? Your daughter, is she well?"

"Very, Masood. She is holidaying in America at the moment. She was instrumental in the development of the bacterium, and I have rewarded her with a holiday before she returns to announce her upcoming wedding and continue working on other projects for me."

"An exceptional young woman then?"

"Absolutely. I am very proud." William found it curious that the man was asking after his daughter and wondered why.

"As you should be. I understand she is very beautiful too. Brains and beauty. You are a lucky man, William."

The thinly veiled threat became clear, and William knew he couldn't leave it unchallenged. He didn't care if Masood did anything to Daniela for her sake. No, his pride alone could not withstand the slight. "As are you, my friend. You have many sons. I am sure that they will be exceptional too. Strong boys you can be proud of."

Masood inclined his glass in silent acknowledgment of the stalemate, and when the doctor returned and whispered into Masood's ear, he watched William as he listened.

"Excellent, William. I am assured that this is everything you have promised. Now we must talk numbers." He reached into the folds of his robe and withdrew a sheet of paper, then handed it to Sterling. William unfolded the page and scanned the figure.

"I have invested significant resources on this product, Masood, as I am sure you can appreciate. As a businessman, I appreciate that you must try to achieve the best deal possible, and so must I. This is not adequate recompense for my investment." He placed the paper on the small table next to his chair.

"William, I would have been insulted had you accepted the number on that page." He smiled, a plastic smile that barely twitched the corners of his mouth.

"Double it."

"That would be unacceptable for me. Perhaps we can meet in the middle, as you Brits say."

"That would be acceptable. Delivery will be to the New York address you gave me earlier. I will contact you with the exact date in due course."

He stood, shook Masood's hand, and left. Smiling, he fiddled with the change in his pocket.

CHAPTER NINETEEN

"What time is your flight?" Finn dropped an armful of clothes next to Pete's suitcase.

"Not until ten. If we leave for the airport at six, we should be fine and miss the worst of the traffic."

"Okay." She folded a pair of shorts and stuffed them into his case. "I can't believe it's been two weeks since I left you in this room. It feels like it was just yesterday that we got here."

"I know, three weeks and the time has just flown!" He wrapped his arms around her and pulled her in for a hug.

"Are you all packed?"

"Nearly, I just need to finish in the bathroom. I can't forget to steal stuff. The concierge will look down on me if I don't."

She laughed sadly at him. "Who told you that?"

"The concierge. He was the guy helping out behind the bar on the first day we were here."

"Ahh, the waiter with the tan."

"And no bikini lines."

"Really?"

Pete nodded emphatically.

"You dog!"

"Woof." He chuckled genuinely this time as she pushed him toward the bathroom. "So the diving's going well?"

"Yeah. I'm loving it. It seems pretty natural too."

"And Oz? You're still getting on okay with her?"

"Yeah, fine. Really good actually. She's a good teacher, and so far I really enjoy working with her. Plus, she'll do almost anything I want if I let her drive my car. Why are you asking?"

"Just checking you're still okay with everything. When we were helping you move in with Mrs. Richmond, I thought I picked up a few vibes between you two."

"Pete, stop. She's my friend and my teacher. That's it. We get on well; that's all. I thought you liked her?"

"I did. I do. I mean, she's great fun to be around. It's just that she's the kind of girl you have a lot of fun with. The kind of girl you climb out of the window to go and see. You're the kind of girl you take home to meet Mum and Dad. Do you know what I mean?"

"She's been around the block once or twice, while I'm all sweet and respectable."

"Exactly. She isn't the kind of person you should be relying on."

"How would you describe yourself, Pete? Take home to Mum and Dad or climb out the window for?"

"I'm definitely a climb out the—" Realizing what she was implying, he sighed and stopped talking.

"I can look after myself. I might be innocent, but I'm not naïve. She has been friendly, supportive, and willing to be my friend. What's wrong with that?"

"Nothing. I just worry about you."

She wrapped her arms around him. "I know. Thank you for caring enough to worry, but you know we have to let go now, don't you?"

He squeezed her harder. "I know. I don't have to like it though. I feel like I'm leaving part of myself here."

"You are. Definitely. The best part of yourself." She felt him chuckling against her. "But I am too. We'd make each other miserable if we tried to make a life together. Turkey basting aside, we'd start to resent having to keep so much of our lives a secret. We'd end up hating each other."

"I could never hate you."

"You don't know that."

"Yes, I do. And so do you."

"Pete, I love you, and I want to keep it that way. You've been my best friend for as long as I can remember, and I really don't want to lose you. You're the only person I know for sure ever loved me. I need to keep that in my heart. I don't ever want you to hate me." The tears welled in her throat making it difficult for her to speak. "I couldn't stand for you to hate me."

"So you push me away instead."

"Pete, you agreed with me that this was the best way." She grabbed his hand. "Has anything changed? Have you suddenly decided that the concierge was just a bit of fun and that you want to be with me for the rest of your life? Would I make you happy? Satisfied? Marriage is about more than sex, I know, but you can't tell me you'd be happy watching porn and jerking off for the rest of your life!"

"Finn!"

"Well, you know my dad would insist on a prenup, so what do you think would happen?"

"I know. But you don't need to be so crude." He lifted his hands to her face and wiped away the tears that slipped slowly down her cheeks.

Finn snorted. "Since when did you become a prude? You're the one who told me what jerking off was!"

"Yes, but we know I'm a slut with a dirty mouth. You, however…"

"Yeah, I know. Sweet and innocent." She patted his back and started to move away. "I think I might have to do something about this reputation of mine. If diving doesn't work out, maybe I should be a streetwalker." She stuck her hand on her hip and cocked it to one side taking on the exaggerated gait straight out of *Pretty Woman*, desperate to take her mind off the sense of loss already invading her heart. "What do you think? I'll get some high-heeled boots and strut my stuff."

"You in heels? You'd break your neck before you got to the first car, baby."

She straightened up. "Gee, thanks. You're just jealous."

"Of what?"

"I don't know. I just thought I'd say it and see what came to mind."

"Nutter."

"I know."

"So should we go and grab something to eat before we go to the airport?"

"Sure, what do you fancy? Besides the concierge?"

Pete stuck his tongue out at her. "Spoilsport. Do you feel like Italian?"

"Yup, I can go for a pizza." She hoisted Pete's rucksack onto her shoulder as he lifted the towing handle on his case. She grabbed the key card as they got to the door, and they waited in silence for the lift. Memories of their shared past bombarded her during the short ride to the pizzeria, only the sound of the engine and the occasional horn filling the silence.

They made short work of ordering pizzas and Cokes when they got into the restaurant, and Finn smirked at Pete as he watched the waiter walk away.

"How's the stitching?"

"Huh?"

"On his bum? You seemed to be examining the stitching very closely." She handed him a napkin. "Just wipe your chin."

"Cheeky mare."

"Yeah, yeah. So tell me the plan for when you land back?"

"Let's see. Night flight back home; tomorrow I'll be sleeping. I have a meeting set up for Monday with John Pritchard. He's setting up that unit I was telling you about to run through financial crimes and needs an IT expert." She tried to ignore the way he avoided her eyes whenever he talked about Pritchard and the new job. She knew there was more to his story than he was telling her, but she couldn't put her finger on it.

"Hacker?"

"To assist him with software development and stuff like that. It's all pretty hush-hush so it shouldn't get back to your dad until it's a done deal."

"Sounds exciting."

"Yeah, it's more what I thought I'd be doing. Using my cyber skills to catch the bad guys, not make them richer." He realized too late what he had said. "Sorry, Finn."

"So you see yourself as some sort of computer Robin Hood?"

"Yep, always did like those men in tights."

"Pete, tell me the truth. What's going on with this Pritchard guy? Every time you talk about him, you're all vague and I know you're hiding something. Please just tell me what it is."

Pete twisted his napkin around his fingers. "I'm not sure it's a good idea."

"What are you talking about?"

"John Pritchard works for MI6."

"Wow. You're going to be a spy?" Finn grinned and took a sip of her drink.

"I guess."

"Didn't you say he approached you?"

"Yes."

"I didn't realize your reputation was that good."

"It's not. He approached me because I have inside knowledge of one of their investigations."

"Pete, please don't tell me you've been doing anything illegal."

"Not knowingly. I got involved with something, and before I knew what was going on, I was too far in."

"I don't understand. You're talking in riddles."

"He's investigating Sterling Enterprises."

"Don't be ridiculous."

"I'm serious."

"Why are they investigating my dad's company? What do they think is going on there? What do you think is going on there?"

"I know there's a lot going on."

"Don't be so obtuse. Just spit it out. What do they think is going on in my dad's company? I mean that thing is his life, how they can think something is going on under his nose—" The realization hit her like a sledgehammer. She gasped and covered her mouth, trying to hold the words back.

"Finn, I'm sorry."

"Why didn't you tell me?"

"I didn't know anything for certain for a long time. I just had suspicions. Heard rumors. That kind of thing. I couldn't tell you those kinds of thing. He's still your dad, whatever kind of bastard he is."

"It's not suspicion or rumor now, is it?"

"No."

"So tell me. I think I deserve to know. He is my father after all."

"Finn—"

"Tell me!" Her heart thundered in her chest as she tried to calm her breathing. "Please, Pete, tell me what you know."

"I know that Sterling Enterprises is laundering money. Huge amounts of money."

"From what?"

"That I don't know. I swear."

"Carry on."

"There has to be more to it, because MI6 wouldn't be investigating if it was just money laundering, but I swear I don't know anything else."

"So why do they want you, if you don't know anything?"

"I designed the company's computer systems. I have files of evidence proving the money laundering, and I said I would testify that your dad knows this is happening."

"You're sure he knows?"

"Yes. I found e-mails from him to Jack about it. I'll give all this to Pritchard when I meet him on Monday."

"Then what? Are they going to arrest my dad?" The thought crossed her mind that it would ensure that he left her alone, and that with him out of the picture maybe she could return to her work, to finish her research with the E. coli bacteria protocols. She didn't find the thought appealing. She knew she would miss Florida and the diving too much already. More than that, she knew she would miss Oz, and she didn't want to lose the fledgling connection she could feel developing between them. The idea of her dad actually doing something illegal didn't surprise her as much as she thought it should, nor did the prospect of him going to prison upset her. Her only concerns were the unanswered questions, which suddenly seemed endless.

"I don't know. It depends if they can make a case, I suppose. Listen, I didn't want this to be our last face-to-face conversation for I don't even know how long. I'm sorry, Finn."

She shrugged. "I wish you'd told me sooner."

"I wasn't supposed to tell you at all."

"Why?"

"Official secrets act. I had to sign a disclaimer before we left the UK."

"Wow. So telling me was treason."

"Great, now I feel better."

She laughed and held up her little finger. "I won't tell. Pinkie swear." She wiggled her finger.

"Finn, we aren't kids anymore."

"I know."

He laughed and hooked his little finger with hers. "Okay, now what?"

"Don't tell me you don't remember?"

"I'm not singing that stupid song. No way."

"Then it's not binding."

"I don't care."

They finished their meal, paid, and left. Finn caught a flash of light out of the corner of her eye as they settled back into the car and headed for the airport. Almost certain that it was a camera flash, she looked around, but couldn't find its source, so she pushed it to the back of her head. *I'm getting paranoid now.*

CHAPTER TWENTY

H ey, are you okay?"
Finn was staring out across the ocean, hugging her coffee cup, the brew long cold and unnoticed. Oz's voice broke her reverie, and she looked up with a wan smile.

"I'll be fine."

"I know you will. But that wasn't what I asked. Did Pete get to the airport okay?"

Finn wiped her hands across her face as the tears welled in her eyes, and she found herself unable to speak.

"What time is he due to land?"

"He should be landing any time now. I was going to give him a call tonight, if he hasn't already beaten me to it."

"Well, in the meantime do you want something to take your mind off him?"

"Definitely. What do you have planned?"

"Well, you passed your rescue diver test with flying colors yesterday so I thought we'd move on with logging your dives for your Divemaster certification. We've got plenty of time today. No reason why we can't get three dives taken care of. There's a boat going out with some tourists in about thirty minutes. Can you be ready?"

"My gear's all boxed. I just need to grab my wet suit."

"Perfect. I'll get Carlos to put the tanks on the boat for us, and I'll see you there in a few minutes."

Finn watched her go, grateful that Oz had found the perfect way to take her mind off things. Not only was she reeling from Pete's departure, but the discovery of her father's nefarious activities and the subsequent interest of MI6 left her with more questions than answers. Why MI6? They wouldn't be investigating simple cases of money laundering unless there were international or terrorist connections. Why hadn't Pete trusted her with his suspicions in the first place? She felt cold inside and tried to push the troubling thoughts away, knowing there was nothing she could do about the situation. She tried to focus on the diving ahead of her and the time she'd be spending with Oz. She felt the chill in her bones begin to thaw as she pictured Oz in her wet suit with the top half rolled down to her waist, just high enough to cover the scar on her belly most of the time. Every glimpse of it piqued Finn's curiosity, and she wanted to ask her about it but found her courage failing every time. So she focused again on the image of the strong, tanned shoulders covered with only the thin straps of the bikini top she always wore underneath. She found herself hoping for the aqua blue top today, loving the way it made Oz's eyes stand out. She hurried to grab her gear and flipped through her own swimwear, mentally casting aside one after the other until she spotted her dark green bikini and hurried to the changing room. Oz had said that green brought out her eyes. She thought about her conversation with Pete. The truth, even if she didn't admit it to him, was that she had a major crush on Oz. She made her feel good, she made her laugh, and more importantly, for the first time in her life, she felt sexy. Oz made her feel like the new woman she wanted to be, and she was going to keep doing whatever it was that made Oz look at her like a woman.

The more time they spent together, the more she liked Oz as a person. She had told Pete Oz was a good friend, and it was true. The more she watched her interact with the crew and customers alike, the more fascinated she became with the woman behind the snorkel. She held the green bikini top to her chest and grinned before rushing to finish getting ready.

Twenty minutes later, Finn passed her crate to Carlos and stepped aboard the dive boat.

"Hey, Finn, are you going out with Oz today?"

"Yup. Where are we off to?"

"Key Largo. She didn't tell you yet?"

"Nope. Should I be worried?"

"Well, it's a beautiful spot. She asked me to put three tanks each on the boat for you so she must have a good plan. Clem's taking out a group of six, and Mac's got a group of five. Different levels in each group, so Oz will probably want you to listen in to the dive briefings of both before she does the briefing for you."

"Does that mean you are our captain today?"

"No, my dad is the captain. I get to run around doing everything he tells me to do."

"Carlos, stop chatting up the pretty girls and get the rest of the gear on the boat! We don't have all the day to be playing Don Juan, you know." Oz joined them, smiling.

A furious blush colored Carlos's cheeks. He turned quickly and almost tripped over the box he had put down for Finn, causing his blush to deepen further.

"I told you. He's smitten." Oz was grinning at her from the dock, her hair glowing against the shining sun. It was easy to see her eyes sparkling with mischief, even covered by the dark glasses. She wore shorts over her bathing suit and had a backpack slung over her shoulder, one arm securing her dive crate to her hip. Finn felt her pulse speed up as she stood looking at her. She wanted to reach out and run her fingers through her hair, stroke her fingers down her cheek, and feel the soft, smooth skin for herself. She shook her head in an attempt to clear her thoughts.

"Stop teasing and pass your crate over."

Oz handed the crate over and stepped aboard.

"So tell me about today's dives."

"We're going to do a deep dive and a couple of wreck dives. We're going to dive on the Spiegel Grove. We'll be doing all three dives on it and start off with the deep one first. That means we're going in and straight down to ninety feet. That's thirty meters in English."

Finn smiled sweetly at her. "I can do the sums, thanks, Oz."

Finn watched as Carlos cast off the boat and then she headed to the top deck where Mac was giving his briefing. He nodded to Finn as she sat at the back of the group and listened intently.

"The Spiegel Grove was a five hundred and ten foot long naval vessel that was eighty-four feet wide and could carry more than three hundred combat troops, twenty-one landing craft, and eight helicopters at any one time. It lies between fifty and a hundred and thirty feet deep. It was scuttled in two thousand and two to create an artificial reef. This wreck is so big that you could easily dive it twenty times and still see something different every time."

He held up a picture of the wreck. "This is how the wreck lies currently. We're going to descend and stay on the shore side of the vessel. We get better protection from the strong currents there, making dives easier and therefore much more enjoyable. We'll be down about forty minutes, depending on air usage, and we'll stay around sixty feet. We'll have a three minute safety stop at fifteen feet as we ascend. Now, there are sections we can swim through. Everyone here has their advanced dive certifications, so if you want to, we can go on the swim-through. Does anyone feel uncomfortable going inside the wreck? Nope. Cool. Okay, we'll be going onto the bridge. The doors are missing so you can't get stuck behind closed doors or anything. This will be a drift dive due to the strong currents. Does anyone have any problems with any of that?"

Clem tapped Finn on the shoulder and motioned her to follow him. "I'm going to start my briefing now, if you want to come and listen."

"Thanks." She followed him downstairs.

"Okay, guys, if you'll all gather around, I'm going to start the dive briefing." The group congregated quickly and settled into their seats.

Finn listened and learned a bit more about the wreck itself, but not much more about instruction. The styles were different, but the information was virtually the same.

"That's it, really. If we have to come up, we'll do it as a group, take care of whatever the problem is, and then decide on the course of action from there. Does anyone have any questions?"

Finn set off to find Oz when the talk ended.

"So tell me what you know about the wreck," Oz said, sitting with her back to the sun, her bathing suit showing off her tanned, toned arms. Finn took a breath to steady herself.

"It's underwater." Finn grinned cheekily as Oz laughed loudly.

"Can you tell me how deep?"

Finn fed back the information from the other dive instructors almost word for word. "And since they said their dives are drift dives, I'm guessing ours is too. How'd I do?"

"Not bad. A little short on details, but the main points are definitely there. Let's see if you can still tell me when we come back up." She made the T sign with her hand "What's this?"

"One hundred bar." She made a fist herself. "Fifty. And each finger is ten bar. Always tell you the number lower if I'm in between and let you know when I get to one hundred bar so you can plan ahead."

"I'll make a diver of you yet. So we'll go in and drop to what depth?"

"Ninety feet."

"Then we'll just drift along nice and steady. We won't be going in the wreck on this dive. We'll save that for next time. Just follow me and keep breathing. Oh, and here, put this on your BCD." Oz tossed her a coin-like medal.

"What is it?"

"It's your wreck medallion. All divers who go on the wrecks out here have to have one to show they're allowed to dive the wrecks. You can get annual medallions or lifetime ones. I got you an annual one. It covers this wreck and two others that you'll be diving pretty regularly. We'll be down a shorter length of time than the others."

"Because we're going deeper so our air will run out faster."

"Exactly. But I'm not going to set a limit on the dive. I want to see how long you get at depth, then we can gauge what work we need to do to maximize your dive times."

"Cool."

They got their gear ready and went through their buddy checks. The boat came to a stop and Mac led his group in first. When they had descended, Clem led his group below the surface of the water and Oz stepped off the back of the boat. Finn watched the waves tossing the small dive boat, planted a hand over her mask and regulator, crossed the other over her body, and stepped off the boat. She signaled her okay to Oz and pointed her thumb down. Foot by foot, they descended into the blue-green depths of the ocean, and at one point she pinched her nose to help equalize the pressure in her ears. Oz asked if she was okay, and she signaled that she was fine.

A shadow appeared slowly below them, the coral-covered hull rising out of the depths. A shoal of sergeant majors with their yellow and black stripes swarmed in front of her, dancing one way, then shifting to the other as the current flowed around the ship.

So beautiful. Finn slid into an aerodynamic swimming position and maintained the position naturally, Oz occasionally pointing to interesting fish or plants.

A parrot fish was pecking at the coral attached to the hull, and Finn swam slowly around it, mesmerized by the vivid greens and pinks against the blue water and buff-colored coral. Oz was shining her flashlight into a crevice ahead of her. She swam over and balked at the sight of a moray eel. Its fearsome prehistoric features splayed as it bared its teeth, its warning to any who would invade his territory. They floated along watching angelfish with blue and yellow stripes, squirrelfish, with their distinctive red-orange bodies and thin white stripes weaving in and out of the coral formations, along with tangs, groupers, snapper fish, and even a few porcupine fish. As they neared the end of the dive site, a turtle raised its head and swam out of the porthole just ahead of them. It seemed almost curious as it swam toward them before dropping down, only to reappear behind them and pass them easily, before disappearing into the vast blue ocean. Finn looked at Oz, wide-eyed with amazement. She made a general gesture with her hands in an attempt to signal her amazement and nodded when Oz threw her an okay sign.

She found her attention drifting to her left, watching the great blue abyss for shadows that could become creatures she had only dreamed of seeing in this environment before. The enormity of the space beside her shocked her for a moment, the true vastness of the ocean hitting her all at once. A small part of her had been worried she might feel some sense of fear when she was down here, but all she felt was the calm Oz had told her about. The pure and simple wonder of being surrounded by the power and magnitude of the ocean and all its inhabitants, from the smallest fish to the largest mammal and everything in between. It was so easy for her, floating along beside Oz. It felt so natural it was hard for her to believe that this was not the world to which she belonged.

Finn saw Oz check her gauge and noticed that she had just hit one hundred bar so she signaled Finn to check hers. She signaled back straight away with a T sign and two digits. Oz shook her head and signaled again. Finn repeated the sign. Oz reached for Finn's wrist and looked at the air gauge herself. She pointed to her own chest and gave the T sign for one hundred bar and the signal that they would be starting their ascent to the surface. At fifteen feet, they held their position for the required three minute safety stop and watched as a shoal of barracuda eyed them warily. They broke the surface a few minutes later and located the dive boat about twenty feet away. A short surface swim and

Carlos's help had them on deck in no time. He lifted the tank as Finn unstrapped her BCD and he placed it in the rack, reaching Oz just in time to help her rack the tank.

"Wow. That turtle was incredible. And the colors in that parrot fish? Oh my God. Stunning."

"Finn, I'm sorry."

Finn frowned at her. "What for?"

"Making you repeat yourself over the air thing. I can't believe how light on air you are. I've never, and I do mean never, dived with anyone who came up with more air than me at the end of the dive. I thought it must be a mistake. I'm sorry."

"Oh. It's okay. I kinda like surprising you. So was that okay?"

"No problems at all. We need to do a surface interval now before doing our next dive. What's a safe time limit before we go down again?"

Finn thought for a moment. "Recommended after a ninety-foot dive would be forty-five minutes to an hour. The longer the better. I could use a drink, though." She grinned at Carlos when he handed her a bottle of water. "You're a mind reader."

"Not really. Everyone else wanted drinks when they came up too."

Oz waited until Carlos wandered away. "So what did you think?"

"It was amazing. I wish I'd had my camera with me."

"You'll be here plenty more times with your camera. Juanita will be here tomorrow and you can talk to her about it all then."

"Oz, thank you so much. I'm enjoying this more than I ever thought I would."

"You're welcome. Feel like Chinese food tonight?"

"Sure, I'll see if Emmy wants anything when we get back to shore."

"I was thinking that you might want to come over to my place? I can pick up takeout when I leave here and then you can come over when you're ready."

Finn's excitement grew at the prospect of being invited into Oz's home for the first time, and she tried hard to control her reaction and not scare Oz into retracting the invite. Something told her that this was a big deal for Oz, but she couldn't keep from smiling. "That sounds perfect. Gives me time to jump in the shower and let Emmy know where I'll be."

"Anything you don't like?"

"Not a huge fan of Chinese soup, but I do like duck."

"Duck, got it."

"And crispy wontons. I love those."

"Duck and wontons, no problem. You might want to write up your dive log while we're waiting." Finn grabbed her backpack and fished out her log book. Oz smiled at her before going to talk to the other divers, and Finn felt it to her toes. Dinner with Oz. The perfect end to a perfect day.

CHAPTER TWENTY-ONE

Sterling grabbed the dressing gown before he strode angrily from his bedroom and down the stairs.

"This had better be fucking good, Jack."

"Sir, I'm so sorry to wake you. But I really thought you would want to know about this as soon as—"

"Spit it out, you fucking idiot."

"Sir, Peter Green is on a plane back to London. I believe he is meeting with Pritchard from MI6 on Monday."

Sterling stood stock-still and stared at him. "How reliable is your source?"

"Very."

"How close is our Mr. Green?"

"Initial approach, sir. I believe that he has yet to give them anything detrimental to you or any of your dealings. We've got the information in time."

"When they land—"

"Sir, your daughter's not with him."

"What?"

"He's returning alone. Daniela is still in Florida."

"Still at the hotel?"

"I believe so, sir."

Sterling nodded. "Tail him when he lands. If he shits, I want to know about it. I'll visit him myself."

"Very good, sir." Jack started to make his way out of the room.

"And, Jack? Call our friends in America. I'm concerned about my daughter. I thought they were looking out for her at all times."

"Yes, sir."

He poured himself a drink and sat heavily in his chair looking around the room, his eyes landing on the picture of his wife and daughter. The decorator had placed it on the bookshelf more than ten years ago. It was expected, so he left it there. He finished his drink and slammed the glass on the desk before crossing the room and picking up the picture. He studied the faces looking back at him. Studied the way the light played in their eyes as they smiled.

He stared into his wife's eyes and wondered if she'd been planning her escape even then.

He didn't care that she was gone. It was what he intended in the long run anyway. It was the fact that *she* decided when she was going. How she was going. *The bitch could've left me a fucking body to make my life a bit easier, torch the car rather than push it off a fucking cliff.* He despised having to spend the money to pay off the coroner to get the case closed and the estate finalized, but there was no way he was going to wait seven years with all the money tied up. No body. No money. He still couldn't believe that she had the audacity to fake her own death. *Fucking bitch, I will find you. I don't care how long it takes; I will find you. Then I will enjoy making you suffer.* He stroked a finger along the glass covering her face, then threw it against the wall, smiling as the glass shattered and fell to the floor. He crossed the room and poured himself another drink, swallowing it down in one gulp before picking up the phone.

CHAPTER TWENTY-TWO

F inn showered and changed quickly, wanting only to be with Oz. She thought back to her reaction when she saw Oz on the dock earlier that day. The way her heart had jumped in her chest and her breathing had quickened and she knew there was only one explanation for it. *Innocent, not stupid. I want her.* She found herself thinking back over the conversations they'd had. The way Oz acted around her, the flirty little comments, the compliments, the rambling. *Does she want me too?* She checked her reflection in the mirror, quickly applying a new coat of lipstick. *Do I want her to want me too? Or do I just want the fantasy? She's made no secret of her past, or her reputation. Do I want to be another notch on her bedpost?* She ran her fingers through her hair. *If that was what she wanted, she would have tried something by now. Wouldn't she?* She flipped off the bathroom light. *She said that she thinks I'm beautiful. Was she just being kind?* She laughed to herself as she closed the door to her room behind her. *I'm driving myself crazy with this. She's just being a good friend. Pete told me I was beautiful too. He didn't want to sleep with me either.*

"Emmy, I'm going out now."

"Okay. Are you off somewhere nice, dear?"

"I'm just going round to Oz's. She's trying to cheer me up, what with Pete leaving and all."

"That's nice of her. See you in the morning."

"Bye." She almost ran the short distance to Oz's house and took a deep breath before she knocked. *This isn't a date, no matter how much I might want it to be.*

❖

Oz pulled open the door and grinned as Finn held out a bottle of wine.

"I was taught to always bring something when you visit for the first time."

"That's really sweet. Thank you." Oz took the bottle noting the label, a 2010 Selbach-Oster Anrecht Riesling. "I'm afraid I don't know very much about wine."

Finn shifted uncomfortably, regretting her decision to bring the wine. "It works really well with Chinese food."

"Then it should be perfect, and you can educate me on the finer things in life. Come on in, but you have to promise to be nice. I haven't had a house guest before."

"Are you serious?"

Oz shrugged sheepishly.

"How can that be possible? I thought you said you lived here for years?"

"Yeah, about four years. Since I got out of the navy."

"So why no house guests?"

"This is my personal space. It's where I escape from everything out there."

"Oz, I don't want to invade your space. We can go and eat at Emmy's."

"No, you're not invading. I invited you. I want to show you. Please. Follow me." Oz led her down a spacious hallway into an open plan living and kitchen area. Swaths of white muslin draped the floor to ceiling windows and doors along the back of the house. Brown leather overstuffed sofas called invitingly from their position in front of a wall mounted flat screen TV. Glass shelves holding slender glass vases with a single flowering orchid in each adorned the walls seemingly haphazardly until you stood back and looked at them as a whole, and they became the branches of a tree.

"Did you design this yourself?"

Oz shrugged, embarrassed and desperately hoping Finn liked her design and wouldn't find her lacking. "Yeah. It seemed like a good idea at the time."

"This is so beautiful. It looks like an uber modern tree with these delicate flowers tracing each branch. It's amazing."

"You can see it?"

"Of course."

"I thought it would just be me."

"It's not just you. It is amazingly beautiful, and I can't wait to see anything else you want to show me." Her smile was so genuine and heartfelt that Oz found herself grinning as she tugged her into the kitchen.

"Not only did I design it, I did the work too. When I bought this place, an old lady had lived here for about thirty years. She'd been struggling to keep it up, and it was really dated. So I started ripping out walls and opening up the space. I love nature and outside stuff, but I wanted to make it a bit different. Hence the glass branches and orchid leaves. I wanted the kitchen to flow from it but be different again. So this is what I came up with. I like it."

"Your home is beautiful. I hope I can live somewhere as gorgeous as this eventually. I love what you've done here too. The work surface looks like water. The blue is so intense it looks like the ocean. That's what you wanted wasn't it?"

"Yeah, it was."

"Didn't you say you did all the work yourself too?"

"Yes."

"And you tried to tell me you weren't butch. You're such a fibber, Oz."

"Hey, be nice or I won't feed you."

Finn mimed zipping her lips closed.

"Are you ready to eat?"

"Hell, yeah, I'm starving."

Oz headed straight for the sofa but dropped in front of it letting her back rest against the seat. She started pulling cartons from the bags. "We've got crispy wontons. Duck in plum sauce."

"My favorite."

"Sweet and sour chicken, crispy chili beef, fried rice, soft noodles, prawn crackers, and fortune cookies."

Finn followed and sat next to her, accepting the glass of wine Oz handed to her as she did. Oz handed her a pair of chopsticks and raised her beer toward her in salute. "Welcome to my humble home, Finn." Oz clinked their glasses together, her stomach flipping at Finn's shy smile.

"It's gorgeous."

"Thanks. I haven't been sleeping very well, so I thought I might as well do something useful and managed to get the kitchen finished quicker than I thought I would."

"Why couldn't you sleep?" Finn said around a mouthful of rice.

"Worrying about you."

"Me. Why?" Finn frowned.

Because I read the file on your father and I think he killed your mother. Because I'm scared that you've bitten off more than you can chew, but I admire you even more because of it. Because I really want to be able to protect you, and I don't really understand why. Oz shrugged, and decided on the easier path. "Since Pete left, I guess I was a bit worried that you'd be upset and stuff."

"I was, and I cried myself to sleep after I took him to the airport." She pulled some rice from the carton before quickly transporting it to her mouth. "You don't need to worry about me."

"You can't help worrying about your friends, Finn. It's the natural order of things." *And I really can't seem to stop.* "I've got movies, if you want something mindless to distract you?"

"Sure, what do you have?"

"Well, I don't know what you like, but my collection is extensive. I'm pretty sure I could scare up something in every genre." She pulled open a cabinet and flipped through a few before she held up one of the plastic cases. "*Avatar* for the sci-fi action genre." Then a second case. "*Blind Side* for the Sandra Bullock genre." She raised one eyebrow as she wiggled the case before grabbing another. "*Harry Potter* for the English genre."

"Do you have any real genres in there or are they all like this?" Finn was grinning at the look of mock outrage on Oz's face.

"Madame, I don't know what you are talking about, but I think I take offense. May I continue?"

"Please, do."

"Well, thank you. Now, where was I?" She rummaged around the bag again and grabbed another case. "Oh yes, here we go. *Salt* for the Angelina genre. *Knight and Day* for the Cameron Diaz genre." She dropped them both back into the bag and spoke while still looking inside. "And finally, we have *Shrek* for the funnies genre."

"You have interesting genres for films; that's for sure. Is there by any chance a little fishing involved here?"

Oz feigned indignation. "I don't know what you mean."

"Of course you don't." Finn flipped through the cases and selected one. She crawled across the floor to the DVD player and slid the disk into place. Oz watched her backside the whole way, loving the way her shorts pulled tight with each movement. She burst out laughing when Finn clicked the button and a grumpy green ogre filled the screen. Finn grinned as she crawled back to her place and began happily munching on her duck.

"Will you not even give me a clue? Sometimes I think you're straight, and I think you're flirting with me, but then you seem to realize and stop yourself."

"Does it really matter?" Finn knew she was being coy, but couldn't help it. Part of her was worried that if Oz did know she was gay, and still didn't find her attractive, it would blow a grapefruit-sized hole in her self-esteem.

"I guess not. I'm just curious and it's bugging me that I can't figure you out."

"So it won't bother you whatever happens to be the truth?" Finn winced inwardly. She wanted it to bother Oz if she wasn't gay, and that bothered her.

"Not in the slightest."

"Okay." Finn moved over to the cupboard and looked around before tossing a DVD over to Oz. "That one would be my preferred genre." Oz opened the case to see the *Gia* DVD staring at her. The smile that spread across Oz's lips lit up her whole face, and Finn found herself unable to breathe as she watched.

Finn kept her eyes focused intently on her rice as heat suffused her cheeks.

"Good genre. So when did you come out?"

"I haven't, really."

"Huh?" Oz's eyes locked on Finn's lips as she spoke. Finn couldn't help but lick them in response and the flare of answering desire in Oz's eyes nearly made her groan out loud.

"You're the second person I've told." She poked her chopsticks at the bottom of the carton. "Pete was the other one."

"That must have made relationships awkward."

Finn chuckled sadly. "Try impossible."

Oz stared at her and Finn waited for the obvious question, nerves churning up her Chinese food.

"Impossible?"

"Yup."

"Like totally impossible? Like, even casual flings?"

"Yup. Totally"

"Never?"

Finn shook her head. "Never."

"So how do you know that you're a lesbian?"

"Are you seriously asking me that question?" She looked at Oz with both eyebrows raised. "Have you ever slept with a man?"

"No."

"So how do you know you aren't straight?" Finn crossed her arms. Pete had asked her the same thing, and it stupefied her that people who were already out would ask something so inane.

"I *have* slept with women."

"Okay, before you slept with the first one. Did you think 'oh, I'll just give this a try and see if it's for me,' or did you know that you were attracted to women?"

"Okay. I get the point. But you're twenty-eight."

"With an overbearing father, a very busy career, and a major fear of looking like an idiot."

"Why would you look like an idiot?" Oz frowned, her confusion obvious.

"Hello. Twenty-eight-year-old virgin. Of course I look like an idiot."

"No, you don't. I think it's really sweet."

Finn snorted and stabbed her carton with her chopsticks. Her hand trembled when Oz took it in her own, but she couldn't bear to look at her and see the pity in her eyes.

"Finn, listen to me. You are a beautiful woman. You're kind, generous, smart, funny, sexy, and I think it is amazing that someone hasn't come along and swept you off your feet. When you meet the right person, you won't feel stupid or awkward. You'll be glad you waited to share something so special with her. If she's the right person for you, she'll make sure you know that. She'll do everything she can to show you just how special and amazing you are. Sometimes I wish I had waited for someone special."

Finn looked up at her and saw that Oz meant every word she said, and her mortification melted away under her warm, caring gaze.

"You're so beautiful, so amazing, Finn. The woman you choose to share yourself with will be the luckiest woman ever, and she damn well better appreciate that."

Oz was so close. Her lips were just inches away. It would be so easy to learn forward, to taste them, to suck on them and feel Oz's hands. No. Oz was her teacher, her friend, and there was no way she was going to risk complicating life more than it already was. She grabbed her chopsticks again and put some space between them.

"Can I ask you something?" Finn asked, staring into her rice container.

"Sure."

"What's it like?"

Oz almost choked on the mouthful of rice she had just taken. "Huh?" Finn just stared at her, the question hanging between them. "Sex?"

Finn stabbed her chopsticks into her rice, heat flooding her cheeks. "I've read books. Romances and stuff. And I can imagine. But I don't—I mean, I've thought about it and fantasized and stuff. What's it like to make love to a woman?"

Oz picked at the rice in her carton as she thought. "Well. I can't really tell you that."

Finn looked back at her food, disappointed. She had hoped Oz would be open with her.

"I can't really tell you because I'm not sure I've ever made love."

Finn looked up at her. "But you said that you had."

"I've slept with women, sure. It was just sex. There was no emotion or feelings involved. It was fun. It was different every time, because every woman was different. Sometimes it's passionate. Sometimes it's nothing more than a release. Satisfying physically, but never anything more. It's different than what you're talking about."

Finn wanted to ask her more. She wanted to know what Oz felt the difference was. She wanted to hear her put words to the thoughts running through her own head. She could feel her cheeks burning, her heart pounding, and her mind racing. She tried desperately not to picture Oz with another woman. Holding her, kissing her, making love to her. She wanted to feel Oz's hands on her own skin, and she knew that given half a chance, she wouldn't care if it made their friendship difficult; she wanted Oz. Food lost its appeal and she put her carton down on the table.

"Sex was always something that came easy for me."

Finn glanced over and saw that Oz looked almost as uncomfortable as she felt. She didn't dare speak or move, desperate as she was for Oz to keep talking.

"Women seem to like me and I enjoy giving them pleasure. I love to see a woman writhing under me when I'm touching her. I love to see her face when she comes for me, because of me. It's the most amazing feeling for me, I feel so alive and powerful, I suppose. That probably sounds arrogant or something, but it makes me feel complete in a way nothing else outside of diving does. It's simple and beautiful and pure. In that moment, there's no pretense, no hiding or games. We're just there. Living and giving and taking pleasure. I would do anything to keep that look on her face. Whatever she enjoys, whatever pleases her, that's what I want to do. Like I said, every woman is different in what she likes, what pleases her, but what pleases me is finding those things and giving them to her."

Finn found it difficult to swallow. She wanted to reach out and take Oz's hand, just to feel her skin. She wanted to lean against her body and feel her heartbeat, hoping that it was thundering in her chest as hard as her own. The silence stretched thin between them until it felt like it had a heartbeat of its own, and Finn knew she had to say something. She swallowed hard before licking her lips and willing them to work. "I want to be in love with the woman I finally sleep with. I've waited this long; I might as well wait for the right one now." She turned her attention back to the TV. "Have you ever been in love?"

"No. I thought I was, once. But it was just lust. Full-blown, hormones raging 'got to have her or I'll die' lust." She laughed sadly. "I was sixteen. She was eighteen. Sarah Matthews. Dark hair, green eyes, amazing breasts, and I swear I thought I'd die if I couldn't be with her."

"What happened?"

"Her parents caught us in her kitchen. We were making out pretty good. She'd gotten my shirt off, and I had my hand up her skirt. Her dad chased me out of the house, sans shirt, with his belt in hand. Needless to say, I could live without her."

"You're joking?"

"Nope. So I'm tearing down the street, tits jumping up and down, and I ran straight into my dad. He just took his coat off and wrapped it around my shoulders. Sarah's dad came straight up behind and started screaming at me. My dad stepped in front of him and started talking really quietly." Oz rested her head against the sofa, a wry grin on her face. "Now, you gotta picture my dad here."

"I got it."

"My dad says to him, 'I know it's a shock, and the girls should show you more respect, but chasing a half naked young girl down the street with your trousers falling down, isn't the best way to go about that now, is it? You go on back and talk to your daughter, and I'll do the same with mine.' Then he turned to me and told me to go inside the house. It must have been ten minutes before he came in. He never raised his voice. He never grounded me. Not a thing. He just sat and pointed to the chair next to him. When I sat down, he looked at me for the longest time, then he said. 'Well, you look the same as you did this morning. You still sound the same as you did this morning. And I love you just as much as I did this morning. But if I ever hear of you disrespecting someone I work with again by having his daughter in the kitchen, I'll let him take that belt to you, you hear?'" She was laughing as she recounted the memory.

"Your dad sounds wonderful."

"He's not bad. Oh, that reminds me. Uncle Charlie invited you to Thanksgiving dinner next month. You're welcome to come with me."

"Really?"

"Yeah."

Finn took a deep breath and gathered her courage, and she knew it was a bad idea. She knew it might complicate the relationship between them, but she knew she wanted Oz. She wanted to touch her, to just reach out and run her fingers through her hair. So she took a chance. "As your date?"

Oz's smile faltered and her eyes grew wide.

"I think I'd like that." Finn turned back to the TV and tried to keep from smiling at Oz's reaction.

"Are you serious?" Oz's voice was barely above a whisper.

Finn turned back to her, trying to decide which way to go. To admit the truth, that she really wanted it to be a date, or fall back on the relative safety of teasing flirtation. The flickering emotion in Oz's eyes held her captive. The longing she had seen there before, but the uncertainty was new. *Is she really as unsure as me? Does she feel it too?* She watched as Oz's pupils dilated, her chest heaved, and a pink flush darkened her cheeks, all telling her Oz was teetering on a knife edge, just like she was. She took a deep breath, gathered her courage, and took a chance.

"Yes, I'm serious." She reached out with a trembling hand and gently touched her fingertips to Oz's cheek. "Will you take me as your date?"

Oz curled her fingers around Finn's palm and brought it to her lips. Finn's breath caught in her throat as Oz's lips brushed across the back of her hand.

"I would love to take you as my date. On one condition."

Finn cleared her throat before she spoke. "What's the condition?"

"You let me take you on a date before then. Can't have our first date on Thanksgiving, at my uncle's."

Finn grinned. "Just tell me where and when."

"Tomorrow night. I'll show you some of the sights."

Finn's skin tingled as Oz's thumb stroked back and forth over her wrist. She could feel her heart racing and couldn't drag her eyes from Oz's lips. Her stomach flipped when Oz licked her lips and she tried to control her shaking hands. It wasn't fear that made her tremble; it was her desire. The desire to feel Oz holding her close to her body and kissing her was all-consuming.

"Are you going to kiss me now?"

"Is that what you want?"

Finn knew her ability to speak had deserted her and barely managed to nod in response. Oz shifted until she was kneeling in front of Finn, tugging gently on her arm to bring her closer. Finn moved quickly into the same position, her eyes never leaving Oz's.

"Tell me." Oz let go of her hand and stroked the tips of her fingers down each cheek. "Tell me what you want."

Finn placed her hands on Oz's hips, desperate to feel her solid body, to anchor her as she gathered her courage and managed to croak out the words expressing her desire.

"I want you to kiss me."

Then Oz's lips covered her own, gently brushing at first, then tenderly pressing against her. She felt fingers slide into her hair and a soft moan escaped her lips at the exquisite contact. Exploring, dancing around her mouth, discovering lips, teeth, and tongue. One hand slid from Finn's hair and caressed her back, locking securely at her waist and pulling her tighter into the embrace.

Finn found her own hands sliding up to Oz's shoulders, trying to pull her in closer. Slowly, the kiss eased to a stop, and Oz rested her forehead against Finn's as they waited for their breathing to return to normal.

"Wow." Finn still had her eyes closed. "Does it always feel like that?"

"First kiss too?"

Finn shook her head, trying to hide her embarrassment. "No, but it never...I never..." She took a deep breath and tried to calm her racing heart. "I've kissed a few people, but it never felt the way I thought it would. The way I read about in so many books. I thought there was something wrong with me."

Oz hooked a finger under her chin and raised her head until Finn met her eyes. "No. There is nothing wrong with you. Nothing. It doesn't always feel like that. That was amazing." She placed a small chaste kiss upon her lips. "I've kissed some women and shouldn't have bothered." She dotted kisses across Finn's cheeks. "I want to kiss you again, to make sure that was real. To make sure I haven't dreamed you."

Finn caught Olivia's lips between hers. This time she wasn't tentative or shy. She hungered to feel Oz's lips move against her own. She pressed her tongue inside Oz's mouth, teasing gently before retreating back. Oz's hand rested at the nape of her neck as the other, still locked behind her back, pulled her body tighter into Oz's, then relaxed as the hand moved down and cupped her butt. A gentle squeeze brought a gasp from Finn and powered her hands into action. One slid down to Oz's backside while the other cupped her neck. It was Oz who broke the kiss, pulling back and placing her hands on Finn's shoulders.

"Okay. I'm convinced. You're real."

Finn blinked as her breathing slowly returned to normal. She felt the rise and fall of Oz's chest against her own, pleased that she had affected Oz so much, and longing for more. "I'm not convinced. I think you should kiss me again." Finn moved toward her, but Oz stopped her.

"I need a minute here, Finn. I don't want to rush anything with you, but you're driving me kind of crazy." She took a deep breath. "Can you just give me a minute?"

"I'm sorry, I just—"

"Don't apologize. I would love to go on kissing you all night. But I know myself well enough to know that I can only take so much before

I want more of you. All of you." She stroked Finn's cheek. "I already know I want you, Finn. I could take you to bed and have sex with you all night. But you already told me that sex isn't what you want. You want more. You deserve more." She wrapped her arms around Finn's shoulders and pulled her into a tight embrace. "I don't know if I have it in me to give."

Finn pulled back and stared deep into Oz's eyes.

"Why do you say that?" The pained look in Oz's eyes made her heart ache, and she knew that Oz was trying to decide just how much she was going to share. The battle to keep her shutters down was clearly written in the frown marring her beautiful face.

"I've never had much trouble finding women to keep me company when I wanted some."

Oz let her go and sat back against the sofa, and Finn was instantly aware of the distance she put between them. She sensed that Oz needed the physical distance to say the things she needed to, so she sat next to her, careful to maintain the distance.

"I've been with a lot of women and not always treated them very well."

"In what way?"

"Well, I'd go out sometimes looking to hook up with someone, then I'd go back to their place and we'd have sex. I couldn't even tell you half of their names now. I never dated anyone; it was always just sex. Even if I saw them more than just once, like the tourists here on holidays, I never wanted anything else from them."

"And they wanted more from you?"

"They deserved more from me."

Finn cocked her head to the side, considering. "Why?"

"Because no one deserves to be used. But I never thought of it that way until I met you."

"I agree, but weren't they using you in exactly the same way? You were all consenting adults." She shrugged. "Oz, I know the reputation you have. I've known that since the day on the dock when you were joking around with Clem and Mac. Let me ask you something. Did you ever lead any of those women to believe that you were looking for a relationship beyond that night, or however long it was?"

"No."

"Did you ever lie to get anyone into bed with you?"

"No"

"Did you ever force anyone to go to bed with you?"

"God, no. I would nev—"

"I know, Oz. Did you mistreat any of them while you were in bed together?"

"No, they always seemed to enjoy it."

"It was a one-night stand, or a holiday fling for them too. They may have wanted more." Finn stroked her cheek. "I know I would, but I'm also pretty damn sure they knew what was on the table before they even kissed you." She leaned forward and kissed Oz softly. "I don't think you used those women any more than they used you, and if you all got what you were looking for out of the experience, a night of pleasure, then I don't see anything wrong with that."

"Finn, I never wanted anything more than that. When I was in the navy, it was too difficult to even contemplate. I could've lost my commission, and I was away so much on assignment it didn't make sense to look for anything more. But I think that was a convenient excuse. I think that I'm just not cut out for it. For a relationship."

Finn couldn't hide the disappointment she felt, and she turned her head away to hide the tears filling her eyes, willing them not to fall.

"I still don't think that, Finn, but I really like you. I don't know if I can do this, but I want to try."

Suddenly, she didn't care if Oz saw the tears in her eyes; she had to see her face. "What are you saying?"

"I guess I'm asking you to give me a chance. To give us a chance. Even if I can't make any promises."

Finn couldn't find the words to say everything she wanted, to tell Oz that she wouldn't have said no even if she could have. She closed the distance between them and kissed her, slowly pressing her body against Oz, until the need to breathe pulled them apart.

"I'm going to take that as a yes."

Finn smiled as Oz tucked her against her body and wrapped her arm around Finn's shoulders."Does it bother you?"

Finn frowned slightly in question.

"My reputation? Does it bother you?"

"Does my being a virgin bother you?"

"No!" Oz answered quickly. Too quickly. Finn began to pull away from her, so she wrapped her arms around her and pulled her close. "It doesn't bother me. Nervous, I suppose, is the best word to describe it."

"Why?"

"It makes me nervous wondering why you would want someone like me. Nervous, that I've never been in a relationship before. I don't know that I can be someone's girlfriend, or partner, or anything but someone to warm a bed."

"Yes, you can. You just don't know it yet." She smiled gently. "Everything you've done for me. Helping me find somewhere to live, helping me move. What you did today, taking me out to distract me, and taking the time to cheer me up tonight. These are all thoughtful little things that I always thought a wonderful girlfriend would do. You might not believe that just yet, but that's okay, because I do."

Oz laughed. "You're very sure of yourself, aren't you?"

"No. I'm sure of you. Your reputation doesn't bother me, Oz. Everyone has a past. And that's what your reputation is based on. I don't for one minute believe that you would get involved with someone and then continue to play around. You have too much honor for that." She cuddled in close before she dropped back to her place on the floor. "I've missed all this so far. Can we restart the film?"

Finn pushed herself off the floor and settled on the sofa as Oz restarted the film and sat next to her. She grinned as Oz took her hand, and barely resisted the urge to move closer, as she didn't want to push further than Oz was comfortable with. She wanted to cuddle up next to her and feel Oz's arms wrap around her, but was content to feel Oz's thumb stroking the back of her hand. She refused to let fear control her decisions. She refused to let her own past taint the magical feeling of their first kiss. The whole point of coming here was a fresh start, a new beginning, and that meant letting go of past fears and losses. She trusted Oz. She believed in her enough to push everything out of her head and enjoy the feeling of Oz pulling her closer and holding her through the rest of the movie.

CHAPTER TWENTY-THREE

William Sterling saved the document he was working on and shut down his computer as his cell phone started to ring.

"Yes?"

"William, my friend."

"Masood, it is good to hear from you. How can I help you?"

"I have a question or two for you."

"Of course."

"The vaccination is prepared also, is that correct?"

"Yes, but we need a few more days to produce the quantities required—"

"That is your concern, William. Not mine. All I want is the quantity we discussed. There would be very little point in using the bacteria if I am not around to enjoy the deaths of my enemies."

"The quantity we arranged has been produced." William smiled as he thought about how he planned to deliver a defective batch of vaccine to Masood and watch him perish like everyone else when he unleashed Balor on the world. The correct vaccine would be sold by Sterling to the rest of the world, after an appropriate amount of time had passed to develop the vaccine, of course. Not a cure. There was no hope for a cure or an effective treatment for those infected either.

"Very good, William. I am looking forward to seeing this in action."

"As am I."

He hung up and tossed his phone on the desk. The 'development' of the vaccine for Balor would make Sterling Enterprises a fortune overnight. He couldn't even fathom the full extent of the wealth he would accumulate after this event. The power that would be at his fingertips when the world looked to him as he held in his hands the only way to stop Balor.

CHAPTER TWENTY-FOUR

O z knocked on the door of Mrs. Richmond's house and waited nervously, pulling slightly at the collar of her black shirt, before smoothing her hands down the front.

"Hello, dear. Finn's nearly ready. Do you want to come in?"

"That'd be great, Mrs. R." Oz followed her inside and sat on the edge of the sofa.

"Relax, dear. She might be a few more minutes."

Oz smiled and tried to sit back a little. She couldn't believe how nervous she felt, and the amused smile on Mrs. Richmond's face was not helping.

"Hi."

Oz spun around and watched as Finn walked toward her. Casual wedge sandals graced her feet with black laces crossing her ankles. Her legs were bare to just above the knee where a sapphire blue dress started and caressed each curve of her body. Finn had piled her hair up high on her head, a few loose curls escaping around her face.

"Oz, are you okay?"

Oz smiled and stood, quickly crossing to kiss Finn's cheek. "You look great. Are you ready to go?"

"Yeah, the cab's here." A honking from outside alerted them to the arrival of the taxi.

"You planned ahead."

"It's my Girl Scout motto."

"Where are we going?"

"To Pearl's Patio."

"Are we going to a garden party?"

Oz laughed as she led Finn outside, waving at Mrs. Richmond as she closed the door behind them. "Pearl's Patio is a lesbian bar that has karaoke every Saturday night."

"Are you going to sing for me?

"I think not." She directed the taxi driver before she sat back and caught Finn's hand in her own again. Bringing it to her lips, she whispered against her skin. "You look incredible. I knew you were beautiful, but I really didn't realize how beautiful you are."

Finn blushed deeply. "I'm glad you think so."

"Trust me, Finn. I'm going to be beating them off with a stick."

"You said that when we went to Turtle Kraal's, and not one person said or did anything even remotely inappropriate."

Oz placed her arm around Finn's shoulders as she whispered in her ear. "That's because when you went to the bathroom I stood up on the table and told everyone that you were mine."

"You're so full of crap."

Oz laughed, kissing Finn's hand again before moving slightly away from her. Finn's teasing was already easing her anxiety. She was so focused on making sure Finn had a good time, she realized that she hadn't thought at all about her own expectations of the evening. She only cared that Finn enjoyed herself and enjoyed them being together. Oz didn't want to think about why this was so important to her. The possibilities were far too daunting for her to comprehend. The cab ride was short and they could hear the slightly pitchy tones of the vocalist as they opened the door. Oz looked around for a table. Spotting one toward the front, she pointed at it.

"Do you mind sitting near the front?"

"No, that's fine.

Oz couldn't help thinking that they'd have to stay close together to talk, and the prospect both thrilled and terrified her. Her desire to be close to Finn, to touch her, warred with her fear of failure and the possibility that she would disappoint her.

"I'll go grab us a drink. Would you hold the table?"

"Of course."

"What can I get you to drink?"

"Red wine if they have any. If not, vodka and cranberry juice please." Oz headed to the bar. Finn had only been sitting a few moments when someone sat next to her. "That was quick."

"When I see what I like, I don't like to hang around. It wastes too much time." The stranger was leaning close enough that Finn moved back slightly.

"My friend has just gone to the bar. She'll be here any second."

"But she's not here now, so I'll just sit here and talk to you for a while." The woman had a military style haircut with a barcode tattoo on the side of her neck and another of barbed wire around her bicep. Her hair was so short it was difficult in the low lighting to determine its color. Her leather biker pants and black vest topped off the heavy biker boots and strong odor of alcohol.

"I don't really feel comfortable sitting here talking to a stranger."

"I'm Maggie. Now I'm not a stranger." She stretched her arm along the back of Finn's chair.

"Look, I'm here on a date."

"Then she really should stay closer to you." Maggie's hand moved to Finn's shoulder and started to slide toward her neck.

"Maggie. It's nice of you to come over and say hi, but I'm really here on a date. Oz will be here any second."

"Oz?"

"Yes."

"As in Zuckerman?"

"Yes, she's my date." Finn's retort was sharp.

"Dive girl, Oz? I'm sorry, honey. Oz doesn't date. She'll buy you a drink before she screws you. Sometimes. But she doesn't date."

"Well, you're mistaken."

"Honey, I've known Oz a long time. Trust me. You'll be better off with me. I can show you a really good time."

"Moose, get your hands off her." Oz felt anger welling in her chest at the sight of another woman with her hands on Finn. Jealousy she had never felt before blossomed in her chest and she fought hard not to grab Maggie and yank her away. The physical urge to come to Finn's rescue was so foreign it made her hands shake.

"If it isn't the Wizard of Oz. I was just saying hello to your little friend. What's your name again, honey?"

"I didn't tell you. Oz, it's fine. Maggie was just leaving."

"Do you know how she got the nickname Wizard of Oz?"

Oz glared at Maggie, but she didn't back down.

"Because she's supposed to be magic. But you know what I think? I think she turns out to be a fraud just like the real Wizard of Oz. That's why you haven't ever had a girlfriend for more than five minutes, hey, Ladyfish?"

Oz put the drinks on the table and sat in the chair on the other side of Finn. "The bouncer will probably get her to leave any second now. Please, just ignore her."

"What's the matter, Oz? Worried your little date will get a better offer?"

Oz continued to ignore Maggie and leaned in closer to Finn. "I told you I'd have to beat them off with a stick." She placed a tender kiss on Finn's cheek.

"I think I'm going to throw up." Maggie grabbed Finn's hand and placed a rough kiss on it. Oz was about to stand up and take care of things when the bouncer showed up.

"Maggie, shut up and go home." The bouncer placed a large hand on Maggie's shoulder and the other under her armpit. She hoisted her out of her seat and away from the table in one swift movement. "Sorry about that, Oz. You know what she gets like sometimes."

"I do."

Finn turned back to Oz. "Why did you call her Moose?"

"It's her nickname. Maggie Moose. Her last name is Caribou. I think she's had that nickname since she was a kid." She took a long pull of her drink. "Dance with me?" Oz held her hand out. Finn simply took it and allowed herself to be led to the dance floor a few feet away. As she held Finn in her arms, Oz felt the tension coiled in her body begin to recede. She knew it was irrational, but she couldn't seem to stop the feelings of jealousy and anger that had exploded within her. She knew she had no right to demand anything of Finn, but she wanted to be the only woman to touch her. She tried not to think about the pleasure she had felt when she heard Finn clearly telling Maggie that she wasn't interested because she was with Oz. She held on to the feeling of pride that rippled through her and smiled as she pulled Finn's body closer to her own.

Oz could feel her desire growing, and as the last notes faded away, she lowered her lips to Finn's, before leading them back to their seats. They sat and sipped their drinks.

Oz leaned forward in her seat, worrying the label from her beer bottle.

"Are you all right? You've gone all fidgety on me. Are you angry?"

"Angry about what? Maggie?"

"Yeah."

"No, I'm not angry, not with you or with her. I am a little bit worried though."

"About what?"

"Well, everything she said to you was true."

"No, it wasn't."

"She didn't lie to you."

"I don't think for a moment that she did. That still doesn't make everything she said true. She said that I'd be better off with her. That isn't true, clearly."

"You don't know that."

"Yes, I do, Oz. I wasn't interested in her in any way. I didn't look at her and want to talk to her or hear what she had been doing all day, and I definitely didn't want to hold her hand and sit next to her just watching TV. I had no desire at all to cook for her, just to see her smile. And I definitely didn't want her to drive my car." She trailed her finger down Oz's neck as she continued speaking softly. "I had no urge whatsoever to do that to her. Or this." She planted her lips against Oz's neck and left a trail of kisses in her wake. "Or this." She flicked her tongue across the skin below her lips, and Oz shivered and tried to keep still. "And I definitely didn't look at her and want to do this."

Finn pulled her face closer and pressed her lips hard against Oz's, taking her mouth with an intensity that surprised them both. Oz moaned as Finn probed her mouth. Finn plunged her tongue deep into Oz's mouth, searching, exploring, and teasing. Oz battled down her urge to take control, balling her fists against her thighs to stop herself from wrapping her arms around Finn's back and tugging her closer. She wanted to feel Finn's breasts pressed against her own. Only the desperate need for oxygen forced them apart. They were both breathing heavily as Finn placed kisses across Oz's cheek and whispered into her ear. "You haven't lied to me either, Oz. I might not have any experience, but I'm not stupid. Nor am I a child." She kissed Oz's ear and sucked gently on her earlobe, making her tremble. "I've always wondered what it would be like. I know what I'm getting into here." She trailed her tongue along the outer edge of Oz's ear. "Do you?"

Oz grasped her shoulders and, unable to take the teasing anymore, she held her still as she moved to whisper in her ear.

"I'm pretty damn sure that I don't have the first clue what I'm getting into here." She sucked Finn's earlobe, returning the favor and delighted at the sensation of Finn shivering beneath her lips. "It feels delicious, doesn't it?"

"Yes." Finn's voice was barely more than a whisper, a fact that pleased Oz immensely.

She trailed her tongue along the edge of her ear. "You feel like you're burning even as you shiver, don't you?"

"Yes."

"I think we should dance."

Finn seemed dazed as she pulled away and led her back on to the floor. They started moving to the beat, and Oz found herself mesmerized as Finn relaxed and let her body move to the music. The gentle sway of her hips in time to the beat was hypnotic, weaving a sensuous spell around her. Oz watched, barely moving as Finn's own hands ran across her torso, her hips, through her hair. Oz struggled to keep her feet moving in time to the music, since all she wanted to do was watch Finn's body move.

Her breath caught in her chest as Finn took hold of her hand and pulled them closer together. She wrapped one arm about her waist, and the other hand slid from Oz's shoulder into her hair. Her fingernails scratched gently at her scalp as she continued to move against her.

Several dances and drinks later, they walked out of the bar and waited outside for a cab. Finn ran her hand down the length of Oz's spine.

"Thank you."

"What for?"

"A wonderful first date."

"You're welcome. But it's not quite finished yet."

"No? What's left?"

"You'll see." Oz helped her into the cab and cradled her against her side as Finn leaned her head on Oz's shoulder. The rocking motion of the car soon had Finn dozing against her, and Oz couldn't help replaying the evening in her mind. Her anger when Maggie had her hands on Finn, and her desire to forcibly remove them. She'd worked hard for a long time to avoid any situation where she wasn't in control. Her career in the navy had taught her the importance of that, if nothing else. Nightmares of the few moments where she had lost control still haunted her. It didn't matter that she'd been cleared by her superiors and that her actions were deemed necessary. What mattered were the blood-covered faces of the men she had killed and the comrades she had lost along the way. That was what losing control meant. It meant losing people, losing friends. It meant losing people she cared about. She laid her head on top of Finn's and acknowledged that she already cared too much to stay away from Finn. Her reaction to Maggie was all the confirmation she needed to prove that. She closed her eyes and took a long breath. *What the hell am I going to do now?*

"I think I had too much to drink."

"Ah, so my plan to get you drunk and have my wicked way with you is working."

Finn laughed. "Is that the plan?" She stumbled sleepily toward the house. Oz caught up with her at the front door.

"No, that isn't the plan. If the time comes when we sleep together, I want you to be completely aware. No alcohol involved. I want you to know every time I touch you. I want you to feel every kiss and caress, but most importantly, I want you to feel every emotion that goes with it. Both of us. I want to make love to you, Finn, when we are both ready. Not when you're drunk."

"So if that isn't the plan, what's left for our first date?" Her voice was husky with desire and emotion.

Oz moved closer and lowered her head. "The good night kiss, of course." She closed the distance between them and let her hands slide up Finn's arm, smiling as goose bumps erupted under her fingertips. She loved the way Finn trembled as she skimmed across her shoulders and slowly traced the length of her throat and the underside of her jaw before she kissed her. Gently at first, and then Finn moaned and wrapped her fingers into Oz's hair, pulling her closer. The fire ignited in Oz's belly as Finn moaned into her mouth and threaded her arms about Oz's neck. She pressed Finn against the door, one hand went to her waist and the other her shoulder. She couldn't resist the urge to explore a little and trailed her fingertips upward, brushing the material of Finn's dress against her ribs, stopping just below her breast. She slipped her other hand softly into Finn's hair and caressed her scalp, loving the way Finn moved against her as she scratched her fingernails over the sensitive skin.

She needed to touch Finn everywhere; her hands were greedy in the desire to explore as she traced her fingertips down Finn's neck, across her chest and slowly along the edge of the plunging neckline. Finn trembled against her and started to move her hands down Oz's back. Oz tore her mouth from Finn's and trailed kisses down her throat while her fingers closed the distance to Finn's breast. She drew one fingertip across the raised bump of her hardening nipple and smiled against her skin as Finn moaned and arched into her touch. The hands at Oz's back drifted lower, squeezing her ass and pulling her closer. Finn's apparent desire only served to further enflame her own until she couldn't stop herself from pushing her thigh between Finn's legs and pulling their hips flush together. Oz moaned as Finn's hips moved slowly against her leg. It was sheer willpower that kept her from lifting Finn's legs and wrapping them around her body. She wanted to feel Finn's desire on her skin. To smell the sweet musk that she was sure would be waiting for her.

Finn tugged Oz's shirt out of her pants and traced patterns over the small of her back; teasing up and down her spine, along her sides, stopping short of the outer edge of her breasts every time. Oz drew her fingers across Finn's shoulder, her lips trailing in their wake until Finn grabbed her hand and laid it upon her own breast. Oz gladly took the hint and gently squeezed, flicking her thumb over the hard nipple. She pulled back slightly and the hungry look on Finn's face made her breath catch. She could neither stop nor gentle the kiss she wanted, her tongue plunging into Finn's mouth, exploring every inch of her, eager to know every ridge and valley. She pushed her hands down Finn's sides, gripping her hips and pulling her tighter against her thigh; her knees threatened to buckle under her when Finn ground down on her and trembled. Oz knew she was at her own limit; they were both breathing fast and hard, desire mounting, and the need to feel skin was becoming more and more difficult to deny. Oz was determined to keep her promise though and began to reduce the ardent passion of their kisses until they broke apart gasping and Oz wrapped Finn in a strong embrace and waited while they both caught their breath.

"Good night, Finn." She pulled away slowly and backed down off the porch. Their eyes locked as Finn stood with her back to the door. She was gripping the handle like it was the only thing keeping her on her feet, her breathing was still ragged, and her hand visibly trembled as she lifted it to wave.

"Good night, Oz." Finn's voice was husky, her desire clearly evident as she pushed the door open behind her and disappeared inside. Oz stood staring, unable to make her feet move as fear gripped her. She cast her eyes heavenward and sucked in a deep breath before doing something she hadn't done since she was a small child. She prayed for patience.

She slowly managed to turn around and walk to her own house, knowing sleep wouldn't come easily to her. Arousal coursed through her veins, each beat of her heart only making the situation worse. Walking away from Finn, even just until the morning, was so much harder than she had expected. Despite her words, what she really wanted to do was walk Finn to her bed, slowly peel away her dress, and cover her body with kisses. She wanted to feel Finn's skin react beneath her tongue, to taste her. She wanted desperately to please her and hear her name whispered from Finn's lips as she came. Oz changed into her running shorts and quickly tied on her sneakers before heading out the door again, uncertain if she was running to conquer her desire or her fear.

CHAPTER TWENTY-FIVE

The incessant ringing of Finn's cell phone woke her up. She cracked one eyelid and stared blindly at the alarm clock beside her bed as she grabbed the handset and brought it to her ear.

"What time is it?"

"Daniela, it's nine o'clock in the morning."

"Dad!" She shot bolt upright in bed, her eyes wide open. She glanced at the clock again. Four a.m. "It's actually four in the morning here. Is something wrong?"

"Not at all. I just thought I'd give you a call. Is that a problem?"

"Not at all. It's just unusual. Normally, you have Susan call me."

"I noticed that you checked out of the hotel, and I wondered if there was a problem."

Finn sighed. She should have guessed that someone would have their eye on those little details. "No, Dad. I've been spending a lot of time with some friends over here and it just made more sense to stay here. We weren't utilizing the hotel so it made no sense to spend the money just to leave our bags there." The silence hung in the air. *Shit, he knows I'm lying. Always does. I am the world's crappiest liar ever.*

"That's fine, Daniela. You must let me know where you're staying, however."

"Sure, it's sixteen—"

He cut her off. "I'll have Susan call you to get the details from you. I must go now. I have a meeting shortly."

"Bye—" The line went dead. "Dad." She threw herself back against the pillow and smacked the phone to her head. She knew Susan wouldn't call until just before she was leaving the office to make it around lunchtime for Finn. She was kind that way. Finn had never figured out why she worked for her father.

Since sleep was out of the question, she switched on the bedside lamp and grabbed one of her diving books, intent on reading until she felt ready to go back to sleep. But as the cooling sheets covered her body again, memories tugged at the edges of her mind.

Every scene was different. The school nativity aged five. The nanny came to watch that one. And every event after that, from school plays to graduation, included some employee of her father's paid to attend. But never her father.

Every memory had the same constant, lingering empty space. The empty space where a parent should have been, filled with a seemingly endless stream of interchangeable strangers.

She folded over the corner of the page and placed the book on the nightstand, knowing full well she would have to read the passage again, having taken in nothing for the past half hour. She looked at the clock beside the bed, the dark red numbers burning into her brain as she turned out the light, closed her eyes, and watched as the digits changed in her mind. 4:30. 4:31. 4:32. 4:33.

Her thoughts drifted slowly away from the loneliness, coming to rest on Oz. What was it that made her so sure she could depend on her? A track record for one-night stands and holiday flings? *About as likely as Pete, based on that history.*

A cocky smile and a killer kiss. *What a kiss, though.*

She touched her fingertips to her lips, needing to feel the pressure against her skin, the tactile reminder of the desire and pleasure as Oz had kissed her good night, and tenderly caressed her skin. She had longed for it to never end even as her breath faltered and she had to pull away.

I want her. Does it need to be more than that? Even as she posed the question to herself, she knew the answer. She wasn't naïve, and she wanted people to take her seriously. And she needed to take her own desires seriously now.

She knew the reason she had waited was more about making sure she could depend on her lover. She needed to know that the woman she loved would be there for all those silly little occasions that meant everything and nothing. The next birthday. And the one after. And the next fifty. Moving homes. Holidays. Laughter. Tears. A hug.

She needed someone to want to be part of those things for her, who wanted to hold her through tears of joy and pain. She needed someone who wanted to watch her sleep, just to be near her. She wanted someone who would bring her tissues when she had a cold, and flowers just because it would make her smile. Just one person in her life, one woman was all she wanted. Not an interchangeable face for each different occasion. She already had a lifetime filled with that, and all she wanted now was one face to memorize for the rest of her life. One face to be with hers in every photograph, accompanying each memory for the rest of her life. She needed one face beneath her fingertips, and one mouth to kiss, one single body to know, better than she knew her own. And just one person beside her, beneath her, above her, one person inside her skin. All she wanted was one single name on her lips. She would wait for that person.

CHAPTER TWENTY-SIX

Finn was sitting on the porch swing reading as Oz approached. Finn had on a pair of charcoal gray shorts and a pale blue tank top. Her bare feet were slapping on the tiled floor as she swung back and forth, humming to herself. Oz leaned against the rail and smiled.

"You've been shopping." She placed a gentle kiss against Finn's neck. "I definitely like the new disguise."

"I'm glad. I was aiming for lesbian-in-training. My other top has the letter L embroidered on it."

Oz chuckled. "I think that's a look that could take off. We'll start a new trend at Pearl's. Do you have any plans, or can I tempt you to join me for the day?"

"I was only going to do some reading. What do you have in mind?"

"It's a surprise, but it's beautiful where we're going so you might want to grab your camera."

"Sure, I'll go get it. Emmy's in the kitchen if you want to say hello."

"I'll just wait for you here, if that's okay?"

"Sure." Finn hurried inside and Oz could hear her telling Mrs. Richmond that she was going out. When she returned, Oz couldn't resist pulling her in close for a long, lingering kiss.

"We have a small errand to run on the way out there."

"Okay." Finn followed her back to her car and settled in for the ride, a slight frown marring her brow.

Oz started the car and pulled away from the curb. "Are you okay?"

"Yeah, why?"

"You're frowning. We don't have to go out if you don't want to."

"I do want to. I was just thinking. That's all."

"Do you want to talk about it?"

"Not really, but it might help." She shrugged. "My dad called me this morning. At four in the morning to be precise."

"Is something wrong?" Oz knew a call at four a.m. was never a good thing.

"He said everything was fine and he didn't seem to realize the time difference. I find that hard to believe since so much of his business is international."

"So what did he want then?"

"He said he was just checking in on me. He knew that Pete and I weren't staying at the hotel anymore. He seemed concerned." She snorted.

"You don't believe that?"

"No. I don't."

"Why not? He's your dad."

Finn shrugged. "He was never there."

Oz waited, knowing that Finn needed to tell her in her own time. She worked to keep her face neutral, her own disgust and suspicion of the man growing with everything she learned about him.

"He never seemed to remember he had a child. I was left to a series of nannies, tutors, and various other staff members to be looked after. They made sure I had everything I needed, as you can imagine. Daddy's money always bought the best. Best clothes, schools, coaches. Whatever. But they were all employees. You know?"

Oz smiled sadly. "Not really."

"They all took care of me because it was their job. He's my dad, but he never was. More like an open checkbook."

"So today's phone call was really unusual?"

"Very. I actually can't remember the last time he called me. It's usually his secretary who calls and passes a message or something."

"So what do you really think it was about?" She watched as Finn chewed her lip, clearly debating whether or not to say any more.

"I think he knows that Pete's gone and he was trying to find out if I knew the reasons why."

"What do you mean? I thought you said it was always the plan that Pete would go back to the UK?"

"It was. There's just a lot more to it. I think part of the reason Pete pushed me to stay in the States was so that I was away from my father when things get complicated."

"I don't understand."

Finn sighed heavily. "Pete told you he had a new job to go back to, right?"

"Yes."

"Well, what he didn't tell me until he was leaving is that the job is with MI6."

"Wow. He must be very proud, but I still don't understand what that has to do with your dad. I thought you were convinced he'd fire Pete anyway?"

"He would. Pete was recruited to MI6 by this Pritchard guy because they're investigating my dad, and I think Pete by extension. It seemed like Pete didn't have much choice about going to work for Pritchard, to be honest."

"Why is MI6 investigating your dad?"

"Pete said they were looking at money laundering and that he has proof that it's going on and that my dad knows about it."

"Wow. And you think your dad is trying to find out how much you know?"

Finn shrugged. "It's the only thing that makes sense to me. He never calls me, so why now? What's different?"

Oz felt the cold grip of guilt, knowing she should tell Finn that she had her own file on her father. She knew she should share her suspicions, but the look of confusion and anguish in Finn's eyes made her keep quiet. She wanted to take the pain away for her, to help heal the wounds written so clearly on Finn's face. She wanted to weep for the child that had been left alone, and protect the tender heart that was still evident in Finn. She tried to figure out the consequences of keeping the damaging things she knew to herself, but the situation stayed murky. She tightened her grip on the steering wheel, frustrated and worried.

"Can we change the subject, please? There's nothing I can do about any of it, and I'd really just like to forget about it all for a while. Enjoy spending the day with you. And who knows, maybe we can talk about you for a change."

"Sure."

"So where are you taking me?"

"Well, we're going to the mall first. I need to pick up a few things, and then I thought I'd take you kayaking on the Everglades."

"Wow. Tell me about the Everglades, then."

"The Everglades was called the River of Grass by the Native Americans who lived in Florida. It's about eleven thousand square miles of slow moving water that creates all these ponds, wetlands, swamps, and mangroves, as well as some forest areas too. It's a huge refuge for wildlife and has some species unique to the area, and some more that are endangered and others still that are just plain spectacular. It's like a patchwork quilt of different habitats. It's amazing. One part of it is called ten thousand islands, for obvious reasons." Oz pulled into the parking lot at the Dolphin Mall and turned off the engine.

"You can come with me or wait here. It's up to you. I'm only going to one store, but these places have a habit of swallowing me whole. I may need you to rescue me."

Finn was already out the door.

"I guess you're coming with me."

"I can't have you getting lost. So what shop are we heading for?"

"You'll see."

Oz led them through the labyrinth of stores and kiosks to a camera store specializing in underwater camera equipment. Finn barely seemed to notice as Oz led her inside. She seemed awestruck by the sheer size of the store.

"Don't they have malls in England?"

"We have the Trafford Centre Mall in Manchester. But that's maybe half the size of this."

Oz chuckled and left her looking around at the cameras while she made her way to the counter.

"Hey, I'm Olivia Zuckerman. I have some items reserved."

"The Ikelite 6801.70 underwater housing for a Nikon D7000. The lens port and strobe light are also in there. I've also included the arm and cables for the strobe light, a spare set of O-rings and some silicone, so it should all be good to go." Oz paid for her purchases quickly and found Finn staring into one of the cabinets.

"You ready?"

"I think I should talk to these guys about my camera case."

"Why don't you speak to Juanita? She'll probably be able to get you a discount or something." Oz headed for the door, smiling as Finn followed grumbling under her breath.

"Come on."

"You know it was cruel taking me in there don't you?"

Oz climbed back into the car and waited until Finn had fastened her seatbelt before she handed the bag to her. "This is for you."

"What is it?"

"You won't know until you open it." Oz grinned as Finn pulled open the bag and started to lift out the boxes inside. She stared, slack-jawed, as she peered at the unopened boxes. "Do you like it?"

Finn nodded her head slowly, tears filling her eyes. "But I can't accept this, Oz. It's too much."

"No, it isn't."

"Oz, the housing alone costs more than a thousand pounds. That's more like two thousand dollars, and the rest…it's too much."

"Finn, I can afford it. There are some things I need to explain about all that, but I can afford to do this. I've seen you under the water. Did you know that your fingers twitch when you see something amazing? It's like you're trying to take the picture even without the camera there. You want to be able to capture all those things, and this will let you do that. Then you can show me all the wonderful pictures you'll take, and I can enjoy it too."

"How can you afford this?"

Oz blew out a long breath and ran her fingers through her hair.

"Well, when I was in the navy, I lived in the barracks or with my parents. I was at sea a lot so I lived really cheap. I saved almost every penny I earned and made some good investments, and when I decided to get out, I really wanted to work for myself. I didn't like the idea of taking orders from anyone else." She threw a small grin in Finn's direction. "Anyway, long story short. The dive center, the boats, they're all mine, and they're all paid for. I don't like all the paperwork, so Rudy runs the office for me. I also like just being one of the guys, so they don't know that I'm actually Rudy's boss. It sounds complicated, but really, we've never had any problems. Rudy phrases questions like he's asking for my opinion in front of the guys, or just makes the decision and we deal with it later. He's a really great guy. Anyway, that's how I afford the house and how I can afford to do this for you. Please." Finn still looked skeptical. "Technically, I am your boss, so I could insist on it and make you take pictures for work." The words froze on her lips as Finn stretched over and kissed her.

"I still say it's too much."

Oz took a deep breath ready to begin on the next prepared speech until Finn put her hand to her lips.

"But we'll argue about that later. Thank you. This is the most wonderful, thoughtful gift anyone has ever given me." The tears rolled down her cheeks. "Now take me to the Everglades. I need to take pictures so we never forget today." She sat back in her seat, slowly pulling open the boxes and examining their contents.

"I'll never forget." *Nor will I forget the look on your face right now.* She cast her eyes upward as she turned on the ignition. *Please don't let me screw this up.*

❖

By the time they had reached Cape Sable, Finn had her camera encased in the housing and was taking shots to get used to the controls. Oz found a parking space close to the water to make it easier to launch the kayak.

"So what's the plan, Captain?"

"Well, me hearty." Oz assumed an exaggerated pirate-type gravelly voice but started coughing and ruined the effect, making Finn giggle. "Thanks for the sympathy."

Finn shrugged, still laughing.

"Care to give me a hand getting the kayak down?"

"Sure." They worked together and quickly had the boat floating at the edge of the water. Oz held it steady as Finn climbed in.

"I figured we could find a good quiet place and go snorkeling for a while. Give that new housing a try. How does that sound?"

"Can we go swimming here? What about crocodiles and stuff?"

"I'm not planning on getting near any crocs. Don't worry, I'll keep you safe."

"I didn't bring my stuff."

Oz pointed to a bag in the bottom of the craft. "I took the liberty of packing madame's swimsuit and snorkeling apparel. I hope you don't mind. They were at the dive center so I grabbed them."

"You are so sweet."

Oz put a finger in front of her lips. "Shush, don't go telling anyone. It's a very closely guarded secret."

Finn kissed her tenderly on the lips. "Your secret is safe with me. Besides, if other women found out, they'd want you too much. I don't think I want the competition."

Oz wrapped her arms around Finn's waist. "There wouldn't be a competition. You'd win hands down."

"See what I'm talking about? Sweet."

"I try. Are you ready? I'll push us off."

Finn set her paddle in the water and waited for the kayak to move. They paddled together, letting the quiet envelop them, only occasionally stopping to take pictures, until they came across a manatee cow and her calf.

Oz couldn't help but laugh as Finn grabbed her camera and slipped into the water to follow them around, taking picture after picture, even though she was still in her shorts and T-shirt. She kept the boat close by in case Finn needed to get out, but the gentle nature of the heavy beasts made it unlikely. She shuddered at the sight of their scarred backs as they played in the water, the battle wounds of survival in a marine world where man was the only predator, yet professed to be a protector.

She rubbed at the scar on her stomach subconsciously as her mind wandered. The scent on the wind was no longer the salt water and mangrove trees, but rather the pungent iron of blood congealing on the blade in her hand. The weight of the knife was reassuring as she stalked the corridors of the cargo ship, searching each room systematically as they tried to gain control, and summon help. Shots reverberated around her, and she knew time was running out. For her and for Rudy. Her heart rate picked up as she kicked open the last door and dropped to roll inside, anticipating the gunfire aimed at the open doorway. She took cover behind an overturned table then peeked around the edge to gauge the shooter's position. One look. Two. And throw the knife on three. Then the crash of a body hitting the floor and the clatter of the gun.

Splashes in the water startled her back to the present and she watched as the calf swam close enough to Finn for her to stroke it, and she marveled at the instinctive trust the animal felt, his natural wariness gone in the face of Finn's gentle nature. It shouldn't be surprising, though. Finn had a sense of tranquility about her that made it easy to trust her. It made her comfortable to be with and terrifying to get close to. Finn grinned up at her as the hulking gray bodies finally disappeared and Oz helped her back into the boat. "Thank you."

"You're welcome." Oz couldn't keep from smiling, the shadows of her past fading in the wake of Finn's happiness. "Did you get me a picture?"

"Perhaps. One or two thousand."

"See? My investment has paid off already."

"Are they endangered?"

"Yes. In two thousand and three, there were only around three thousand left. After Katrina destroyed so much of their habitat, followed by the BP oil spill, I dread to think what the numbers are like now."

"That's such a shame. They're so beautiful. And gentle."

Her excitement was catching, and Oz's grin widened at the wicked thoughts running through her mind as she passed Finn a towel and watched as she tucked it around her and secured it under her arm.

"Do you want me to hold that towel up so you can change?"

"Can you be trusted?"

Oz cocked an eyebrow and shook her head. "Probably not."

"Well, I suppose you've been very well-behaved so far. I'll give you the benefit of the doubt." One corner of her mouth lifted as Finn scrunched her lips together to weigh her options.

"You don't know the kind of things I've been thinking about you."

"Back at ya, hot stuff." She stood and reached under her towel, managing to remove her panties and put on the bikini bottoms Oz had passed her without putting herself on display.

"Very impressive." Oz reached into the bag and pulled out the matching top. "A little disappointing, but impressive. Now. What are you going to do with this one?"

Finn reached for the garment and let the towel fall. Oz's eyes widened as they fixed on the perfect, full, firm breasts before her. It was only seconds before they were covered again and Finn was smirking at the wide-eyed look of shock and desire Oz was sure was firmly planted on her face. Her arms stretched up her back as she tied the string securely.

"Oz?" She waved her hand in front of Oz's face. "Hello, earth to Oz, anyone there?"

"You're trying to kill me aren't you?"

Finn knelt in front of her and placed a hand on either side of the narrow craft for balance. "No, darling, I definitely don't want to do that. Should I say I'm sorry?"

"For what?" Oz grinned and kissed her soundly. "That little peep show should keep me going for at least, I don't know, maybe the rest of the day." She kissed her again, deep and long. "Just be glad I'm not the one with the picture taking fetish!"

Finn laughed as she picked up her paddle again.

"You told me you'd tell me more about you today."

Oz grimaced and looked around, hoping to find a distraction. But there wasn't one. "What do you want to know?"

"Tell me about the navy. What did you do?"

Oz closed her eyes, wishing the topic was one she could avoid but knowing that, eventually, Finn would need to know. If they stood any chance at making this work, she needed to find the strength to share some of her deepest fears. "I was a navy diver. It was pretty varied from day to day. It might be working with explosives or mines, repairs, rescues. Pretty much anything you can think of."

"Rescues? I bet that was pretty exciting."

"No, not really. Sometimes it was pretty scary."

"Really?"

"Yeah."

"Do you want to tell me?"

"Yeah. But not today. Today I want to enjoy the Everglades with you and not think about all that other crap." Oz hoped Finn would drop the subject. She wasn't sure how long she could speak without lying to her. She didn't want to admit to the blood on her hands.

"Thank you for today, Oz. I'm really glad you brought me here."

Oz didn't know if it was intuition or something else that made Finn see her need for the subject change, but whatever it was, she was grateful and more than happy to let it drop. She wondered why a woman as wonderful as Finn was even interested in spending time with her, let alone interested in anything more.

They paddled for a while longer, sticking to safer topics, for which Oz was grateful. The shadows weighing on her shoulders were lightened by Finn's smile, her laugh, her beauty. Oz sighed inwardly, careful to keep her smile in place so Finn wouldn't know just how much it hurt to be so close to something so perfect but know she could never have it.

CHAPTER TWENTY-SEVEN

The knock at the door woke him. Pete glanced at the clock as he made his way through the flat, a persistent fist announcing its owner's presence again.

"Yeah, okay, I'm coming." He pulled open the door and found himself knocked back into his own flat as William Sterling strode into the room. He was a short man with balding hair and a protruding stomach. His well-tailored suit hid the protrusion, but even lifts in his shoes could do little to affect his height.

"Good evening, Peter. Are you well?" He didn't wait for an answer before he continued. "Where is my daughter?" He began wandering from room to room. "Daniela? Come and say hello to your father."

"She isn't here, Mr. Sterling." Pete looked again at Sterling and marveled at Finn's resilience and the courage she showed in escaping from him.

"Then where is she? I've already been to her house and she isn't there."

"She's still in Florida."

"I see. And why are you here, then?"

"I had some matters to attend to here at home. Daniela was enjoying herself. She's made some new friends and so we thought she could stay there a while longer."

"And when is she returning?"

"We haven't really set a date. I may decide to return there for a while first. It depends on what happens here."

"With John Pritchard and his team?"

Pete stared at him. *Fuck.*

"Yes, they've approached me about a position on their team."

"I will double your current salary and give you a promotion. As soon as you and Daniela marry, of course. That should make you very comfortable and ensure you have no need to be speaking to Pritchard and his cronies."

Pete took a deep breath and steadied himself. "That's a very generous offer, Mr. Sterling, but it isn't about money at all. After Mr. Pritchard approached me, I decided to talk to him to see what I could find out from him. That way I could give the information to you, of course." Pete knew his only chance was to convince Sterling he wasn't a traitor. The small smile that twitched at the corner of Sterling's lips set Pete's mind at rest.

"How very enterprising of you, Peter. I must say, I was surprised when I heard you were meeting with Pritchard about the position. This makes much more sense. Why didn't you tell me about it sooner?"

"I wanted to, Mr. Sterling."

"William, please."

Pete inclined his head. "William. As I was saying, I wanted to. However, I suspect that Mr. Pritchard is watching me. Coming to you straight away would have roused his suspicions against me and cost us the opportunity to find out what he knows. I was counting on how well you know me to convince you that my intentions in this matter are only to better assist you."

"Very good, Peter." Sterling headed for the door. "I trust you'll keep me informed now? Discreetly, of course. We don't want this blowing up in our faces."

"And your daughter is fine," Pete said to the closed door. "I'll let her know you asked after her, you selfish old prick." *Fuck!*

Pete picked up the phone and hit the speed dial. He paced the room as he waited for her to answer.

"Hey, Pete. How was the flight?"

"Not bad at all. The reception here wasn't great though. Your dad was just here."

"He called me last night."

"Really?"

"Yeah, at four in the morning. It took me an age to get back to sleep."

"So he already knew you weren't here?" *Double fuck.*

"Pete? Are you still there?"

"Yeah, I'm here. He knows about my meeting with Pritchard. I tried to convince him that I was going to the meeting to see what Pritchard was up to and make sure it wasn't going to cause any problems for your dad. He went for it pretty easily." *Too easily.*

"So when is the meeting with Pritchard?"

"Monday at ten. My body clock's all screwed up. That's tomorrow, right?"

"Last time I checked."

"Good, I'll let you know how it goes. How's everything at your end?"

"It's really great actually. Oz took me out on the Everglades today in a kayak and I went swimming with a manatee."

"What's a manatee?"

"It's like a huge seal. They're also called sea cows. They're really gentle and amazing, and there was a cow and a calf, and the calf let me touch him. It was incredible. I'll e-mail you one of the photos if you like?"

"You took your camera in the water?"

"Yeah. Oz got me a waterproof housing for it." She fell silent.

"I can hear you thinking, Finn. Spit it out."

"I went on a date."

"Really?"

"Yeah."

"Oh my God! When? With who? Where did you go? So many questions."

"Saturday night at Pearl's Patio, a lesbian bar, and there was a great singer with a lovely voice."

"Finn, honey, tell me who."

"Oz. Are you still there? You didn't faint did you?"

"Yeah, I'm here. I thought you said you weren't sleeping with her—"

"I'm not sleeping with her." Finn's voice hardened and he froze. "We had our first date last night, and she kissed me good night at my door and then left me. Nothing inappropriate."

"I'm sorry, Finn. I didn't mean it like that. I guess I'm just surprised. Is she there?"

"Yeah, she's here."

"Can I speak to her?" He heard the rustling as she covered the microphone and spoke to Oz.

"Hi, Pete, how are you?"

"Yeah, Oz, I'm good. I'm a little surprised I guess."

"I know. So am I, to be honest. It wasn't something either of us planned."

"She might not tell you this, but she's not exactly worldly."

"She already told me, Pete."

"She did?"

"Yeah."

"And you're okay with that?"

Oz laughed, but he could hear the edge in it. "I'm terrified. I'm eight years older than her, and I can barely remember being on a date. I understand what you're trying to do here, Pete, and I think you're a great guy for trying to protect her. She hasn't had enough of that. But I promise I'm not trying to take advantage of her. I have no intention of hurting her."

"I'll fly back over there and kick your ass if you do, Oz."

"She did tell you that I was in the navy, didn't she?"

"Yeah, yeah, I realize I might break a nail doing it, but hell. She's worth it."

"I agree, Pete. I'll make you a deal. If I do anything that causes her a moment's pain, I'll come to you. Save you the airfare. No need to add insult to injury."

"Well, that would make things easier. Seriously, though, I'm worried about her. I don't know if she's told you much about her dad, but—"

"Pete, can you hear that?"

"Hear what?"

"That echo on the line."

"Yeah, I noticed that before. Probably a dodgy line. It is an international call, after all."

"Yeah, maybe." She paused while she composed herself and thought. "Listen can you do something for me?"

"What?"

"Get out of your place and find a pay phone. Use your cell phone and text the number to Finn. I'll call you on it."

"I don't get it—"

"Please, Pete." Something in her voice added to his own uneasiness and made him listen to her.

"Okay. I'm going now."

Five minutes later, he was waiting in a call box around the corner from his house as the handset began to ring.

"That echo means your phone has been tapped and someone was listening in."

"Fuck."

"Tell me what I need to know, Pete. Is this her dad?"

"Is she there?"

"I asked her to make me a sandwich. We have a few minutes."

"Her father is a very powerful man with a lot of nasty friends. Well-armed friends. He's involved with people all over the Middle East and North Africa. I know for certain that he's using the company to launder money. I can prove that. What I'm not sure about is where the money is coming from. His legitimate business dealings cover his travel itinerary, but not even close to the wealth he has. There are rumors that he's using the bio labs to develop biological weapons, but I can't prove that. The guy I'm going to meet is MI6."

"How dirty are his hands?"

"At the moment, the police would have a hard time charging him with anything. Suspicions are all well and good, but they won't stop him."

"What do you know about Finn's mom?"

"Again, there are rumors, suspicions. I've read police reports about her disappearance, witness statements, and the coroner's verdict of suicide. I hacked a few government systems I shouldn't have, a bank or two, and found a bank statement for the coroner who ruled it suicide. He was definitely paid off. But I can't trace it back to her dad."

"Pete, are you in danger?"

Pete let out a long breath before he spoke again. "Yeah, I am. After I hang up, I'm going to call Pritchard and go straight in. It's Finn I'm worried about now."

"I'll take care of her, Pete."

"How?"

"I was in the navy for a long time. They trained me well. I won't let anything happen to her."

"I'm probably just being paranoid. She doesn't know anything about all this. Nothing. I've known her practically her whole life, and mostly her dad's just ignored her. It wasn't until she started to show some serious brains that he paid any attention to her at all. She's ignorant to whatever the fuck he's doing." He exhaled loudly. "He may just decide that there's enough going on and leave her alone."

"I don't believe that, and neither do you, Pete."

"I wish I did though."

"Yeah, me too. Is he good? This Pritchard guy?"

"Yeah, I think so. I don't know much about him, but he's got a good record."

"What else can you tell me about her father?"

"They think he's linked to terrorist training camps in North Africa, but they don't really know how, and they can't prove it at the moment."

"Al-Qaeda?"

"Yeah, probably."

"Are you going in by choice?"

"They approached me, but I'm not being forced. I haven't done anything wrong. I want to be a good guy I suppose."

"Okay, when you go in he's gonna have to keep you low for a while. Then he'll give you a new number. Call me on this number, 555-4309. It's a satellite phone and it's secure."

"Why do you have—"

"It's my uncle's. He's an admiral in the navy. Please just call and we'll get the message. Finn will worry otherwise."

"Yeah, I know. Tell her I love her and try to make her believe that this isn't her fault."

"I will. Take care, Pete."

"Take care of her for me."

"Always. That's a promise." He hung up and flipped open his mobile phone to search for Pritchard's number. He looked up just in time to see the car slow down across the street, the barrel of a gun peeking out of the half-open window, the silencer already in place. He felt the air rush from his lungs. He heard the glass wall of the cubicle shatter. He felt his hands move to his stomach of their own volition and saw them come away red. The coppery tang of his own warm blood hit his nostrils as he slid to the ground, the bright red blood seeping away from him, mixing with the shards of glass he lay in. He closed his eyes and laid his head on the ground. Each breath bubbled crimson on his lips as his vision narrowed to a pinprick of light before going dark altogether.

"Fuck, that hurts."

❖

"Sir. It's done," Jack said when Sterling answered the phone.

"Did he place the call to Pritchard?"

"No, sir, but there may be another issue."

"I don't like the sound of that, Jack.

"Sir, after you left, he called your daughter as you expected. She's in Florida—"

"That's what she told me when I spoke with her this morning. What is the problem?"

"Mr. Green alluded to the fact that he was stringing you along. Just as you told me. However, it appears that your daughter has no intention of returning to England. She also seems to have some relationship with the woman she's befriended."

"What are you telling me, Jack?"

"Sir, the woman's intentions toward your daughter are definitely of a sexual nature."

"And does my daughter share this inclination?"

"It would appear so, sir." The silence stretched along the line. "Sir?"

"Do we still have eyes on her?"

"Yes, sir, but she checked out of the hotel and is living with an old woman who rarely leaves the house. We have no phone number or devices in the house."

"Trace the number Green called."

"He called her mobile phone, sir."

"Fuck." Sterling covered the mouthpiece and yelled to his secretary before coming back on the line. "Susan is going to call her and get her information. I'll get the details to you. I want her watched. I want to know exactly what's going on with that little bitch!" He disconnected the call and threw the handset at the wall. So much for marrying her off and keeping her on track. The perversion must be genetic. He'd have to see to her. Regardless of her intelligence, she wasn't worth keeping around if she was going to be like her mother.

CHAPTER TWENTY-EIGHT

Finn walked into the study, placed the sandwich on the table in front of her, and sat in the chair opposite Oz.

"Okay, unnecessary task done. Now will you tell me what's going on?" She watched the guilt wash across Oz's face before she rubbed her hand over her eyes and nodded.

"I'm really sorry about that, but we need to talk about your dad."

"I know. I understand if you don't want to get involved." Finn's head sank to her chest.

"Finn, stop. That's not what I mean." Oz retrieved the envelope from her desk and held it out to Finn.

"What's this?"

"It's information I got from my uncle. It's about your father. I know you're probably going to be pissed off that I did this, but I needed to know what I was getting into after everything you told me about him. I'm sorry." She watched Finn fight back her annoyance and peel open the envelope.

Oz watched as she read page after page. Each business portfolio. Property details. She noticed every time her hand trembled when turning the page. Finn read the police report about her mother's disappearance. The witness reports, the coroner's verdict, and his bank statement. Tears wet the pages in her hands.

"He killed my mother, didn't he?"

"I don't know, baby, but it certainly looks very suspicious."

Finn wiped the tears from her eyes.

"Why? If he wasn't happy in the marriage, why not divorce her and be done with it?" Finn jumped to her feet and began pacing the room, anger clearly replacing her heartache.

"It looks like there was a prenup." Oz shrugged. "The money that started his business came from your mother. He would have lost everything, since he was the one cheating."

"So he killed her instead?"

"It does look that way, but there's no way to prove it. Her body was never found. Without a body, it's very difficult to prove death, never mind murder." Oz crossed the room. Gently, she held Finn's shoulders, hating the pain and confusion in her eyes. "Finn, there's more I need to tell you. Sit down?"

Finn paced a little more before sitting down again.

"Pete has given me a bit more information. You know about this Pritchard guy and the MI6 stuff Pete's involved in?"

"Yes."

"Well, apparently, they've been tracing connections to al-Qaeda training camps in North Africa. Your dad is—"

"Is this a joke? He's my dad, not some kind of terrorist!" She jumped up and started pacing again, and Oz could see her hands shaking as she ran them through her hair.

"Finn, I'm sorry. It seems like it's all true. I wish it wasn't." She grasped Finn's hand as she passed her, bringing her to a stop. "I really do." She looked deep into Finn's eyes, needing her to believe, to know how serious, and potentially deadly, the situation was. "Pete is in danger. His phone was bugged. There's a chance MI6 bugged it, but we can't be sure."

"You think it's my dad?"

"I do, yes."

"Oh, God. Oz, I told Pete about us. Does that mean my dad knows?"

"It doesn't matter."

"If he can kill my mother he—Oh God. I'm going to be sick." She ran for the bathroom. Oz followed and held her hair back as she heaved until her stomach was empty.

"It's okay, baby." She stroked her head as the tears fell, waiting patiently for them to subside. "Are you okay?"

"No."

"Sorry, stupid question. I'm going to call my uncle and see if he can get any more information." Finn didn't move, her eyes fixed on a spot only she could see as Oz walked quickly out of the bathroom.

She grabbed her cell phone and dialed the number Charlie had given her. He answered on the second ring.

"Uncle Charlie."

"Hey, squirt, you okay?"

"Not really. I need some help. William Sterling."

"I've been digging, sweetheart. I'm on my way over now. Your dad is here with me. He's gonna crash our party."

"Uncle Charlie, nothing in life could ever be that bad that we need to bring in my dad."

"True, honey, but you know he hates to be left out."

So they're both worried about me. "Okay, you bring him around to play."

"See you soon, squirt."

Oz knelt next to Finn and stroked her back.

"My dad and Charlie are coming over. They'll be here in a few minutes. Are you up to seeing them?"

"Do they know?"

"Know what, baby?"

"Do they know about my dad?"

"Some of it. Does that matter?"

"Of course it does."

"I'm sorry."

Finn washed her face and walked back to the papers she'd left on the table. She picked up the picture of her mother sitting on a swing with a young Finn on her lap. They were facing each other, Finn pinching her mother's nose.

"Your mom was beautiful." She brushed Finn's hair behind her ear. "You look just like her."

Finn traced her fingers over the face in the photograph. "You think so?"

"Yup." She kissed Finn's head.

"Oz, I wanted your family to be happy about us."

"Honey, I'm sure they will be. You do know that you're the only person in my life who has ever been invited to Thanksgiving dinner, don't you? Ever."

"This will probably change all that."

"Finn, my family knows that everyone is responsible for the things they do, and the decisions they make. I'm not to blame for the things my father has done, and he isn't to blame for the things I've done. Despite what I might have told him when I was a kid." She grinned as Finn chuckled. "You are not to blame for what your father is involved in. Whatever that may be. Nor will I allow you to be vilified because of it."

The doorbell rang and she got up from the sofa. "Are you coming?"

"I'll just be a minute."

Finn's pain was terrible to see, and knowing she couldn't do anything about it made it worse. *This was why I didn't want a relationship.* The need to comfort, to protect another human being was foreign to her, and Oz realized that whether she had wanted it or not, Finn was her responsibility now. And she wasn't about to let her down. She could deal with the relationship question later. Right now, she just had to keep her safe.

❖

"I'm surrounded by giants."

Finn looked at Oz and her father and uncle and gave them a small smile. Charlie was looking around with a mischievous frown.

"Did you two hear something? I'm sure I heard a squeak, but I can't see anything."

"Watch it, Uncle Charlie. She's got a pretty mean right jab."

Billy pointed at Finn. "You've been abusing my girl here?"

Finn looked at him seriously. "Yes, sir, I'm afraid it was necessary."

"I always thought I let her off with too few beatings. Thanks for picking up the slack."

"You guys want coffee?" Oz put the kettle on the stove and reached for cups as everyone assented.

Billy looked at Finn. "How much do you know about your father?"

"Just what Oz and my friend Pete have said. Basically, he's a bastard. It looks like he killed my mum, is some kind of terrorist, and is on MI6's most wanted list. All-round nice guy, really."

Billy looked Finn in the eye. "Are you ready for this?"

"No, but best not let that stop you."

"I really like her, Oz. She reminds me of your mother. Okay, here goes. Charlie?"

"My sources tell me that Sterling has a lot of very legitimate businesses. Very easily covers all his traveling, but not his income. The funds we know about exceed a couple hundred million. That's personal.

Not from any company." He took a sip of his coffee and looked Finn in the eye. "My sources also tell me that MI6 is looking at him in connection to al-Qaeda. CIA is looking at him in the same way, mostly because of the whispers around his biomedical labs. Rumors suggest he's developed bio weapons and he's got buyers ready to take them."

"Oh, God." Finn bolted from the room, her hand over her mouth.

"Is she okay?" Billy asked.

"Would you be?" Oz shrugged. "She'll be throwing up again. I'll just go check on her."

They sat sipping their coffee until Oz came back.

"Finn'll be back in a minute."

"She throw up?"

"Yeah."

"She don't take after her old man then."

"No."

"Glad to hear it. How'd she react when you told her about your last mission?" Charlie asked.

Oz blanched. "I haven't yet—"

"What haven't you told me yet?" Finn slid back into her seat next to Billy and smiled at him as he wrapped an arm around her shoulders and squeezed her in a quick one-armed hug.

"Uncle Charlie's talking about my last mission for the navy. The one where I got shot." She took a deep breath, already hating the look in Finn's eyes. The shadows of pain grew with every new detail she learned, and Oz's self-loathing ratcheted up another notch as she spoke the words she knew would only add to Finn's pain. But with her dad and Charlie there, she felt strong enough to tell Finn the truth. A truth she needed to know because she was about to depend on Oz and her family for her safety. It was now or never. "It went wrong. Rudy lost his leg, but a lot of other people lost their lives." Silence filled the room. Charlie and Billy were watching Finn, waiting for her reaction. Oz white-knuckled her coffee cup.

"You killed people?"

Oz felt trapped. But she finally looked at Finn and answered. "Yes."

Finn looked at Billy and Charlie, and then at Oz before tears started sliding down her cheeks. "I'm sorry. I need to—" She left the room again. Oz stood to follow.

"Give her a few minutes, Oz."

"But, Dad—"

"No, everything for her has just changed. Give her a few minutes."

"He's right, Oz. She'll be okay. She needs a little time to adjust."

She desperately wanted to follow Finn, to hold her, reassure her, to make sure that they were still okay. She knew, deep down, though, that her relationship with Finn had just irrevocably changed. Suddenly, she felt queasy too.

"Oz, we need to decide how best to deal with this. How close is she to her dad?"

Oz pushed her feelings aside and focused on the problems they had to deal with to keep Finn safe. As long as she was safe, everything else could be dealt with later. She hoped. "Not very. He seems to think she's a trophy more than a daughter."

"Does he know where she's staying?"

"Her friend Pete called earlier. She told him about us. I was speaking to him and heard an echo on the line. I'm pretty sure it was bugged by her dad's guys."

"She hasn't given him any other details though?"

"No, just referred to me as 'Oz' and there was no mention of Mrs. Richmond."

"Well, that gives you a little anonymity."

"I asked her to avoid giving the address to either place if she can. She agreed."

"Good. How long is she planning on staying in the States?"

"She has no plans to go back."

"How?"

"She's here on an American passport. Her mother was from Sarasota Springs."

"Well, that makes life a bit easier, baby girl. About time you did me a favor."

"I can get you a place on the base for a while if you need it. I've got a base full of sailors, armed guards on the gates. Doesn't get much more secure than that."

"Thanks, Uncle Charlie. I might take you up on that. If Finn speaks to me again."

"You're not getting rid of me that easily." Oz jumped from her seat and ran the three steps it took her to cross the room, then kissed

Finn full on the mouth. Finn was blushing deeply when she pulled away. "We need to talk about this, but there's something I need to know right now."

"Anything?"

"The people you killed, they were trying to kill you, weren't they?"

"Yes."

"Then you did what you had to do."

Oz stared deep into her eyes, wishing she could read her mind before she closed her eyes and nodded.

Charlie cleared his throat. "I was just offering you both an alternative place to stay. If you think it will help, I can get you accommodation on the base. I can't think of anywhere safer. As I was saying, armed guards on the gates, a base full of navy men. Think about it. If you need it, it's there."

"Thank you, Charlie. I really appreciate that. Please don't be offended if I tell you I hope we won't need to do that."

"Not offended at all." He smiled kindly. "I have a few questions for you, if you don't mind?"

"At this point, I'd be surprised if you didn't. What do you need to know?"

"You worked at the bio lab in London, correct?"

"Yes."

"What did you do there?"

"I was a researcher. My dad wanted me to eventually take over the running of the lab, but I wasn't ready. I didn't want it either, but that didn't seem to matter. The promotion was meant to be my wedding present."

"What were you researching?"

"I was looking at a new treatment protocol using the E. coli bacteria as a vehicle to introduce material into the host that would either be eradicated or rendered ineffective if introduced in other ways."

Oz laughed. "In English, Finn."

"Sorry. E. coli is a bacterium we all have in our gut. It's harmless and it's part of the normal flora of the gut. What I was working on was incorporating other substances, medicines, into the bacteria that would then treat the person. I was trying to incorporate cancer drugs into the bacteria. If it had worked, then it would have made treatments like chemotherapy much simpler and far less harmful to the patient."

Oz stared at her. "Did it work?"

"I managed to develop a way to get the substances into the bacteria's genetic code, and it was stable. It worked and test subjects in the lab responded to the protocol and were eventually cured. The survival rate in the test subjects was incredible. Long-term, it became problematic because the bacterial replication was unstoppable, and the progeny also created the compound. In most cases, the progeny were actually more prolific in the generation of the substances."

"And why does that matter?"

"Well, we don't want to keep treating the patient after they're cured, and the continued creation of medicine in the gut caused the test subjects to become ill. Eventually, they all died, not from the cancer, but from the cure."

"What medicine were you using?"

"I started with Avastin. It's a typical drug used to treat colon cancer."

"Is that the only chemical that would work?"

"No. The protocol I created could be used to incorporate just about any foreign substance into the bacteria."

"Such as?"

"The list is huge, Charlie. Almost anything you can think of. Anti-inflammatory drugs, medicines for leukemia."

"And can your work be replicated by someone else?"

"Well, yes, of course. The protocol was patented by my father's company. He can give the research and data to anyone he likes. But it's really not worth anything. Like I said, it doesn't make a good medical treatment because of the replication issues."

"But that makes it perfect for a biological weapon."

"What? No. I didn't build a weapon. It's a treatment—"

"I know, Finn, but what you've described sounds like it could easily be adapted." Oz wanted to wrap her arms around Finn again as the horror of what they were saying made sense.

"It was supposed to be to help people."

Charlie grasped Finn's hand and waited until she looked at him. "If I bring you some more information, can you look at it and tell me what you see?"

"Of course. Is that what he's done? Taken my work and used it as a weapon?"

"I don't know, Finn. I really don't. Like I said before, most of what we know is coming from Pete, and a good portion of everything else is just rumors."

"Maybe I should just go and see him—"

"No!" Oz knew the last place Finn should be was anywhere near her father. If even half of their suspicions were true, she knew Finn was in danger, especially if Pete was as compromised as she suspected. She tried to find the words to explain to Finn, but the wide-eyed look of terror on Finn's face made it hard for her to think clearly.

Billy cleared his throat. "Finn, I think we all agree that seeing your father right now is probably not the best idea for you."

"But he's my father; he wouldn't hurt me—"

"We don't know that, baby, and I can't take that chance." Oz hadn't moved. She didn't think she could. Her heart was racing, and sweat trickled down her back as the fear started to become panic. She turned her back on them and leaned against the kitchen counter, not wanting them to see her lose control.

"Come on, Billy, let's leave these two alone. We'll go get a drink."

"Now I know why you got the higher rank. Full of good ideas, aren't you, brother?"

"Yup." They drained their cups and headed for the front door.

"Oz?"

Oz didn't move. She couldn't, not until Finn gently turned her around to face her. The pain had gone from Finn's expression, and there was no trace of the fear either.

"Oz, I think I've taken all I can for tonight, but I need to know that you're all right."

Oz couldn't help but smile. In the midst of so much turmoil, Finn cared enough to check that she was okay.

"I will be. Let me walk you home." Oz wrapped her arms tightly about Finn, wishing they could stay that way, but knowing the rest of the world would intrude far too quickly, she led Finn home.

CHAPTER TWENTY-NINE

Oz draped her towel over her shoulders and reached for her cell phone. She stumbled slightly as the dive boat lurched beneath her feet. She cursed her inability to concentrate on anything but Finn all day. Finn had been adamant that she wanted to carry on as normal, and just as adamant that she didn't want to talk about anything yet. But she'd been distracted enough that Oz had kept a careful eye on her every time they went in the water.

Oz noted the UK phone number as she connected the call.

"Is that you, Pete?"

"Who is this?" The voice on the other end of the phone was harsh and gritty, as though the speaker was a heavy chain smoker.

"I'm Oz. Who are you?"

"Oz? What the bloody hell kind of name is that? I'm looking for Olivia Zuckerman."

"The only kind you're going to get till you tell me who you are."

"Pritchard. My name is John Pritchard."

"Why are you calling me? Is Pete okay?"

"Who the hell are you?"

"Olivia Zuckerman. I'm a friend of Pete's, and Daniela is here with me."

"Daniela, as in Sterling's daughter?"

"Yes. Is Pete with you? When I last spoke to him he was on a pay phone and about to call you."

"He told you about his involvement with me?"

"Yes, he did. I heard an echo on his home line and told him to call me from a pay phone. Surely he told you all of this. You must have spoken to my uncle to get this number, and you could have only spoken to him if Pete gave you the number."

"He didn't call me. I need you and Daniela to come in and give me a statement."

"What do you mean he didn't call? How did you get the number?"

"It was written on the back of his hand. His body was found in the early hours of the morning. He'd been shot outside a telephone box."

Oz's knees went weak and she sank into a crouch, resting her back against the side. "Fuck."

"Precisely. Do you have a pen handy? I'll give you an address to come and give me a statement."

"Not possible."

"Okay, I'll send a car to pick you up."

"Not possible. I'm in the Florida Keys, and Daniela is here with me."

"Ah. I expected she would return with Mr. Green."

"That was never her plan."

"I still need to speak to you both at length."

"I can organize a face-to-face sat link if you can give me an hour or so to get back to land."

"How exactly are you going to do that? Look, I'll call you in thirty minutes with a flight for you and Ms. Sterling."

"With all due respect, sir, if Finn goes back to the UK, she's in danger."

"I'll protect her—"

"I'll protect her here. My uncle is the base commander here at Key West. I'll have a satellite video link available within the hour and then we can talk face-to-face."

"Who are you?"

"I'm a diving instructor. I'll call you in an hour on this number with instructions." She disconnected the phone call and ran to Jose. "Jose, we need to get back ashore. Now."

"The last team is just coming out of the water."

"Good. As soon as they're aboard, get us back to the dock. As fast as you can."

Jose picked up the radio. "Carlos. We've got an emergency. Get the divers seated and then help them get their gear off. As soon as it's stowed, tell me and I'll open up the engine. I'll be at three-quarters before that." Jose started calling in their plans to the shore patrol, and Oz left him to it. She made her way quickly across the upper deck of the boat and placed a call to her uncle.

"Hey, pipsqueak, I was expecting you to call. I just had a call from a guy named Pritchard. Said he was MI6."

"Yeah, he got me. We have a problem. I need to set up a video sat link to MI6. Pete was killed last night. Shot in the call box before he could contact Pritchard."

"Damn it. I've just made a couple of calls regarding Agent Pritchard. He checks out so far. How long before you can be here?"

"We're out past Key Largo at the moment. I'll be back on the dock in about thirty minutes."

"I'll have a chopper waiting to get you and Finn."

"Thanks, Uncle Charlie." She looked down the ladder and watched Finn helping remove tanks and BCDs from the divers and pass them to Carlos. They worked efficiently, and within two minutes, all the gear was stowed and the divers were making their way inside the cabin to warm up and change. The news she needed to give Finn broke her heart. She closed her eyes at the pain she was about to cause the woman she had come to care for more than anyone outside her family.

"Oz, what's the problem? Why are we heading to shore?" Finn looked up at Oz, shading her eyes against the sun.

Oz descended to the lower deck, thinking fast. "Pritchard called me. We need to get to the base. There'll be a chopper waiting for us when we get to the dock. We need to talk to him, and the best way to do that is face-to-face over a video satellite link."

"Why?"

Oz caught people watching them out of the corner of her eye and knew this was neither the time nor the place to give Finn the news about Pete. She hated lying to Finn, even if it would only be until they got to shore, but she wanted Finn to have some privacy when she learned about Pete's death. "I'm not sure. We'll find out more when we get there. It won't be long." She grasped Finn's hand, giving it a little squeeze before she went to the cockpit, knowing the only way she could keep her silence was to keep a little distance from Finn and the worried look in her eyes.

Jose took them into the quayside stern to, and Carlos quickly jumped off the boat and guided it in, securing the stays as he went. He was still securing the lines when Oz led Finn to the stern and helped her off the boat. Rudy pointed to the parking lot, where they could hear the whirling blades of the awaiting helicopter.

Oz turned to Finn and took her hands after making sure they had privacy. "Before we get on the chopper, I need to tell you something. I didn't want to tell you on the boat with everyone around. The reason Pritchard needs to speak to us is because of Pete."

"I thought so. How else would he know to call us here?"

Oz shook her head. "No, Pete didn't call him."

"Then how?"

"Pete had Charlie's number written on the back of his hand." She held Finn's hands. "Pete couldn't call him. They found him in the call box."

Finn froze, her eyes wide. She shook her head as realization began to sink in, tears welling in her eyes.

"Finn, Pete was killed, and you're in danger."

"No. No. No, no, no, no, no." Finn sank to the ground, her face in her hands.

"Finn, listen to me, honey."

"How?"

"He was shot, baby." Oz wrapped her arms around her and held her as the sobs racked her body. "I'm so sorry, baby."

"It was my dad, wasn't it?"

"I don't know, baby."

"Oz, you've never lied to me before. Don't start now."

"I'm not lying to you, baby. I don't know that it was your dad. I think so, but I could be wrong. I'm sorry, baby, but we need to get going."

"So we're going in the helicopter. Then what?" She continued to sob, even as she stood.

"We get to the base and we talk to Pritchard. Then we decide if we're going to stay on the base or go home."

"I need to talk to Pete's parents. Find out when the funeral will be so I can get a flight back. Oh my God."

"They won't release the body for a little while. They have to get all the evidence first, but I don't think it's a good idea to go to the funeral."

Finn pulled away. "The body? Evidence?" She wrapped her arms around herself as though trying to keep from flying apart. "It's not a body, Oz. It's Pete…" She started sobbing again, bent over her arms, her body taut with grief.

"No, baby, stop please. Listen to me. I'm sorry. We have to assume that your dad knows about you and me." She pulled Finn to her and felt her sag against her. "We also know that he is a very dangerous man." She let go of one hand and cupped Finn's chin in order to raise her head from her chest. "Pete loved you, and the last thing he said to me was to look after you. He wouldn't want you to go, knowing that it was potentially dangerous for you. I need to keep you safe."

"You think he wants to kill me too?"

"I don't know.

"He's my dad. He wouldn't want to kill me." She ripped her hands from Oz's and bent over, clearly trying to keep from vomiting.

"Finn, baby, how well do you actually know your dad?"

Finn stepped back and turned cold eyes on her. Eyes that had shown her tenderness and desire now held nothing but pain and fear. She felt her anger growing as she saw the light in those beautiful green eyes dim.

"Do you really think he wants to kill me?"

"I don't know, baby, but I'm not going to take that chance. If we get to the base, he won't know where you are. Please don't be angry with me for wanting to protect you."

"He's my father, Olivia." The tears fell from her eyes again. "My own father. I can't believe he would want to hurt me."

"Maybe I'm wrong. I hope I am. I really hope I am, baby. But please." She kissed her cheek. "Please don't ask me to take that risk." She tightened her grip around Finn's shoulders again. "I only just found you. I don't want to lose you now." Oz took her hand and led her to the helicopter. "Have you ever been in one of these things before?" Oz asked, pulling Finn into a crouch as they ran.

Finn shook her head and they climbed up, the wind from the blades blasting their wet swimwear dry instantly. Oz passed her a helmet with ear protectors and a microphone attached to it. Finn fastened it under her chin as Oz secured straps around her waist and shoulders.

"Everyone good to go back there?"

"Yes, sir." After a ten-minute flight, they landed on the enormous base, but Finn didn't seem to notice anything around them. An officer greeted them and escorted them through a maze of corridors before leading them into a room with a huge video screen, computer screens with radar, satellite, and map images covering them. Charlie handed a clipboard to another officer before he walked over to them.

"Oz, Finn, I hope I don't have to tell you that everything in here is classified."

Oz held her hand up to stop him. "You're right. You don't have to tell us. Is everything set up?"

"Yes, I just had the call placed to Pritchard, and they should be coming online any second." He turned toward the large screen as it filled with the ruddy, stubble-covered visage of the man himself, his suit visibly wrinkled with the jacket and tie discarded. His thinning hair was sticking up at odd angles.

"Agent Pritchard. I'm Rear Admiral Zuckerman. This is my niece, Olivia Zuckerman, and Daniela Finsbury-Sterling."

The man nodded. "Thank you for your help in this, Admiral."

"Not a problem. I'll hand you over to Oz now."

"Agent Pritchard." Oz stepped forward.

"Ms. Zuckerman."

"Please call me Oz. Now, where do you want to start?"

"Very well, Oz. How are you involved in this matter?"

"Daniela is here training to be a dive instructor at my dive school. While she has been here, we have become very good friends."

"You had no prior connection to the family or Peter Green?"

"No, sir, I did not."

"Are you aware of Sterling Enterprises?"

"Yes, sir. Since meeting Finn, I have made it my business to find out about Sterling Enterprises and William Sterling himself."

"And what have you learned?"

"That the legitimate businesses are extensive and well run, but the wealth he has amassed far exceeds what you would expect. There are many unsubstantiated rumors as to connections with terrorists, ostensibly in relation to his bio labs. The feeling is he's ready to start selling biological weapons on the black market."

"Oh God." Finn's voice was barely a whisper, her face paled and her hand shook as she covered her mouth.

Charlie wrapped an arm about Finn's shoulders and led her to a chair.

"Ms. Zu—Oz. Is there anything else?"

"I don't know if you've seen the evidence regarding the disappearance, and the subsequent coroner's report, in regards to Finn's mother. There is compelling evidence that the coroner was paid off to find a verdict of suicide and therefore halt the investigation, and rendered a verdict within weeks of the disappearance rather than the seven-year legal requirement for cases when a body is not recovered. I believe that Sterling killed his wife."

"How did you come by all of this information?"

"Some of it I got from Mr. Green, some of it from my uncle."

Pritchard nodded. "Ms. Finsbury-Sterling."

Finn had her head between her knees, clearly trying to catch her breath. She got up slowly when Pritchard said her name. "Finn."

"How did you become aware of all this information?"

"Pete told me some things before he left, and Oz told me the rest of what I know."

"And what did Mr. Green tell you?"

"That you were investigating money laundering at Sterling Enterprises."

"Anything else?"

"Not really. What happened to him?"

"He was shot. We've traced the call logs of the phone box he was in. It was less than a minute after he hung up from speaking to Oz. His death was quick. Three bullet wounds all center mass. It was professional."

Finn swallowed convulsively and wrapped her arms around herself again. Charlie placed a hand on her shoulder and squeezed. Prichard turned his attention back to Oz.

"After speaking with you earlier, we checked Mr. Green's flat. There were no listening devices, but there had been a very obvious break-in. All electronic devices, computer, laptop, mobile phones, were missing. The place is a mess. We suspect that they removed any such devices at the same time. We suspect it was Sterling's operation that had them planted. What else was discussed during the conversation that Sterling would have heard?"

"He'll know that Pete was planning to betray him to you. That Finn isn't planning to return to the UK, and that we are involved."

"Romantically?"

"Yes."

"Is this a new discovery for your father?"

"Yes. He wanted Pete and me to marry."

"Was he aware of Mr. Green's preferences?"

"Yes. It didn't matter."

"I see." Pritchard signaled to someone out of the view of the camera. A figure moved into the shadows of the shot and handed Pritchard a file. "We do know that Sterling is still in the country and has not filed any flight plan for his private jet, nor has he booked any tickets on commercial flights. Where will you both be for me to contact you again?"

"I've made it possible for them to stay on the base for the duration," Charlie said.

"No place safer, Admiral. Very good."

"What are we expecting the duration to be, Agent Pritchard?" Finn asked

He looked at Finn. "A very good question. I'm afraid we're still trying to get evidence together to prosecute your father. With Mr. Green out of the picture, and your father now alerted to our interest in him, that will be more difficult."

"Is that your way of telling me you have no idea?"

"Yes. I'm sorry. We're working as quickly as we can, given that Sterling is aware we're watching him. Is there anything you can think of, Ms. Sterling, any person your father might confide in? Someone we could contact for information?"

Finn thought for a moment and shook her head. "I'm sorry, Agent Prichard. I wasn't really involved in my father's life or businesses. I've never seen him close to anyone."

Prichard nodded. "Our records show you didn't spend much time with him. But if you think of anyone, please let us know."

"What do you know about the biological weapons?" Charlie asked.

"I'm not at liberty to say, Admiral. But if you have information, I'd like to hear it." Charlie turned to Oz and motioned for them to leave. She took Finn's hand and led her from the room.

"Ah, not in front of the civilians?"

Oz nodded. "Something like that, baby."

"So we just wait?"

"It won't take long." The door opened two minutes later and Charlie stepped out. He motioned them to follow him and led them through the maze to an office, his name stenciled on the door.

"Would you girls like a drink? I've got water here. I can get coffee brought in or…" He opened one of the drawers in his desk and waved a bottle of Jack Daniels at them. They both agreed and waited as he poured three shots and raised his in salute.

"To Pete." They repeated the toast and Oz and Charlie stared as Finn tossed back the whiskey and slammed the glass back down on the desk.

"So what are they doing about my dad?"

"They aren't going to do any damn thing at the moment. We know more about the biological weapons than they do. With what they do have, they can't do a damn thing. He is, and I quote, looking into the matter further. In other words, he'll take the information I've given him and decide what to do next."

"So what are we doing?" She looked at Oz. "We can't hide on the base indefinitely."

"I've got my source looking into the bio stuff further," Charlie said. "If we can get more intelligence on that angle, then Pritchard will have to move on it, or the CIA will."

"That doesn't sound good." Finn's brow furrowed.

"No, it's not likely to be a good outcome. Give me a couple of weeks. I'll get you set up with some housing on base, and I can get your boat authorized to dock here if you want to keep diving. It will keep you occupied while we're digging."

"Thanks, Uncle Charlie. I need my laptop and some other stuff off the boat. Can you get them clearance to dock today?"

"No problem. Just get me the name of the boat and make sure any passengers they have stay on the boat when they dock."

"Will do."

Finn watched them organize the business, the boats, and her dive training from the base in a few short sentences. "Oz, surely this isn't really necessary."

"I'm probably being paranoid, but I'd rather be cautious." Oz stepped close to her and placed a gentle kiss against her brow. "I'd also prefer it if you stayed here while I go to the house. I'll pick up anything you want me to get for you."

"Oz, that's rid—" Finn put her hands to Oz's chest and pushed her back.

"I think she's right to be cautious, Finn. Your father has long arms, and it only takes a phone call to the right person…" Charlie left the rest unsaid. Finn looked from one to the other.

"You really think my dad would kill me?" she whispered.

Their sidelong glances answered her question.

"That answers that, then." She pushed a hand into her hair and eased out of Oz's embrace. She needed a bit of distance, a bit of control. Everybody was taking over, making decisions. No one asked what she wanted, and it didn't seem to matter anyway. "And where exactly do you want me to wait?"

"There's a house here on the base for you both. I can take you over there now or you can wait with me while Oz goes to get your things."

"I shouldn't be much more than an hour. Two tops. Can you lend me your car, Uncle Charlie?"

"Of course."

"No offense, Charlie, but I really think I'd like to be alone for a while," Finn said quietly, feeling like she could drop to her knees any second.

"None taken, darlin'. Should I show you to the house?"

Oz took Finn's hand and she gently pulled it away, not acknowledging the flash of hurt in her eyes.

"It's only a one-bed house, but it should be enough for the time being. It's only temporary, after all." He pulled a key from his pocket and opened the door. A dank odor permeated the air as they stepped inside. The living space and kitchenette were small, and the furniture, a small table with a single chair against a dingy wall, a dirty beige couch with a multitude of stains on the cushions, and a rug of indeterminate color, made the space seem like something from a bad vacation movie. Not a place to live while they hunted her psychotic father.

Finn wandered into the bedroom. The mattress was bare on the bed frame. There were no curtains, and the light shining through the grimy glass highlighted the dust in the air. The walls were the same dying magnolia color throughout. She went into the bathroom. Toilet, sink, shower, all uniform white and functional, all surprisingly clean.

"I'm sorry, Finn."

"Charlie. Stop. Don't say you're sorry. There's nothing wrong here that a little air and a pair of curtains can't sort out. Thank you for your help." She turned to Oz. "You ready for the list I'm going to give you?"

"Will I need a pen and paper?"

"Probably. My camera. Everything I need is in the case. My laptop and the books on the desk in my room. If you take the curtains from my room and bring those, they should fit the windows in the bedroom. I don't think Emmy will mind, but you might want to ask her first. The bedding from there should be fine for in here too."

"Of course it is. What clothes do you want me to get you?"

"Shorts, T-shirts, underwear, jeans, just the usual stuff. My suitcase is in the closet." She turned to Charlie. "Is there somewhere on base that I can get some food?"

"I'll take care of it, baby." Oz said.

"Sweetheart, I can do it. It'll give me something to do while you're away."

"I'll take you to the store once Oz leaves." Charlie said as he handed over his car keys.

"Thank you, Charlie."

Oz left quickly and Charlie led Finn to the commissary. She was quiet as she filled her basket, not paying attention to what she was taking off the shelves. She was grateful that Charlie seemed content to let her be; she couldn't take any more bad news. Her head felt like it was going to explode as questions pummeled her with no answers in sight. The few answers she did have terrified her.

The pain of Pete's death felt like it was crushing her, stopping her from breathing and making her dizzy. The possibility her father was responsible was a thought she couldn't bear. She didn't want to accept that the man who had fathered her was capable of killing her best friend. She didn't want it to be true, but already the reality of the situation, the reality of the man, was becoming clearer to her. He would stop at nothing. He didn't care who he hurt or who he killed. If they were in his way, they were a target.

She began to see exactly what Oz had meant when she said that she was in danger. Finn realized that her lack of involvement in her father's illicit dealings was not a safety net, because she knew far too much to be outside of his control. She knew too much about the development of the bacteria, and if it was intended as a weapon, her knowledge could lead to a cure for it, making it far less valuable on the black market. Slowly, as though she were watching a film, everything became clear.

At thirty, she received full access to her trust and was independently wealthy of her father, so he couldn't control her financially anymore. Marrying her off to someone he felt he controlled was another level of control, another jailer that she would have to break away from before she could think for herself. He didn't know Pete had never wanted that kind of control over her. She realized that anyone around her who wasn't in his control faced the same risk that Pete had. *And we didn't even know it. Not again. I won't be the reason anyone else gets hurt. I can't do that to Oz.*

CHAPTER THIRTY

"Honey, I'm home." Oz walked into the house, her fists full of trash bags, backpacks over her back, Finn's camera and laptop cases over her shoulders. Finn walked out of the kitchen area and kissed her, taking some of the bags from her. "I missed you." They kissed again and Oz pulled her closer to her. The whole time she had been gone she had been worried about Finn's frame of mind. She had looked so small and fragile when Oz had left the base, and it broke her heart to know there wasn't anything she could do to fix it.

"I missed you too. I've made dinner. It just needs to go in the oven. Are you hungry?"

"Yeah, but I think we should get some of this sorted first." Oz pointed to the bags. Maybe if they got some of their own stuff in the house, it wouldn't seem so awful. Maybe it wouldn't feel like Finn had put some distance between them. "Then we can sit down and relax."

"Okay."

Together they put the house in order, slowly making it more homey. Herbs and sauce, along with open windows, helped dissipate the musty smell. They worked in silence, and with every minute, Oz felt more panic churning in her stomach. They'd left a beach house and moved to an ugly base house. Finn was quiet, clearly lost in her own thoughts and pain, and Oz couldn't figure out how to make anything better.

"Dinner's almost ready. Charlie found another chair earlier, so I thought we could sit at the table."

Oz sat down as Finn put the baking sheet into the sink and came back with a bowl of salad and a bottle of wine. Finn's voice trembled slightly, and tension stretched between them like a rubber band stretched too tight.

"This is wonderful." She caught Finn's hand and kissed it. "Just like you."

Finn smiled sadly. "Oz, we need to talk."

Oz's stomach lurched. "Those have got to be the most feared words in any relationship. Baby, I know this place isn't great, but it's temporary."

"It's not that, darling—"

"Oh." Oz's voice was flat as she racked her brain for another problem. "Does being on the base make you think about my past? About what I've done?" She felt the bile rising in her throat, anger and guilt playing an equal part.

"Oz, it's nothing like that. It's about me."

"It's not me, it's you? That is such crap, Finn." Oz frowned, desperation and panic combining into an angry parcel.

"Oz, will you let me speak? Please?"

Oz pressed her lips together and sat quietly, folding and unfolding a napkin, shredding it into pieces.

"I don't know how to thank you for everything you've done. You and your family. I don't know how I can ever thank you enough. But I don't want to put you all in danger any more. I think it might be best if I went back to England and faced my dad. That's the only way you can be safe."

She doesn't want me. She wants to go. I don't know how I've done it, but I've fucked it up already. She thinks she'd be better off without me.

"You can't go. Finn, he's going to hurt you. I'm sure of it. Please don't—"

"I don't think he will. If he thinks he doesn't have anything to fear from me, he'll leave me alone."

"I've known men like him before. Everything I've learned about him tells me he doesn't care that he's your father. All he cares about is himself! If you go to him, you're making it easy for him. Do you want to end up like Pete?"

"Don't be ridiculous. I don't want anyone to get hurt."

"Then don't go."

"I have to."

"No, you don't. Stay. Here, with me. I'll protect you—"

"If he's the man you say he is, you can't protect me from him."

"Yes, I can. I will."

"I have to go, Oz. Don't you see?"

"See what? That you're choosing to leave me?"

"That I'm trying to protect you!"

"Me? I don't need protection. He's not after me."

"Pete didn't think he did either."

Oz leaned forward, desperately wanting to touch her but afraid something would break inside her if Finn rejected her. "What happened to Pete was not your fault."

"No? Because from where I'm standing, the only reason he was involved in any of this mess is because he was my friend."

"It was your father's fault, not yours."

"He was my best friend. He was the only one who was always there for me. Now he's dead, and it's all my fault."

"Finn—"

"No. I won't risk it again. I won't let anything happen to anyone else."

"Finn, you can't stop him."

"I can stop him hurting you. If I'm not with you, he has no reason to hurt you."

"I'll take the chance."

"I won't. Don't you see? I can't. I've lost everyone. Everyone I ever cared about is gone. He's taken my mother and Pete. I won't let that happen to you too."

"So you're just going to give up? Walk out on me, on us?"

"That's not what I'm doing."

"Isn't it? It sure looks like it to me."

"You don't understand."

"Then make me understand, Finn. Explain it so that I can understand why you're okay about walking out of here and straight back to the life you were desperate to escape." Her hands were shaking as she clenched and unclenched them at her sides. "When you came here you were certain you were never going back. That your father wasn't going to be a part of your life anymore. You dreamed of living your own life, making your own choices."

"This is my choice."

"Is it? Because I don't think this is a choice you're making. I think it's a reaction." She took a chance and took Finn's hands in her own. "I think you're in shock and that you'll see what a bad idea this is when—"

Finn ripped her hands away. "Don't, Oz. Don't patronize me."

"I'm not trying to patronize you. I want you to stay. I need you to stay here so I can protect you. I need to look after you, Finn. I can't do that if you're not here."

"I told you, I'm going back to London. I'm going to see my father and I'm going to stop anyone else getting hurt."

"I can't let you do that."

"What?" Finn whirled around, her eyes blazing in her anger. "What did you say? You can't let me? And what exactly are you going to do? Lock me in? Are you going to put bars on the window so I can't climb out?" She pushed against Oz's chest, pushing her away. "I won't let you hold me here."

"That's not what I meant. I just want you to think about this calmly and rationally before you do something we'll both regret."

"I think it's too late for that, don't you?"

"Finn—"

"Just stop. I'm going back to London. End of story."

Oz felt like an abyss had opened beneath her feet and was swallowing her whole. Finn had walked into her life with her oversized clothes, cute accent, and beautiful eyes, and Oz had let herself believe in the possibilities. She had let herself believe she was worthy of being with someone like Finn. She had let Finn's innocence soothe her demons, and her joy at all the simple wonders she had seen had brought Oz so much pleasure. She had wanted so desperately for it all to be real, for it to last, that she had forgotten that she didn't belong here. It was time to let go of the fantasy, the dream, and let Finn go her own way.

"Is that really what you want?" Oz tried to keep her face blank and her voice calm, holding back the tears that threatened to spill down her cheeks.

"Yes, that's what I want. I want to go to London. I want to go and talk to my dad. It's my decision, and no one else's." Oz got to her feet and went to the front door. She slowly pulled it open and spoke without turning.

"Stay here as long as you need to. I can organize a ride to the airport for you whenever you're ready." She closed the door behind her and let the tears fall. If Finn wanted to leave, she wasn't going to beg her to stay. She was a grown woman, and she could do what she wanted. Maybe she was right. If her father didn't think she was a threat, he'd leave her alone. Oz had no right to make her live in a military base just because she wanted to protect her. She had no right to expect Finn to stay with her. She would let go and pray to whoever was listening that she had done the right thing.

CHAPTER THIRTY-ONE

O z didn't know where she was going. She just knew she couldn't stop. It hurt too much, and she only stopped walking when she came to the obstacle training course. The blood was pumping through her veins, and the need to run was making her muscles twitch. She didn't think about the darkness descending around her. She didn't think at all. She just needed to outrun the pain.

You always knew you weren't good enough for her, Zuckerman. It's not a surprise. You knew she would need to get away from you. You have nothing to offer a woman like her.

Her feet pounded the hard-packed dirt as she started running, her pace fast and furious. She attacked each obstacle with the fury building inside her. Each wall surmounted, and every bridge crossed. Every single inch of the course scoured.

She dragged herself through the half submerged tunnel and continued running, covered in the foul smelling mud that had lain in the pits for years. Years of doubts and fears, of panic and loneliness kept her company as she ran. She carried on, ignoring the sting of the barbed wire, the scrapes to her hands and knees as she threw herself over the wall and collapsed on the other side of the finish point.

What I said didn't matter. Nothing I feel for her matters. It's everything I've done before her that she sees. And I can't erase that.

"What you doing here, squirt?"

Oz opened her eyes to see Charlie looking down at her. She just stared up at him through the haze of self-loathing eating her soul.

"You needed to blow off a bit of steam, huh?"

She closed her eyes again before covering them with her arm, her breathing ragged and sweat running down her neck.

He sat on the grass beside her. "I thought you'd be back at the house with Finn. I know she was planning on cooking you some fancy dinner. You best get over there before it burns."

"She doesn't want me there."

Charlie looked at her before he spoke. "She tell you that?"

Oz shrugged.

"What happened?"

Oz didn't know where to start. She felt the tears well in her eyes again and tried to push herself off the ground, intent on running the course again. Charlie held her arm and pulled her back down on the grass beside him. Then he waited patiently.

"She said we needed to talk. That she thought going back to England and facing her father was the best way to deal with this whole situation." She wrapped her arms about her knees and let the tears fall. "I only just found her, Uncle Charlie, and already she doesn't want me."

"That isn't what she said to you."

"Yeah, it is. She said she thought she should go back to England. Without me. She wants to leave me."

"No, honey. That's what you're hearing. That's your fear and your own insecurities hearing that she doesn't want you. If she thinks facing her father is something she should do, I don't think that's any reflection on how she feels about you."

Oz stared at him like he'd grown a second head.

"Think about this for a minute. Use the damn brain you've got in your head, and just think of what she's going through. What do you think is really going on in her head right now?"

"If I knew that, I don't think I'd be here."

"She's scared. She's just lost her best friend, the only person she's had to talk to, to care about, to lean on in how many years?"

"About twenty."

"Right. And it was, probably, her own father that killed him."

"I think we all know that it's more than probably."

"Right. And she's just found out that in all likelihood her father knows about your relationship with her."

"I know she's scared—"

"Scared? Girl, if I was her I wouldn't even be functioning right now. She's trying to resolve her problems the only way she can think of. Whether that solution is right or wrong, she's got some guts to think of going and facing the old bastard to get him off your back."

"What do you mean?"

"Oz, think. Do you really think she wants to go and see the man she thinks has killed her best friend, her mother, and quite possibly turned the work she was doing to treat cancer patients into a biological weapon? Do you really think she wants to do that?"

"No."

"Then why is she prepared to do that?"

Finn's words came rushing back to her and managed to penetrate the pain. Finn was willing to do it to make sure she was okay. She was willing to sacrifice herself to keep others safe. "Oh, God. I don't deserve her." The tears were flowing freely down her cheeks.

"What the hell are you talking about now?"

"She's going through all of this and still thinking about me when all I can think of is myself and how much it hurt when I thought she didn't want to be with me. I don't deserve her."

Charlie shook his head. "Maybe you don't. Maybe you should just sit here, stinking like a swamp and rotting in your own self-pity."

Oz stared at him.

"What? Isn't that what you wanted to hear?" He frowned at her. "Whether you believe you deserve it or not, Finn wants to be with you, and right now she's terrified that she's going to lose you like she's lost her mom and her best friend. Breaking her own heart is probably a price she's willing to pay to keep you safe. But I can promise you one thing."

Oz listened to him, clarity filtering through her self-pity and making her feel sick.

"You running off *will* break her heart. Now you have to decide. Are you going to let her walk out of your life or are you going to be the woman I helped raise and stand up and fight for what you believe in?" Charlie got up and walked away. He didn't look back as he headed toward the small house where Finn was staying. It was only a few seconds before Oz caught up with him.

"Where are you going?"

"I'm going to try and help a young woman who is suffering, because you don't seem to be the woman I thought you were, Ladyfish." He stretched out his stride and moved away from her.

"Uncle Charlie, please wait." He paused and turned around staring at her hard. "I need to see her. I need to sort this out with her. I love her." Oz sucked in a surprised breath. It was true, and it terrified her.

"Tell her that."

"What if she doesn't want to hear it?"

"Then I'm on the other end of the phone." He pulled her into a quick hug. "Go and take care of her. She needs you."

❖

Oz knocked on the door before she pushed it open. Finn was crouched in the corner of the room with her arms wrapped around her knees, staring blankly as tears ran down her cheeks. Oz fought back another wave of tears and guilt, crossed the room, and pulled Finn into her arms. Finn made a half-hearted attempt to push her away, but Oz felt her clutching the hem of her shirt.

"Let me go."

Oz released her but didn't move away. "I'm sorry, Fi—"

"What are you doing here? I thought you were gone."

"I'm sorry. I shouldn't have left."

Finn shrugged, pushing herself back toward the corner. "It doesn't matter."

"Yes, it does."

"Why?"

"Because I don't want you to ever think I'll leave you. It's just not going to happen."

"Oz—"

"No, please let me say what I need to, and then if you tell me to go, I will."

"Go on then."

"When you said you were going to go back to London, I panicked. All I could hear was that you were going far away from me and there would be nothing I could do to protect you because you didn't want my protection. I was terrified I would lose you. I still am. All I want is to make sure that you're safe. Nothing is more important to me. I didn't think about how much pain you were in, and for that I'm more sorry than I can ever tell you. I was selfish and so wrapped up in my own pain that I didn't actually hear what you were telling me. I only heard that you were leaving me, and that played on my own insecurities. I need to make that right. Whatever you need to do, we'll figure out a way to make that happen. If you need to go to him, then that's fine. I'll come with you—"

"No. The idea of going to see him is to keep him away from you, not to bring you to him."

"Finn, I'm not going to leave your side. If you go to him, we go together. If we stay here, we stay together. If you want to run away and hide, we do it together."

"Why?"

It was the question she'd been dreading, scared that when the time came she wouldn't be able to answer, but now she felt like she couldn't hold the words back. "Somewhere in the past month, I've fallen in love with you. I don't want anything to come between us. Not your father, not my fears, and not yours either." She took Finn's hand. "I need you." She stroked her thumb across the back of Finn's hand. "I really hope you feel the same way about me."

Finn was quiet for a long time, just watching her. Sweat trickled down Oz's back and she fought hard to remain calm. She knew Finn had to decide how far she was willing to trust her. Even scarier, she knew Finn was deciding how much she really cared for her.

"All my life, people came and went who didn't care about me. My mother was dead and my father used me to create a weapon. Pete was the only person who loved me. And now he's gone too." Finn wiped her tears away and leaned into Oz's palm on her cheek. "What I want now is someone who won't leave. A person who wants to be there for all the adventures, who can't wait to see me at the end of the day. I want someone I can depend on, Oz."

Oz pressed her fingers to Finn's lips before lifting her chin. Looking deeply into her eyes, sparkling with unshed tears and emotion, Oz knew with all her heart that she wanted to give Finn everything she needed. All the things she wanted. She felt the emptiness that had settled in her soul dissolve and the sense of belonging that had always been missing fill the void.

"But I don't want you to get hurt. If anything were to happen to you, I don't think I could live with myself."

She brushed Finn's lips with her own. "Nothing's going to happen to me. I was in the navy, remember? I can take care of both of us. Just say you'll let me stay with you. Please."

Finn wrapped her arms around Oz's neck and cried against her. She mumbled something Oz couldn't make out.

"I'm sorry, baby. I can't tell what you're saying."

Finn pulled back slightly. "I said, I love you too."

Oz held her close, smiling even as tears of relief coursed down her cheeks. "Then we'll figure it out."

"How?"

"Do you trust me?"

"Of course I do."

"Then here's my plan. We stay here. On the base. We carry on exactly like we were planning to do before. We go diving, you finish your courses, and we spend more time together. You're going to tell me everything you remember about Pete, and we'll have a memorial for him if you like. And we're going to wait."

"But—"

"We're going to wait until Charlie has more information. We'll talk to him and my dad, and we'll work together to find the best way to keep us all safe."

"So your great plan is to do nothing?"

"No, it's to bide our time and not run off without all the information. The last mission I went on was a fairly routine repair to a cargo vessel. They were more than four hundred miles from the nearest port that could handle them. They'd damaged the prop shaft and had to replace it. The onboard repairs were all done, but they didn't have a qualified dive team to do the underwater final fix. The boat I was on was only a hundred miles or so from them so we offered our help. What else do you need to know, right?"

"What happened?"

"Rudy and I were the team that did the repairs. Really simple job. Just welding the new prop shaft in place and connecting the old prop. After the repairs were complete, we went aboard the cargo vessel to make sure the repairs were holding and we didn't need to go back down. Sometimes the tech crew would do that, sometimes we did. Depended on the repair. This time we did. As soon as we got on the deck, we were in trouble. There were guns pointing at us and we had no communications with our own ship. Pirates. The crew had deliberately sabotaged their own prop shaft in the hope of getting rid of the pirates and getting help. Instead, they got me and Rudy."

"Go on."

"We were being taken down into the ship where they were holding the crew as hostages. We knew that if we ended up there…Well, it wasn't going to end well. Rudy made a really quick move and managed to get a gun off one of them. All I had was my dive knife. I stabbed one of them, took his own gun, and shot him with it." She took a deep breath. "There were seven of them all together. We'd already taken out two, but we had to get to the bridge to get help from our own guys. There were two more pirates watching the door where the hostages were being held in the dining hall. We shot them and freed the hostages. They directed us to the bridge and we told them to stay where they were. They'd be safer there. When we got to the bridge they were armed with automatics. Rudy got shot pretty bad but managed to take out one of them. I got another and then got Rudy out of the line of fire."

"Oz, you don't have to tell me—"

"Yes, I do. I could hear our guys over the radio trying to find out what was going on. They'd heard the gunshots and were obviously concerned. I knew we just needed to hold on for a little longer. I dragged Rudy behind a bulkhead. His leg was a mess. There was only one pirate left, and I figured we had a better chance if we waited for help. The guns we'd stolen were out of ammo, and the guy was pinned down in the bridge. Waiting for help was the best option. The problem was that the captain of the ship didn't like being told what to do. He decided that he was going to retake the bridge himself. Before we could even react, the pirate had a gun to his head and was screaming for a fast boat to get away. Where to, I still haven't figured out, but that was what he wanted." She shrugged slightly.

"Our guys were coming now. We could hear the engines of the ribs getting closer. With every single second, that guy was squeezing harder on the trigger. Rudy and I both knew that he didn't have the time to wait for the cavalry. If we were going to save him, we needed to do something now. Rudy was bleeding out and we had no bullets left. Just my knife. We figured if Rudy could create a distraction, maybe I could throw the knife from behind the guy and give the captain enough space to escape." Oz scrubbed her hands over her face.

"Oz, it wasn't your fault—"

"Please. Let me finish." She waited while Finn nodded. "It didn't quite work out like that. When I was in position, Rudy started shouting

ANDREA BRAMHALL

and the pirate half twisted. The twist was just enough to deflect the knife. He turned so that I had a full view before he pulled the trigger. The captain was looking straight at me and there was nothing I could do. I'd played my hand and failed. We should have waited. Maybe then he wouldn't be dead. I started to bend down to pick up one of the weapons lying on the floor, but he pulled the trigger. That's how I got the scar on my stomach. I grabbed a gun as I fell and fired." She rubbed her stomach. "I spent six months recovering after that, and I learned that the best way to get yourself in trouble is to go off thinking you have all the information. We thought we knew what we were walking into. Eight men died and Rudy lost his leg."

"Oz, it wasn't your fault. You found yourself in a situation and dealt with it the only way you could—"

"It doesn't matter. I won't take that kind of chance with you. You're too important to me."

She felt Finn's lips against her neck. "You're important to me too."

"So you'll stay here with me?"

"Yes."

"Excellent."

"For now. I can't hide forever, Oz."

"I know. Just till we find out more, then we'll come up with another plan. A long-term one that we can both deal with."

"Together?"

"Together." The shadows of her past lifted, and even with the threat of Finn's dad hanging over them, Oz felt the warmth of Finn's love and trust burning away the guilt that had been her companion for too long.

CHAPTER THIRTY-TWO

Junior pushed the cleaning cart down the corridor of Sterling BioTech, picking up the occasional bin and emptying its contents as he went. He slowly approached the server room.

"This is Delta One. I am approaching target. Needing a little interference here, boys." He spoke quietly under his breath. The microphone embedded in the button on his collar was sensitive enough to pick up the whispered words. The receiver in his ear relayed the response.

"Everything's in place, Delta One. You're a go to target."

He parked the cart outside the door and quickly attached a cable to his own paltry security badge. He connected the other end to a small computer unit before he slid the card into the terminal by the door and waited for the computer to bypass the security codes and grant him access.

"This is Delta One. I have access."

"Affirmative, Delta One."

He pulled on a pair of latex gloves before pushing open the door and crossing the room. He pulled a small transmitter from his left pocket and an external hard drive from the right. He plugged the transmitter into the back of the router and switched it on before crossing to the main server and sitting at the desk. He quickly brought up the login screen and fished in his breast pocket for the small pen drive full of access programs and codes to allow him to access the secure information hidden on the server. It seemed to take only seconds before the login screen disappeared and the desktop flashed up. He scanned the screen, dismissing each icon before he began scrolling through the computer's files, transferring information to the USB port as he went. His eyes lit on a file labeled "Lyell." He grabbed the whole folder and dragged it to the hard drive.

"This is Delta One. I have found information and am transferring now. Transfer time, two minutes."

"Understood, Delta One."

"Any movement out there?"

"Negative, Delta One. All quiet on the western front."

"Ha ha."

He scrolled through some of the other files as he waited for the transfer to complete.

Ninety seconds.

"Delta One. We have movement on the elevator."

"This floor?"

"Not sure."

Sixty seconds.

"Well, best let me know."

"We're tapping into the elevator system now."

"Why the hell didn't you do that before?"

Thirty seconds.

"They're coming for a visit, Delta One."

"Fantastic."

Twenty seconds.

"Delta One, you need to get a move on."

"Yeah, I know that. Tell me when they get to the corner. Preferably, before they turn into this corridor, please."

Ten seconds.

"Delta One, we have a single male approaching the west corner. Approximately fifty feet from the corner."

Five seconds.

"Twenty feet, Delta One."

Transfer complete.

He pulled the cable from the computer, closing the windows on the screen as he stuffed the drive into his pocket. He logged out of the session and grabbed the pen drive, stuffing it into his breast pocket as he crossed the room and pulled open the door.

"Rounding the corner now, Delta One."

He pulled the door closed behind him and pressed his security card against the reader.

"Hey, what you doing there?"

He turned to face the man coming toward him. "I'm trying to get in here to clean stuff, but this stupid pass don't work."

"That's the computer room. We don't clean in there. It's like top secret security or something."

He looked at the man, his own gray uniform threadbare at the knees, sweat stained under his arms and along his collar. His work boots were scuffed, the sole pulling away from the leather on one, making a slapping sound against the tiles as he walked. His face was round, his cheeks ruddy and smeared with dust and grime. His smile was broad as he approached, though.

"Are you done with this floor? I was just going to take my lunch break and wondered if you wanted to join me. I can show you where the cafeteria is?"

He stepped closer to the small man and clapped him on the shoulder. "That'd be great. I'm still trying to get my bearings."

"Yeah, I know what you mean. It took me a month to get to know everywhere in this place. It still feels weird sometimes, eating my lunch break at two in the morning. I'm all upside down now."

He turned his cart away from the door and headed away from the server room. "How long you worked here now?"

"Three years."

He whistled. "That's a long time. You must like it." They made their way down the corridor, toward the elevators.

"Nice work, Delta One. You actually gonna eat with this bozo?"

He grinned as he pushed the button in the elevator, and they headed for the cafeteria. "So what do they have in this cafeteria of yours then, buddy?"

Junior grinned as he followed his short friend into the cafeteria. Oz would be proud of him.

"Jack, why the hell are you calling me at three in the morning?" William Sterling growled down the phone.

"Sir, there was an incident last night at the US biolab."

"What?"

"Lyell believes that files about the bacteria have been downloaded. Along with correspondence between you and Lyell."

"Has there been any damage to the product?"

"No. All samples and finished quantities have not been tampered with. The loss is purely electronic."

"How the fuck did this happen, Jack? How did you let this happen?"

"I'm sorry, sir."

"I want a full breakdown on what information was downloaded and I want to know how the hell they got into the system. I thought you told me that system was impenetrable?"

"Sir, the guy who developed the network assured me that it was."

"Well, he was lying, then wasn't he?"

"I have already taken care of that particular issue."

"Good. Do we know who orchestrated this?"

"Not yet, sir. But I'm working on it. It originated in the US. That much we've been able to ascertain."

"I want specifics. How close are we to the quantity that we require?"

"The last barrel is in production now. It should be ready tomorrow."

"Good. It's time to make this deal. Take care of Lyell."

"Yes, sir."

"Any news on my daughter's whereabouts yet?"

"She's disappeared, sir. I searched her house and found some information on scuba diving. I'm tracking down that angle at the moment. I'll let you know when I find anything."

"See that you do." He ended the call and dialed another number.

"The product is ready, Masood."

"Excellent, William. There is to be a change in delivery address."

"Where?"

"Washington."

"That's a significant change in our agreement."

"I am aware of that, my friend."

"And where in Washington will I be delivering?"

"William, I will take care of my final destination. I want you to deliver to a warehouse inside the city. I have my people in place to ensure that the president has a holiday he will never forget."

Sterling shuddered at the unpleasant sound of Masood's laughter ringing down the tinny phone line. "There will obviously be a much greater risk."

"I am aware of that too, William."

"The price must be changed accordingly."

"And what do you feel would be appropriate recompense for this increased risk?"

"Make it an even hundred million and I think I can accept the risk."

"Done. When can I expect delivery?"

"Five days. I'll send you the coordinates and the details for the money transfer."

"A pleasure as always, my friend."

The line went dead.

CHAPTER THIRTY-THREE

Jack leaned back against the wall, masking himself in the shadows as he watched the dive boat pull alongside the dock and the passengers scurry to disembark. Backpacks slung over their shoulders, towels draped around their necks, and the breeze ruffling hair that needed the salt washed from it. He watched silently as most disembarked and left the dock, then counted how many people actually stayed back to help.

He mussed his hair before he stepped out of the shadows and walked toward a young woman as she headed for the car park.

"Hi, was the diving good?"

She popped the boot of her car and tossed her bag in before closing the lid and looking at him.

"Yeah, it was really great. We went to see this statue of Jesus at the bottom of the ocean. It was like a spiritual experience for me."

"Wow. That's great. It looks like you were really crowded on the boat. How many people do the guides dive with?" He could see her curiosity piqued as he spoke and decided that he needed to satisfy it in the most realistic way possible. "I'm thinking of diving, but I really hate when the guides have huge groups."

"Yeah, I know what you mean. I hate that. It's just all about the money, and the poor dive guides are worked to death. These guys aren't like that. We stopped at another marina and picked up another couple of people who were helping lead the dives. We had to drop them off before we came back here too."

"That must have been inconvenient."

"Nah. It wasn't that far away, and Oz was a really good guide. She must know everything about the area. The other woman with her, Finn, was really helpful too. She was helping everyone set up their gear and do their buddy checks. Besides, it gave us a bit longer on the boat to sunbathe." She grinned at him.

"Still, I'm not sure I'd like to be setting off earlier just to pick people up who don't want to make it to the dive center."

"Actually, it was really interesting. We picked them up at the naval base. Not many people get to see that, so it was worth the extra time on the boat. I was hoping I might meet a nice sailor while I was there, but it wasn't meant to be." She shrugged. "They were already waiting for the boat and just jumped straight on. I barely had a chance to smile at any sailors, never mind get asked for a date." She smiled. He took the time to look her up and down, noting the dark brown eyes and blond, sun-streaked hair, her small waist and long legs, as well as the clear invitation on her pretty face.

"Well, this must be my lucky day then. Would you like to come for a drink with me this evening?"

"I don't even know your name."

"I'm Jack." He held out his hand and kept hold of hers as he stepped a little closer to her. "Now will you go for a drink with me?"

"I'd love to. I'm Stephanie."

He grinned at her. "Well, Stephanie, let's make this a night to remember, shall we?"

"What do you have in mind?" She cocked her head to the side and looked up at him from under her long lashes.

"What hotel are you staying in?"

"I'm in the Mandarin Hotel."

"How about I meet you in the bar at seven and I'll show you what I have in mind?" Jack smiled, amazed at how easy it was to get the information he wanted.

"I can hardly wait." She stepped back and slid into her car, backing slowly out of the car park and away down the road. She didn't see him grinning as he pulled his cell phone from his pocket and tapped in a number.

"Hi, I'd like to book a dive. Yes, that would be fine. No, I don't have my own equipment. I'm on vacation. Whatever day you can fit me on the boat. I've dived with Oz in the past. Is she still leading groups? She is. Fantastic. I'll drop by early that day to pay for my dive. My name is Steven Morris. Thank you." He rang off and slid the phone back into his pocket.

CHAPTER THIRTY-FOUR

Finn flipped through the pages of a magazine without seeing them, trying to keep her mind occupied. Oz was getting a beer from the fridge when the doorbell rang.

"Hey, Pops, you okay?"

"Yeah, is Charlie here yet?"

"No, why?"

"He's got some stuff he wants to bring over."

"What stuff?"

"I don't know really. Neither does he. That's the problem. He's got a lot of information, but no one who can really interpret it for him. He's almost sure Sterling is ready to move on a deal, but we don't know what the deal is for. There are too many unanswered questions to figure anything out at this point. It's all just conjecture." Oz nodded, playing with a strand of Finn's hair.

"So you're hoping Finn can interpret the data and give you a clue what you're up against with the bio weapons." It was a statement, not a question. "You okay with that, baby? Actually seeing what your dad is selling is different from knowing in the abstract."

"I know, darling. But I think I need to do this. I have too many unanswered questions. If I look at this stuff and it's harmless, then I can put it all behind me. If I look at this and it isn't, well, then at least I'll know what I can do to stop it. To stop him. That means a lot to me. It might help me distance myself from him and the things he's done. It might help me to feel better about myself." She sighed and leaned against Oz. "Does that make sense?"

"Yeah, I guess it does. I just wish it didn't have to be like this."

"You can't protect me from this. I need to know. I need to know what I'm dealing with, who he is. It might help me, it might not. But it can't hurt me any more than the possibility he's selling biological weapons I helped create."

Charlie knocked and came in carrying a laptop case and placed it on the table, booting it up right away.

"When we spoke, you said you'd look at some information for us, Finn. Would you do that now?"

"Of course. Billy said you have some information you can't make heads nor tails of." She sat at the table next to him and looked at the screen he turned toward her.

"Does it make sense to you?"

"You'll have to give me a little while to take a look. I'm fairly quick with this stuff, but I do need to read it first." She began scanning through the data, one file after another.

Charlie chuckled. "Of course, I'm sorry."

"Beer, Charlie?" Billy held up the bottle as he spoke.

"That sounds like a very good idea." He took the bottle from him as Billy handed Oz another. They spoke quietly as Finn studied the files on the laptop, her expression more and more concerned. Oz watched her constantly, noting the set of her shoulders as they tensed, the twitching of her fingers as she hovered above the keyboard. Oz sipped from her bottle, not paying attention to the conversation around her.

Finn scrubbed her hands over her face when she finally looked away from the screen and all eyes were riveted to her.

"There's a lot more I need to read to give you extensive details, but I can give you the outline." She took another sip of her drink. "It's quite simple really. They've been working with the botulinum toxin. It's extremely deadly on its own so they don't actually need to enhance it at all. Most scientists agree that it is the most toxic substance in the world. At least in the biological world, botox is an obvious frontrunner. That particular strain can be isolated from its natural habitat, which is the soil, and then grown in cultures. It is a bit tricky to grow, but not so difficult that it puts people off trying. It grows quickly, and the best ways to produce the most toxic results are well researched and readily available to those in the microbiological community. Purification of the botox protein isn't difficult either.

Quantities could be isolated in a day or less, or even on a continuous-flow basis.

"It's relatively stable and can be stored in crystalline form. The weapon-ready forms are classified, but this material suggests that they're using the same form. It's meant to be absorbed through the mucous membranes in the lungs and nasal passages, so aerosol dispersal is thought to be one of the best ways to deliver as a weapon, but adding it to municipal water or food supplies are also likely ways of introducing the toxin into a population.

"It's tasteless and odorless and, depending on the dosage, it can take from two to fourteen days before the symptoms appear. Symptoms run the spectrum from double vision, difficulty in swallowing and speaking, muscle weakness, vomiting, and eventually respiratory failure. The protein is a neurotoxin, and once the symptoms appear, the damage is irreversible. There are several unique strains, which means that the only effective treatment involves passive antibody shots against all strains; the assumption being that a mixture of strains would be applied. Immunization of a large population is not feasible."

"Why not?" Charlie took notes while Finn talked.

"One of the advantages of the toxin is that since its symptoms are delayed, the damage is done before victims realize they've been infected, so by the time the victim exhibits any symptoms, it's too late to save them. Add that to the fact that the amount of antiserum required to treat hundreds of thousands of exposed people simply isn't available."

"Shit," Charlie said under his breath.

"Is there any good news at all in there, baby?" Oz asked.

"Not really. The known disadvantages are that the toxin is unstable in the air if exposed to sunlight and dry conditions. It can also be destroyed by brief boiling, which means that effective exposure is limited by a small window of lighting and humidity conditions, the same conditions that destroy the E. coli bacteria. Even though it's highly toxic, it would still take a large amount to reach a lethal concentration in a large city's water supply. Contaminating a food supply would be even more difficult. Unless they target individual food processing plants."

"How much are we talking about?" Billy rolled a pencil over his knuckles constantly, obviously his way of concentrating.

"For what? A city-wide attack or to kill a few people?"

"Either."

"It depends on the method of delivery and strain, but a decent estimate is seventy micrograms if ingested, and point seven to point nine micrograms if inhaled."

"How lethal is this stuff?"

"It's fatal in at least fifty percent of cases."

"Fuck."

"It gets worse."

"How?"

"Well, up until now there hasn't been a reliable method of delivery for the toxin. That's all changed now. They're using my protocol with the E. coli bacteria. It means that the infected bacteria establish themselves in the intestines long enough to produce a quantity of toxin that would disable the victim before their immune system could respond."

"How could they get this into people?"

"To do this on a large scale, you're talking about adding quantities of the E. coli toxin to either a water source or a major food supply."

"Not airborne?"

"Not using the E. coli bacteria. It's passed on through physical contact, not inhalation. It isn't like a cold or anything, though that does look like the next stage of development. They're trying to incorporate the toxin into a flu virus, but it doesn't look like they've had any luck so far. The toxin is killing the virus before they can get it stable."

"Do you know if he has the quantities required for this kind of attack?"

"He does. But you need to understand that by engineering the toxin into the E. coli bacteria, they have made the toxin communicable."

"What do you mean?"

"On its own, botulinum toxin isn't communicable. The victim has to be infected with it. E. coli is communicable. You can catch it. They've basically made it a lethal tummy bug."

"How lethal are we talking here?"

"The results of their tests show that any infection of the bacteria causes botulism in one hundred percent of cases. Without treatment, ninety-eight percent of cases are proving fatal. With treatment, they show fifty-four percent fatality rate. The forecast is dependent on where they release the bacteria and so on. If they were to target a third world country with poor sanitation, improper water and sewage treatment, they have enough already stockpiled to cause an outbreak that would decimate the entire population of Africa."

"Are you kidding?" Charlie paced the room, his hand on the back of his neck.

"I wish I was. If their forecasts are to be believed, release in the US would lead to millions of deaths with at least twice that number infected."

"How does this kill?"

"Botulism causes muscle weakness and paralysis. That's why it's so popular with aging women. It freezes the muscles, which irons out the wrinkles. It also paralyzes all other muscles to greater or lesser extents. The respiratory system, the swallow reflexes, and the heart are the most common causes of death. If the lungs don't give up, the epiglottis stops working. If that doesn't, then the heart becomes so weakened that it goes into arrhythmia and fails. The awful thing about this is that even those who survive are incurable."

"What do you mean?"

"It is a nerve toxin, making the paralysis and muscle weakness permanent. The victim is trapped in a weakened or paralyzed body. For life."

"You mean that the whole population who survived would be paralyzed?" Oz couldn't get her head around the possibilities

"Then why would anyone want to release it? They would die too," Billy said.

"Not if they had the vaccine."

"And if they create the airborne flu virus?" Charlie said.

"You don't even want to think about that. I certainly don't. This is bad enough."

"Finn, are you sure about this?"

"Yes. As I said, there is more in there I need to read, but I'm sure."

He nodded and stepped out of the room pulling his cell phone from his pocket as he went.

"Finn, baby, this is where we have to be prepared for things to get ugly." Oz took hold of Finn's hand.

"Things are already ugly, Oz. How can it get any worse?" The tears welled in her eyes. "My father is behind all this. He couldn't do it himself. He doesn't have the knowledge. But I do. This bacteria? The E. coli delivery system? This is my work. These are sequences I decoded and methodologies I developed to incorporate other gene sequences. He's made me a part of this. I had no idea what his intentions were. I was working to help cure illnesses, medicinal protocols. I feel so stupid. He used me just like he used everyone else."

"I know, baby, but you didn't put the toxin into the bug."

"It doesn't matter. If I hadn't discovered how to—"

"Of course it matters. You were trying to help people who were and still are dying every day of a terrible disease. You weren't hurting anyone. You had no intention of hurting anyone."

"We have to stop him. I wish I could stop him. Right now, I want to kill him. If I had it in me, I'd do it myself." The tears spilled down her cheeks.

"You're strong enough to do anything you want."

"No, I'm—"

"Baby, listen to me." Oz knelt before her. "It isn't about strength. You don't have to be strong to pull a trigger. It's about courage. And you've got that. To read all that and tell us not only what it says, but the implications of that, knowing what it means for your own father, takes more courage than I will ever have." She wrapped her arms around Finn and pulled her into a tight embrace. "I don't know that I could have done that."

"Yes, you do. You know that you'll always do the right thing. Whatever it takes."

"And that's exactly what you did tonight." Oz ran her hands down Finn's back, soothing her. "Don't belittle what you've done here. This fight was always going to happen at some point. You know that, right?"

"I know."

"You've given us the knowledge to fight on an even playing field and hopefully stop a tragedy from happening."

"Do you really believe that?"

Oz looked at her seriously. "Yes, I do."

Finn leaned forward and kissed her gently on the lips. "Thank you."

Charlie came back in the room. "I can only imagine how difficult this was for you tonight. Thank you." He pulled her into a quick hug before he closed down the laptop and slipped it back into its case. "I really need to go now. I'm going to be in meetings all night." He and

Billy went to the front door, where they stopped for a moment while Charlie took a call.

"Will it be tonight?" Finn asked.

"Will what be tonight?"

"They're going to have to destroy that lab. The research. The bacteria. Will it be tonight?"

"I don't know, baby. It depends on what intelligence they have on the lab and where the stuff is being kept."

"It's in the lab at the moment. It's being kept in a huge refrigerator unit that takes up one whole floor."

"Uncle Charlie, wait."

Charlie ended his call and turned back to them.

"Tell him."

"The bacteria stockpile, it's in a refrigerator unit that takes up a whole floor of the building. It's all there until they sell it."

"How do you know that?"

"There's an e-mail in the documents. It's actually from my father to the doctor at the lab. It says all that, but you might have missed it because it's all in jargon."

"Thank you, Finn. That gives us everything we need to get your father officially brought in."

"Meaning arrested and prosecuted, right?"

"That's what I'm planning."

When Charlie and Billy had gone, Finn rested her head on her arms.

"You okay?"

Finn lifted her head and looked at Oz. "Honestly?"

"Always."

"I'm not even close."

CHAPTER THIRTY-FIVE

William Sterling stepped off the plane into the ninety-degree heat. Flies buzzed around his head. He waved them away and slid sunglasses over his eyes. Jack was waiting with the limousine on the tarmac. The door was open and the air-conditioned haven awaited him. He sat in his seat and took the glass Jack offered as the door closed behind him.

"So where are we, Jack?"

"The information that was copied was extensive, and I'm still waiting for confirmation as to the source of the leak."

"So we're nowhere. Is that what you're telling me?"

"Not quite, sir."

"Three days, Jack. In three days I will be selling off the bacteria in those drums, and you don't know anything. Not who broke into our files. Where they're from. Where my fucking daughter is."

"We've actually had a breakthrough on that one, sir."

"Well? I'm waiting, Jack."

"It seems she has ties to the US Navy."

"The navy? How?"

"The woman she's with has extensive connections, and the number on Peter Green's hand was that of a sat phone to an admiral on the naval base where your daughter appears to be staying."

"Extensive ties indeed. So we know where she is, but this doesn't exactly help me get to her now, does it?"

"I believe they're being picked up by boat from there every day, sir. A dive boat."

ANDREA BRAMHALL

"And how do you know this?"

"I've been watching the dive center. They're taking out far more tourists every day than they can cope with for the number of dive leaders on the boat. So I talked to one of the tourists after they returned. She told me that they went to the naval base and picked up two more divers. The description fits."

"Excellent work, Jack. What are you planning to do about this?"

"I've booked myself on a dive trip. I'm not a diver, but they take tourists along for the ride too."

"That gets you on the boat. Daniela will recognize you as soon as she sees you."

"I'll keep my head down, sir. I'll have Decker standing by with a speedboat to come and pick me up when I have subdued her. She hasn't seen me in a very long time."

"I want them both. Perhaps we can work this navy connection for ourselves. I wouldn't be surprised if this is where our leak is coming from. It's imperative I speak with my daughter. Her knowledge of the mechanics of the product make her and Lyell the only ones who could develop any kind of countermeasure. Lyell won't be a problem for much longer. I need to know if she will be. Her continued existence outside my control is a threat to my profit line. If Masood discovers she's not working for me and can undo this work in any way, he will be a very unhappy man. Am I making myself clear, Jack?"

"Yes, sir, perfectly."

"You'll need to take someone else with you too. To make sure they don't get away."

"Yes, sir."

"When you have them, bring them to the house. I don't want my daughter harmed, yet. I need to know what she knows and what she's done. If there's any chance she has already begun working on a countermeasure, I need to know, and I need to know now. Do what you want with the other bitch."

"I was hoping to convince Daniela to cooperate and come in peaceably."

"And how do you plan to do that?"

"I plan to use Peter Green. If she thinks he's waiting for her, I presume she will come with me of her own volition."

"And if she knows that he has passed away?"

"I'll deal with the situation differently."

"Very well. Just remember, I want her unharmed."

"Of course. I have also located a hacker. I was planning to visit him today to gain his assistance in tracing the leak at the lab."

Sterling smiled. "Jack, there may be hope for you yet. This hacker, can he do what we need?"

"If he's half as good as his reputation, he could do it with his eyes closed."

"Good, good. What kind of persuasion do we need here?"

"The old-fashioned kind, sir."

"Ahh, money."

Jack nodded. "He's young and ambitious. He'll be a valuable asset to your organization, I think."

Sterling leaned back against the car seat. "Very good, Jack. Today just got a little bit brighter."

CHAPTER THIRTY-SIX

Jack watched them step off the back of the boat one by one before disappearing beneath the waves. He checked his watch and set the timer on the stop watch. He'd listened and knew that Oz and Finn we're doing a deep dive and were expected to surface before any of the other divers who were staying shallow and enjoying the top of the reef. He had thirty minutes to get the boat under control, call Decker, and have everything ready when they got back on board.

He watched as Carlos walked into the galley, then he followed him inside.

"Hello, can I get you something?"

"Yeah, do you have any beers on this tub?"

"Yes, sir. I will get you one." He turned around and stooped to the fridge.

Jack reached into his pocket and pulled out the gun he had hidden. He aimed carefully before bringing it down on Carlos's skull. The sickening crack was followed swiftly by the dull thud as his body hit the deck.

The metallic tang of blood hit the air as Jack pulled a large cable tie from the left pocket of his shorts. He pulled Carlos's hands behind his back and used the tie to secure his wrists. He used three more to secure his ankles and gagged him with a dishcloth. He dragged him across the floor of the cabin and dropped him next to the bench seat that ran the length of the cabin.

He made his way to the cockpit. The boat was secured to a mooring buoy. The captain was sitting in the chair behind the wheel, poring over charts and a yachtsman's almanac. Jack gripped the gun tightly in his fist as he approached, raised his fist above his head, then struck.

Jose slumped over the console.

Jack pulled the cable ties from his pocket and secured Jose's wrists and ankles before pulling him from the console chair and rolling him to the edge of the cockpit. He pulled his phone from his pocket and hit the speed dial.

"Yeah."

"Set off now. By the time you reach me, I should have them secure."

"What are the coordinates?"

Jack checked the readout of the GPS console and rattled off the numbers before disconnecting. He went back down the stairs to the dive deck and waited.

CHAPTER THIRTY-SEVEN

Oz and Finn broke the surface of the water and made their way to the boat. When they reached the dive ladder, there was no sign of Carlos to help them from the water.

"Carlos! Are you there?" When he didn't answer, Oz pulled her flippers from her feet and handed them to Finn. "Will you hold these for me? I'll get on board and ditch my BCD then I'll give you all a hand out. Okay?" Finn took hold of the flippers as Oz climbed up the ladder, sat down, and unclipped her BCD. She quickly unfastened the tank and stowed it as she headed back to the ladder for Finn.

"Carlos?" she yelled toward the head. "We could use a hand out here. Hurry it up. Jose, where's that good-for-nothing boy of yours?" she hollered up the stairs before going to help Finn at the back of the boat, the hairs at the back of her neck standing on end. Something was wrong. Very wrong.

She took her flippers from Finn and waited a minute as Finn took off her own gear and handed it up. She pulled herself up the ladder, and Oz helped her out of her BCD when she got on board.

"Where's Carlos?"

"Don't know. I can't actually hear anyone at all. Something doesn't feel right."

Finn's eyes widened and her focus shifted to the left of Oz.

In the next instant, Oz felt cold metal press against her temple and the clicking metallic ring as a gun was cocked.

"Thank you, Decker. If she does that again, feel free to shoot her. Ms. Zuckerman, I presume." The British accent was silky smooth.

"Daniela, you have caused your father no end of heartache over this woman. He has something of a dilemma to deal with now. Peter is so very upset about all this business."

"Communing with spirits now, Jack? I thought you were my father's bodyguard, not a communications expert."

"So you have heard the unfortunate news. He flicked the gun toward the benches lining the back of the boat. "Take a seat, ladies."

Oz didn't move. The blow was quick and hard against the back of her skull. She staggered forward before dropping to one knee. Finn held out her hands to catch her, but Oz shook her head and rose quickly, using the back of her head to connect painfully with the bridge of Jack's nose. The nauseating crunch of bone and cartilage filled the air, and blood poured down his face. She started to turn, ready to face him, but the blow to the head slowed her reaction time.

"Fucking bitch!" He raised the gun and struck the back of her head again, laughing as she stumbled to the deck.

"Oz, no!" Finn reached forward, but Jack grabbed her and shoved her roughly onto the bench seat.

"I said, take a seat."

Finn stared defiantly at him as she reached out and helped Oz to the bench next to her. Oz pressed her hand to the back of her head and winced as blood oozed through her fingers.

"What do you want, Jack?"

"Your father sent me to bring you home." He pointed the gun at her as he moved closer, leaning forward to bring his eyes level with her as he smiled.

"He could have asked me himself. He knows the number."

"He didn't feel you would be receptive to the idea. What with new developments." He waved the gun in Oz's direction, without taking his eyes off Finn.

"That doesn't explain what you're doing here. We're on a boat, if you hadn't noticed?"

"You didn't make it easy to find you, Daniela. Moving from the hotel to that old lady's house and then to a naval base. I should have remembered how much you liked those aquariums as a child, but I'm here now. That's all that matters. Quite a good bit of detective work, if I do say so myself." He sounded proud of himself. His chest puffed out. Just a bit.

"Aren't we lucky." Finn didn't see the blow coming as her head whipped around. Her cheek stung, but she refused to raise her hand despite the uncomfortable heat that grew. "Careful, Jack. Did my dad give you permission to do that?" He blanched and she knew she'd hit a soft spot. "Better be careful. I understand my dad isn't someone you want to cross."

"No, he isn't. You should have thought about that before you decided to desert him."

"Yeah, but I'm not on his payroll. I can afford a thought of my own." She knew if she could keep his attention fixed on her, he wouldn't hurt Oz. It seemed that while her father wanted her unharmed, he didn't have the same concerns for Oz.

"You don't have a clue, little girl."

"Jack, is it?" Oz said. Her voice sounded rough and she spit a bit of blood at his feet.

"Yes."

"What's the plan here? You can't take us back to the marina or the docks since too many people will see you with us."

The blow was vicious. A thin cut opened on her cheek where the butt of the gun struck her. The blood trickled slowly down her skin before dripping onto the deck. Finn heard her own gasp and tried to move toward Oz, stopping only when she saw Oz shake her head the tiniest bit while looking straight at her.

"That was a little unnecessary wasn't it? We're just talking here, Jack."

"Shut up, you fucking bitch!"

A thrumming noise caught their attention. Finn watched Jack as the motorboat pulled alongside them. The man on board slowed, tossed a line to Decker, and they made short work of securing the rib to the dive boat. He climbed aboard.

"What the fuck happened to you?" The man was tall and wiry with tattoos down his arms and a shock of red hair glinting in the sun.

Jack nodded in Oz's direction. "Bitch decided to try and be clever." He tossed a couple of cable ties at him. "Secure her wrists and let's get out of here."

They quickly cuffed Oz's and Finn's hands behind their backs using more cable ties and then dragged them to their feet. Jack kept his hand tight around Finn's arm and led her to the back of the boat.

"Get in." He shoved her toward the edge of the *Eleanor Rose*.

"I can't. I have no balance with my hands tied behind like this. Unfasten them and I'll get in." She screamed as he pushed her roughly and she landed on the harsh wooden deck of the smaller vessel, making her knees take all her body weight. Another set of hands gripped her arms and dragged her to the side of the deck.

"Get the fuck off me." Oz tried to shrug them off her arms.

Finn watched helplessly as Oz was pushed off the *Eleanor Rose*. She twisted during her fall and landed on her shoulder. The sickening crunch and the odd angle when Oz pulled herself to her feet told her that she had dislocated the joint, but she didn't make a sound.

Finn heard herself cry out again as a black hood was pulled over her head and her world went dark. She jumped as she felt skin touch her own, but it took only a second to recognize the warm flesh. It was Oz, her arm pressing gently against her own flesh. They didn't speak as they waited.

Finn could feel the fear rising in her as she sat, blinded by the hood, her cheek throbbing and her head aching. The heavy scent of diesel fumes filled the air as the engine roared back into life and they left the dive boat behind. Every lurch of the boat across the waves stirred corresponding waves of nausea that threatened to overtake her, and she worked hard to quell the bile rising in her throat. She thought she had accepted the truth of the man her father was, but she wasn't even close. He wanted to talk to her, so he had her kidnapped. What about her friends on the boat? Were they dead because her father wanted to speak to her? Or was it beyond that point now? Was it her death he wanted? She felt Oz move beside her, and her tears started falling inside the hood. Her cheek stung like hell and she didn't want to think about the pain Oz must be in. She hated that she had let Oz convince her to stay, knowing that if she had left two days ago like she had planned, Oz would have been safe. She cursed her own foolishness for believing she would ever have happiness in her life. Now that foolishness would cost them both. She didn't want to consider how high that price would be, but images of the gun in Jack's hand were all she could see.

CHAPTER THIRTY-EIGHT

O z felt the boat slowing down. The diesel fumes weren't blowing away like they had before. The thickening air made her stomach turn, and she fought the urge to vomit. A series of bumps and scuffles, followed by the sound of water lapping gently against the side of the boat told her they had docked.

Hands gripped her shoulders roughly and dragged her from her seat. Pain seared through her shoulder, the bones grating against one another, and she tried to keep her feet as she was pushed onto the jetty.

She could hear Finn stumbling and shuffling across the deck of the boat. She heard her whimper and fought back the rage at the thought of one of the men with his hands all over her. She shuffled to her feet, trying to find her footing, but the uneven wooden decking made it impossible and she tripped, falling to one knee.

"For fuck's sake, stand her up." Jack's voice was harsh as he spat the words from his lips. She felt two sets of hands grabbing at her and dragging her to her feet.

"Fuck, have you seen her shoulder?"

"I don't give a shit if her arm falls off, Decker. Just get them both inside."

"No. I won't—"

She heard a sharp slap and then the sound of a body hitting the floor.

"Boss, I don't think that's a very good—"

"I'm surprised you think at all, Decker. Now pick her the fuck up and get them both inside."

She heard Finn groan and assumed one of them had slung her over his shoulder. Then she heard the unmistakable sound of someone throwing up. She was glad the hood hid her smile as she pictured Finn vomiting all over her captor. The hands around her arms loosened and she worked methodically at her cuffs. As painful as it was, the dislocated shoulder allowed her to twist unnaturally and gave her the space she needed to escape her bindings with a little time. She wished she could see, but right now she had to depend on her abilities without vision. With Finn in danger, it was imperative she keep her head.

"That's fucking disgusting. It's all down the back of my trousers."

"Stop being such a girl, Decker. Get her inside."

The hands on her arms tightened again, forcing her to stop working against her bonds, and urged her forward. She listened intently for anything that would give her a clue as to where they were. The gentle lapping of the ocean against rocks and the wooden jetty made her think they were on a private island in the Keys. She felt the spray of sprinklers against her skin as they flung a never-ceasing stream of water across the lawn. She stumbled up some steps, her dislocated arm jerked upward with the awkward movements. The temperature changed, and air-conditioning chilled her skin as they entered a building. She couldn't help the groan that left her lips as she was pushed down onto a chair, her arm twisted painfully against the backrest.

"Fuck, Decker, you stink man!"

"Ha, ha. Very funny, you little prick."

"Decker, go and change." Jack's authoritative voice echoed through the room, and the man scurried away.

"She's here," Jack said and waited a beat before the louder snap of a phone closing rang out. She heard fabric rustle then the sound of someone sitting on upholstery a few feet away. "He won't be long now." He sounded happy. Confident. Cocky.

She felt the tension knotting between her shoulder blades, and sweat trickled down her spine. She managed to get her wrist in a workable position, the movement forcing contact with Finn. Her heart soared to feel her skin touching Finn's and she took a chance that the hood would muffle almost any soft sound she made. "Finn, baby, I've almost got my cuffs off. If you can distract them for a few minutes, I can get us out of this." Her voice was barely above a whisper.

"How?"

"I didn't dislocate my shoulder by accident. It's the only way to get out of these damn ties—"

"Stop fucking whispering!"

She heard movement then the light stung her eyes as he ripped the hood off her head. His face was only inches from hers, and the stench of his breath turned her stomach.

"Did you think I couldn't hear you whispering?" He leaned closer. "Now tell me what you were saying." He wrapped his fingers around her throat and her arms jerked against the ties.

"Jack, I was the one talking."

"Saying what?"

"I was telling her I loved her."

He removed his hand, and she sucked in a deep breath. Her relief was short-lived when he yanked Finn's hood off and dragged her from the chair.

He laughed as he pulled her tight against him, his face barely an inch from hers. "I watched you." He put his nose to her hair and inhaled deeply. "For years, he's had me watch you." He pulled the hair back off her neck and dragged his tongue across her skin before biting down hard.

Oz wanted to wrap her hands around his neck as she saw Finn's body jerk, and she knew Finn was fighting back the urge to scream.

"Could you feel me?" He nipped on her earlobe and slid his hands down to her ass, pulling her tight against him. "Could you feel me watching you?" He turned her around so her back was pressed against him and she was facing Oz.

Oz looked straight at Finn, the anger she felt turning to cold, hard rage. The revulsion in Finn's eyes tore holes in her soul as she tried to control her breathing and focus on the task at hand. There was nothing she could do for Finn until she was out of the cuffs.

"Dear Daddy made me watch you, and all the time he knew." He grabbed roughly at Finn's breast, squeezing her hard through her wet suit until she cried out. "Do you know what he knew?"

Oz watched tears roll down Finn's cheeks. She stared at the wall, her face blank.

"He knew that I wanted you." His hand slid between her legs and he cupped her. "He knew that I was watching you every time you got undressed."

Oz knew without a doubt that she was going to kill him as he reached behind Finn's back and began to unfasten the zipper on her wet suit. She wanted to feel his blood on her hands, hot and sticky and red. She didn't care if that made her a murderer.

"Every time you got in the shower." He slid the zipper down her back and pulled the thick neoprene off one shoulder. "Could you feel my eyes on you?" He licked her shoulder where it met her neck. "I bet you could. Did you like it?" His hands squeezed roughly at her breasts again, and he bit the back of her neck while he pressed his crotch against her. "I'm betting you did." He grabbed a handful of her hair and jerked back hard.

Oz had never felt so helpless. She couldn't control the shaking in her hands, and it was only making it harder for her to break her bonds. She could feel the heat of rage burning her face, and sweat coated her skin. The pain in her head and shoulder were totally forgotten. They were completely irrelevant in her need to destroy Finn's tormentor.

"I think your bitch likes to watch too. She hasn't taken her eyes off you, has she?" He laughed as he pulled Finn tighter against his body, his fingers still wrapped in her hair. He tucked his gun into the back of his pants and started to inch her wet suit away from her skin. His eyes never left Oz's as he slowly bared Finn's torso, trapping her arms more securely by her sides with the wet suit. Every movement dared Oz to speak, both of them knowing his behavior would only get worse if she did. He pushed the scant fabric of Finn's bikini top aside and gave Oz a vicious grin.

Oz strained to lift herself out of her chair as more tears slid down Finn's cheeks when Jack grasped and squeezed her breasts before pulling hard on her nipples. Finn bit her lip, and Oz ached to wipe away the tiny trickle of blood she created.

Jack let go of Finn's hair and wrapped his fingers around her throat, twisting her head away from his and giving him greater access to her neck. He licked at her flesh and slid his hand inside her wet suit. She squirmed in his grasp and fought to pull away from him. "Now, now, Daniela. No need for that."

Oz could see his fingers tightening on her throat, cutting off her air. She could see Finn gasping, and she fought harder, twisting and turning in his grasp.

"Bitch!" He pushed her away from him, cupping his crotch. He lashed out and slapped her across the face, grinning as she stumbled. Oz watched helplessly as Finn fell to the floor, coughing as she tried to drag air into her empty lungs. Jack reached for her again, pulled her to her feet like a rag doll, then he crushed her body against him and pressed his lips hard against her own.

The floorboards creaked, and the air became thick with the sickly odor of cologne. Jack froze.

"Put her down, Jack."

Jack straightened and stepped away from her.

"Cover her up."

Jack quickly straightened the bikini top and began to slide the wet suit back up her arms, struggling with the damp neoprene every step of the way.

"Where is Decker?"

"He had to change his trousers, sir."

"Why?"

"She threw up on him, sir."

William Sterling stepped in front of Finn and looked down at her. "Does that have anything to do with the blow to her head?"

"I don't know, sir. She fell in the driveway and I told Decker to pick her up."

"Fell? Then why does the mark look like a handprint, Jack?"

"She was somewhat reticent to do as she was asked, sir."

"I see. So you gave her a little persuasion."

It wasn't a question, but Jack nodded anyway.

"And you, Daniela, why were you causing Jack so much trouble?"

"He didn't ask me nicely, Daddy." Her voice was rough and she was breathing deeply.

Good girl, Finn. Keep them distracted just a little bit longer. I've nearly got the cuffs off, baby. Oz could feel how close the bonds were to releasing. She knew she would already be free if she wasn't trying to keep her movements from giving her away.

"She seems reasonable enough to me, Jack." Sterling walked slowly to the bar and poured himself a drink. "I must say, though, your behavior of late has given me cause to question your judgment, Daniela. Do you know why that is?"

"Because I've been having cold feet about marrying Pete."

Oz watched her drop her eyes trying to look contrite.

"No, Daniela, this has nothing to do with that sniveling little faggot. This is about you and her. This fucking bitch!" He kicked out and landed a glancing blow on Oz's shin.

She sucked air in through her lips and stifled a moan as Decker and the other man came back in the room. They positioned themselves by the door, one on either side, their guns held loosely in their clasped hands. Oz mentally paced the distance to them. She carefully gauged the distance to Jack, weighing and assessing the best way to approach them when she attacked. Deciding who the biggest threat was and how best to eradicate that threat. Would she have to kill Jack to stop him? Did she care? Who did she need to target next? She saw the fight develop in her mind in a split second and knew exactly where each counterattack would come from as well as where she needed to position herself between Finn and danger. Every decision was already made when her binding finally gave way and she sat waiting, biding her time. Every decision except one. If she had to, could she kill Sterling? Could she look him in the eye and pull the trigger, knowing he was Finn's father? Would Finn ever forgive her if she did?

"You have disgraced me, you disgusting little pervert. I'm just glad your mother isn't here to see this."

"Don't you dare!"

Oz knew the anger had been building in Finn, held back only until the shock wore off a little and simmering until it reached boiling point. *Please, baby, don't push him too far.* Oz was terrified that her anger would blind Finn to the danger signs.

"Don't even think about her! You aren't good enough for that. You aren't good enough for a lot of things, Father."

Oz grunted as the blow to Finn's stomach doubled her over and made her gasp. She took her time getting her breath back, but she straightened her spine and kept speaking.

"You see, Daddy, I know." She spat the words at him as she took a step closer. "I know every diabolical thing about you. You're an evil, despicable bastard."

Oz cringed at the blow that landed across Finn's face, causing her head to snap to the side, before she spat blood on the ground. The adrenaline in her system probably blocked the worst of the pain, and

Oz grinned when Finn took another step forward and he took one back. Her words were quiet, cold, and she was seemingly unafraid.

"I know what you have growing in the bio lab." She took another step toward him. "And I know what you're planning to do with it." She took another step. "I also know that no matter what you do to me today, you will not get away with it."

The next slap caused her eyes to water, but she took another step, and this time when he backed up another step he hit the edge of a chair and sat down. She leaned down so that her eyes were level with his.

Oz wanted to cheer as she watched Finn stand up to the tyrant who had ruled her.

"I always wanted to make you proud of me, Daddy, because I thought I could be proud to call you my father."

Out of the corner of her eye, Oz saw Jack step toward them, only to step back with a flick of Sterling's hand.

"Even though I didn't like you," Finn continued. "Even though I hated what I saw you do to the people who worked for us. For you. What you did to me. That you didn't care that I didn't love Pete. Or that he didn't love me. I still wanted you to be proud of me." She stared at him. "But you're a monster. You don't care about anything or anyone but yourself. Your money. Your power. You tortured my mother, and you tortured me for years, with all your mind games. No more." She stood up and looked down at him. "It ends now. Today. I'm through playing your games, you pathetic little bastard. I know that you killed my mother."

He stood quickly and wrapped his hands around her throat and squeezed until she went quiet, her eyes bulging and bloodshot. Her cheeks reddened, making the blue tint to her lips stand out further. Oz felt like throwing up, but she knew she couldn't make her move yet. If he didn't let go, she'd be forced to move, but she couldn't take out everyone in the positions they were. She swallowed her bile when he let go of Finn's throat and she gulped air.

"Are you quite finished, Daniela?" He let go of her throat and slapped her hard across the face, the force of the blow spinning her round. "Good. I do *hate* a woman who doesn't know when to shut up." He held her jaw and looked at her. "You don't know a damn thing, little girl. I didn't kill your mother. She did it all herself. But do you know what the real kicker is?" He twisted her face from one side to the other. "Do you know I had to bribe the coroner so that I could get the money?"

She nodded. It was all she could do.

"Do you know why that was necessary?"

She tried to shake her head, but his grip was too tight.

"She didn't leave me a body. Very selfish of her. She didn't even leave a note. I had to print one off." His spittle hit Finn's face. "But the real kick in the teeth, the real truth is that she isn't dead. I didn't kill her. She left. She faked her own death to get away from us. You and me, little girl. She didn't want anything to do with either of us. She wanted her own whore." He grinned as the shock of his words was clear on Finn's face. "That's it. Even after everything I've done for you, you still turned out just like her. A fucking pervert." He pushed her away from him and laughed when she hit the floor. "You're right about one thing, though. It does end today. Jack."

Jack looked at him expectantly.

"Kill her."

Jack raised the gun and leveled it at Finn's head.

"Not in here, you fucking idiot. Take them both outside, take the boat, and toss them over the side. For fuck's sake, do I have to do everything myself?" He stepped toward Jack and backhanded him across the face.

Oz threw herself from her seat into Jack's body, her good arm outstretched, snatching at the weapon and then using her momentum to spin away from him and twist the gun from his grasp, finishing with him in front of her. She struck the butt of the weapon down on the back of his skull, and he crashed to the floor as she leveled the weapon at Decker.

"Put your weapons down. I don't want to hurt you."

Decker lifted his arm, his finger on the trigger.

Oz's shot was clean and lethal, hitting him straight between the eyes.

She barely had to move to bring the third man into her sights. "It doesn't have to be like this. Just put the gun down." His gun was already aimed at her chest, but the man's hand was shaking, his face was pale, and sweat was trickling into his eyes. "Just put it down and you can walk away from this alive." She watched out of the corner of her eye as Sterling started to move. He was trying to inch toward Finn, intent on using her as a shield. *Fucking idiot doesn't know how good a shot I am.* She watched as he moved his hand higher. Not being able to tell where he was going to fire, and running out of time, Oz squeezed the trigger.

"For fuck's sake," Oz yelled as she spun and crossed the room in two strides before pressing the burning barrel of the gun to William Sterling's head. The gun felt so good in her hand. It was an extension of her body. Pulling the trigger would be as easy as breathing. She looked at him and knew that pulling the trigger would put an end to so many possibilities. The pain he had caused and the suffering he was willing to cause made it so hard to keep the pressure low enough to stop the gun from going off.

The only possibility she feared in pulling the trigger was Finn's reaction. How would she feel about her if she killed her father? She didn't know if Finn was ready to accept his part in all of this madness yet, despite the fact that he had just ordered her death. She wanted to free them all of this monster, but knew Finn would never forgive her for it. But she wanted to. She wanted to kill him for all the ways he had hurt Finn. She wanted to kill him for Pete. She wanted to kill him for all the innocent lives he was prepared to squander for money. Her hand shook as she battled her own instincts, and she realized once again how easy it was for her to turn killer again. She dreaded seeing Finn's face, fearing that all she would see would be the disgust and hatred she felt for herself, but she had to know. She needed to see that Finn was okay, if nothing else, so she slowly turned to look at her.

Finn's eyes were huge as she looked around the room, clearly amazed at the position they were in now. "How?"

"Training. Baby, are you okay?" She flicked her eyes back to Sterling. "Finn? Baby, are you okay?"

"Yeah, I think so. How did you get the ties off?"

"Trade secret I'm afraid. You impressed?"

"Hell, yeah."

"Oh, for God's sake, please shoot me." Sterling rolled his eyes.

"Don't tempt me."

Sterling's face paled as she stared at him.

"I have about a billion reasons to take you down, right here, right now. And you know what? I'd probably get a medal for it."

She circled around until she stood in front of the chair and aimed the gun at his chest. She crouched and rifled through Jack's pockets until she found more cable ties and a knife, the gun never wavering from Sterling's heart. She quickly cut the tie that bound Finn's wrists and placed a tender kiss to her temple as she handed her a couple of the plastic ties. "Put those on your dad. Fasten them with his hands behind his back."

Finn did as instructed, and when his wrists were secured she pushed him into a seat and then took it upon herself to secure his ankles too. He stared at her with pure hatred in his eyes but didn't say anything.

Oz lowered the gun and pulled Finn into her arms. She kept her eyes fixed on Sterling as she held Finn tight.

"Baby, we need to call Charlie."

Finn nodded against her chest before she pulled away and crossed the room, picked up a phone, and punched in the number.

"Charlie, it's Finn."

"Are you both okay?"

"Yeah, sort of. We're both pretty banged up, but everything's under control."

"Hang tight. The cavalry is almost with you."

She hung up the phone and walked back to Oz's side.

"How long?"

"Just a few minutes."

"I know you got a lot off your chest before, but this might be the last chance you get to talk to him, so is there anything else you want to ask him?"

"Where is she?"

"Who?"

"My mother."

"Why?"

She stared at him. "Because she was my mother. She loved me. Because I loved her."

"The last time I saw your mother, you were twelve years old. She was with her. That bitch she left me for." Oz snapped to attention even as Finn stared incredulously at him.

"Who?"

"That fucking dyke."

Finn slapped him across the face. "I take offense to that, Father."

He stared at her as though she had grown a second head.

"Who was she?"

"Karen Riley."

"My cook?"

"You remember her do you? Did she interfere with you too?"

"Don't be disgusting. She and my mum were lovers?"

"Yes."

"Why did you employ her if you knew who she was?"

"I didn't. The housekeeper did all the hiring in those days. She wanted to be close to you. Isn't that sweet? Little Daniela's guardian angel. Soon put a stop to that one, though." The smile on his face made Oz feel dirty.

"What did you do to her?"

He just grinned.

"What did you do?"

"I paid her a little visit, that's all. After your mother died, so to speak, I thought I'd see what it was that had your mother so interested." He smiled at her, a lascivious twisting of his lips that didn't reach his eyes. "I have to admit, your mum had pretty good taste."

"What did you do to her?" Finn's voice was barely a whisper.

"Nothing she didn't want—"

"You raped her."

"You say tomato." The smile on his face widened. "But this is where I got the real shock. Guess who was there with your precious Karen? Shacked up together, having a whale of a time." He paused, staring at her. "No? Really? Your dear old mum. Have to say, that really threw me for a loop. But in a situation like that, you just have to make the best of things. And I've got to admit, finding them both there together? Well, two for the price of one you might say."

"You son of a bitch." It was all Oz could do to stop herself from striking him.

"You raped my mother." Finn's voice quivered.

"She was my wife! She was the one who left. They had no right to come sniffing around again. She should have stayed dead! I told them both that if they ever contacted you again, they wouldn't be the only ones to regret it."

"You threatened to rape her again?"

His laughter echoed harshly in her ears. "Daniela, I didn't need a repeat performance, and neither did they."

"Then what? You would have killed her?"

"Yes, but there was no need. You see, there was this big old soft spot they both had. An Achilles' heel if you like."

Oz had never felt so repulsed. "You sick bastard."

Finn stared at Oz, her confusion obvious as Oz held the gun closer to his face.

"That just gave me a billion and one." She pointed the gun at his head. "Where are they both?"

He shrugged and leaned a little closer to the gun.

"Tell me." He grinned a little more and the realization hit Oz like a ton of bricks. *He wants me to kill him so that he doesn't go to jail and doesn't have to face what he's done.* She leaned into his face. "I know what you want." She looked him in the eye so he could see the truth of her words. "Tell me what I want to know and I will give you what you want." She pushed the gun against his temple.

"I don't know." He stared at Finn. "I spent years trying to find them again. But every time I thought I had them, they were gone again. If I had found them I would have killed the bitches. I might have been able to use it to turn you into a proper daughter."

"You've been tracking her?" Finn asked.

He nodded.

"Where was she last?"

"I don't know. I just get updates from the investigators. They send me e-mails."

"Where's your computer?"

He stared at her blankly.

"Don't make me ask again." He nodded in the direction of the bar.

Finn grabbed the laptop from the cabinet he pointed to and booted the system. "Password?"

He stalled, looking at Oz. She pushed against him with the barrel of the gun.

"Alchemy."

Finn punched the keys and quickly e-mailed the details to herself. She riffled through the case and found a portable hard drive, which she plugged in. The files transferred quickly and she wrapped the hard drive in a plastic bag she found under the sink before tucking it in the folds of her wet suit sleeve.

"Drop the gun." Jack's voice was rough, the traces of his concussion audible around the edges.

Oz felt cold metal press against her temple.

"I said, drop the fucking gun!"

Finn froze as she watched from across the room.

Oz flicked her eyes toward her threatened temple and looked hard at Finn, shaking her head almost imperceptibly.

"I said—"

"Okay, okay." She pulled the barrel of the gun from Sterling's temple and held the gun out to the side, a good six inches in front of her, and at the full reach of her arm.

Jack reached for it, but her long arms, coupled with his position behind her, put it well beyond his hand. He stepped around and tried to grab it.

Oz knew the blow to the head would slow him down, and she knew she could spin out of his reach and disable him, despite having only one functioning arm.

But Sterling saw his opportunity and wasted no time. He threw all his might into propelling his body out of the chair at her, landing heavily against her body, his weight taking them both to the ground. The impact of landing on her dislocated shoulder dislodged the gun from her grip and sent it skating across the floor.

Jack scrabbled in the direction of the pistol only to find himself staring down the barrel as it shook in Finn's hand. He laughed as he pulled himself to his feet.

Oz grunted from the floor, pinned beneath Sterling's weight. She struggled and twisted, trying to dislodge the body above her.

Jack edged toward Finn. "You can't use that." He took a step closer to her. "You haven't got the balls to pull the trigger." He stepped closer. "So why don't you hand it over to me?"

"Get back, Jack." Her hands were shaking as she pointed the gun at him.

He stopped advancing but didn't back away.

"Or else what? Hmm, Daniela? Or else what? You going to shoot me? To make Daddy proud?" He laughed cruelly. "He's never been proud of you. Never fucking wanted you or that whore of a mother of yours. You know he only married her for the money, right?" He took another step closer.

Oz could see the fear and pain on Finn's face. She knew that she desperately didn't want to pull the trigger, but she could see something else too. She saw resolve. It was the same look in her eyes that Oz had seen when she said she was going to confront her father to keep Oz safe. Her mouth was set in a grim line and the tiny creases at the corners of her eyes were deeper than normal. Oz knew that her shaking hands didn't mean she wouldn't pull the trigger. She was convinced that Finn could, and would, kill him. She wanted to spare her that burden. She pushed at Sterling's body with her good arm while twisting her hips and torso, trying to get her legs in a position where she could roll him off her.

"I told you to stay back," Finn repeated.

He was beyond hearing her. "Married the bitch for her fucking money. Now hold still while I fucking kill you. Then I'm gonna kill that fucking bitch over there."

The shot rang out, echoing through the room. The smell of cordite hung in the air that suddenly felt heavier than the body lying across her. Jack's steps slowed as he looked down at his chest in surprise. The red flower blossomed outward, but still he stepped forward again.

Finn tried to steady the gun, but her next shot went wild, lodging in the ceiling. The third bullet ripped through his shoulder and threw his balance off.

Jack screamed in rage and pain as he tried to lunge for her.

Finn pulled the trigger again and Oz watched as the fourth bullet drilled through his upper chest. Crimson foam bubbled from between his lips as he attempted to pull in a lungful of air.

"I can't believe you actually shot me." He dropped to his knees. "Fuck, that hurts."

The doors burst open and several armed men flew into the room with their guns poised and ready. Two of them quickly dragged Sterling off Oz and helped her to her feet. Finn was staring at Jack's body, her eyes locked on the growing pool of blood that surrounded him.

"Finn, babe, can you give me the gun?"

Tears began to fall down her cheeks, the gun shaking wildly in her hand as she stared at the crumpled body lying at her feet.

"Finn? Give me the gun. Baby, you're okay. We're both okay, but I need you to give me the gun now."

Finn held the gun straight out to her, totally oblivious to the fact that she was pointing a loaded weapon at Oz's chest. Oz quickly clasped her hand over the top, engaged the safety and passed it to the soldier behind her.

"Looks like we got another SEAL in the family, hey?"

Oz turned around, noticing for the first time that it was her cousin standing behind her. She wrapped her arm around Finn, closing her eyes and allowing herself a few moments to revel in the fact that they were both now safe. "Junior, I never thought I'd be so glad to see you."

"I think I should be offended by that. It's a damn good thing you were diving with a GPS thing in your wet suit today, cousin. Your crew called the dive center, and Rudy called Charlie. We tracked your transmitter, but they had a damn good lead on us." He grinned at her, but she could see the concern in his eyes. "Let's get you out of here."

"You saved us, baby." She kissed Finn's temple and continued to whisper to her, trying to soothe her as she trembled in her arms. "You saved us." Her relief at having Finn safe was overwhelming; it almost let her forget the price that safety had cost, but not quite. She knew Finn would need time to deal with what she had done to keep them both safe. The burden of taking a life, no matter how justified, was one she knew too well.

The SEALs were milling around the room, checking bodies for signs of life. They pulled Sterling outside and forced him to his knees while they waited for orders.

"Oh for Christ's sake, Oz! You didn't leave me anything to do!" Junior threw his hands in the air.

Oz grinned. "Sure I did, Junior. The cleanup is all yours." She stepped to the side, keeping her arm around Finn's shoulders, and led her out to the chopper.

CHAPTER THIRTY-NINE

Oz sat in the living room at the navy house and wrapped her arm around Finn's shoulders, placing a tender kiss at her temple, unable to stop smiling. They'd spent two hours in the emergency room before Oz's mom picked them up.

"How's your shoulder?"

"It's fine, baby. Doc just wants me to keep this sling on to rest the ligaments for a few days."

"When do we have to talk to Charlie?"

"He'll be here soon. You know you're going to have to give him that hard drive you copied, don't you?"

"Yes. I just want to know what my father knew about my mum. And I want to see for myself. I need to." Finn didn't know if she could explain why she needed to know the lengths that her mother had gone to remain hidden from him, but she did. She needed to understand what she had gone through. This woman who was both a stranger to her and yet had loved her so completely that she had been willing to give up her life to save her from harm.

"Then we should probably take a look now before he gets here. I'll grab my laptop." Oz kissed her head again before she stood and left the room.

Finn closed her eyes and rested her head against the back of the sofa. She wanted to erase the last twelve hours from her head. The gunshot still rang in her ears, the smell of gunfire filled her nostrils, and the metallic scent of blood was so thick she could almost taste it. The bright red stain growing on Jack's chest as the life seeped from his body, one heartbeat at a time. Her choice. Her decision. Her action. Cause and effect perfectly displayed. One question burned in her mind and she found she couldn't answer it. Did she regret it? Did she regret taking Jack's life? Knowing that he would have killed her and Oz if she hadn't pulled the trigger made it seem clear. Her response was completely logical and understandable. It was self-preservation at its most primitive level. Kill or be killed. Live or die. Intellectually, she accepted it, understood it, and knew that rationally, there was no real choice to make. But she still couldn't decide if she regretted what she had done.

"Hey, you okay?" Oz put the laptop on the table and squatted in front of her, holding her hands.

Finn shrugged slightly and squeezed Oz's hand. "Honestly? I really don't know. I can't process everything yet."

"Maybe we should wait to do this."

"No. Like you said, I need to give that to Charlie when he gets here, and I need to see this. I need to know what happened to her. I want to know where she is, what she went through. I'm angry with her for leaving me. And I need to get past that. The only way I can think of is to find out why she made the decision she did. Why she left me with him."

"Finn, she didn't have a choice."

"How do you know that?"

"Your father told us."

Finn looked at her, confused.

"He was threatening you. To do to you what he did to them. That was how he kept them away from you. They only stayed away to protect you."

Finn felt a wave of nausea and dizziness hit her. Her vision swam until she closed her eyes. She felt Oz's arms wrap around her shoulders, and the sobs started to come, wrenched from the depths of her soul. Her pain was so complete that she didn't think she would ever be able to escape it.

The knock at the door pulled them apart, but Oz quickly pulled her back into her arms when Charlie, Billy, and a third man entered the room.

"Oz, Finn, you remember Agent Pritchard?"

"Yes." Oz shook his hand.

"Oz, a pleasure. Finn?"

Pritchard held his hand out to shake hers, and she hated having to move from Oz's embrace, but manners were manners, and she quickly moved back to the warmth and safety of Oz's arms.

"We need to get a statement from each of you about the events."

Oz's grip tightened around her. "When?"

"As soon as possible," Pritchard said.

"I brought recording equipment with me, Oz. We can do it all here." Billy waved a small recording device in front of him.

"Is there somewhere a bit more private?" Pritchard looked around.

Oz shrugged as she looked about the small room. "Not really. The only other rooms are a bedroom and a bathroom. Which would you like to use?"

Billy nodded toward the door. "Oz, why don't we step outside while Agent Pritchard and Charlie talk to Finn?"

Finn was reluctant to let go of Oz, clinging to her hand. "I don't want you to leave."

"I'm not leaving, baby. I'll be right outside the door. If you need me, you just shout and I'll be back. I promise." She tried to pull away from Finn, but Finn's arms were still locked about her waist. "Finn, the quicker we do this, the quicker we'll be back together and we can figure out what we're doing next, okay?" Oz slowly stood as Finn released her, and she stepped out of the room with her dad.

Charlie set the tape recorder on the small coffee table, turned it on, and smiled at her. "Finn, I need you to take it from the beginning and tell me everything you remember."

Finn took a deep breath and sighed, knowing that her words would never fully convey everything she had gone though. There simply weren't any strong enough to convey the fear, panic, and horror she had felt, but the moment-by-moment account? That, she could tell. Those were the moments she knew she would never forget, no matter how much she wanted to, and in that instant she realized she had her answer. While she knew logically that killing Jack was the only thing she could do, she knew it was one action she would regret for the rest of her life. She looked down at her hands as she began speaking, shocked that they weren't stained red.

❖

Two hours later, Finn sat on the steps outside the house waiting for Oz. Billy handed her a beer and leaned against the rail beside her, seemingly content to keep her company in silence. The door opened, and when Charlie, Pritchard, and Oz exited, Finn pulled herself to her feet and stood beside Oz. She waved at the men as they climbed in a car and drove away before she closed her eyes and allowed herself to feel the cooling night breeze against her skin.

"How did it go?"

Oz kissed her head gently. "It was fine, baby. What about you? Are you okay?"

"No."

"Want to talk about it?"

"No."

Oz chuckled. "It will probably help."

"I don't know what to say."

"Whatever you feel. There is no right and wrong. Just talk."

"So you wouldn't be disappointed if I told you that I regret killing Jack?"

"Why on earth would I be disappointed?"

"Because he was going to kill us both."

"Yes, he was. And I am very, very glad that you did what had to be done and saved us both. I will always be grateful for that, but I'm not disappointed in you. What you feel about what you had to do is understandable. I regret the death of every person I had to kill. I regret having to be the one who pulled the trigger. I close my eyes and I can see every face. I wish it did, but that doesn't go away. But I know that in the same situations, I would make the same choices I did then, every time. That's how I know I didn't have a choice. That my actions were simply reactions. My regret is that my actions, my decisions, got an innocent man killed. That I would change if I could. Now tell me this, if you were in the same situation again, would you make the same choice?"

"I don't know..."

"Don't you?"

Finn closed her eyes and saw Jack stepping toward her. She could hear Oz grunting and straining, trying to get away from her father. She could feel her panic rising again as she saw the look of contempt and loathing in Jack's eyes. The clarity with which she knew Jack would kill her was startling, but she knew that the knowledge alone couldn't make her pull the trigger again. It was her certainty that her death would be followed quickly by Oz's that made her heart ache. This was the choice she would make again and again. To save the woman she loved, she knew she would pull the trigger every time.

"I'd do it to save you."

"And I would do it to save you. I left the navy because I didn't want to be a killer. I didn't want to end up in a situation ever again where I might have to take any more lives. This morning, I shot two men and I would have happily blown away the rest to keep you safe."

Finn tucked her head under Oz's chin and hugged her tighter. Her brain ached from all the thoughts, and her heart ached from too many emotions. Her body ached from the attack. She wanted to forget for a while. She needed to feel the comfort and safety she could only find in Oz's arms. She needed to feel all of her. She needed to tear down any remaining barriers between them and hold on to the trust and love they had.

She smiled before she reached up and kissed Oz. "I think I've done enough thinking for tonight." Her lips pressed against Oz's neck. "I just want to feel." She licked at the throbbing pulse at Oz's throat. "Make me feel, Oz."

Oz searched her eyes for a long moment, and Finn's breath caught when she saw how clearly desire was painted across Oz's face.

"Finn, I don't think this is the right time."

"I love you, Oz. I want you. I need to feel you."

"I love you too, but I want you to be sure."

"I am." She kissed Oz with every ounce of passion she felt. "Make love to me, Oz."

Oz swallowed audibly and licked her lips before she spoke. "Come with me." Her voice was rough with need as she took Finn's hand and pulled her back into the house. She closed the door behind them and led Finn straight to the bedroom and wrapped her in her arms. Her kiss was tender and sweet with a fire beneath it that caused Finn's knees to weaken.

"Oz." Her breathless voice reached Oz's ears and she helped Finn lie down. When she stood up again, she quickly removed her shirt and shorts before lying down beside Finn.

"We stop any time you want to, okay?"

Stopping was the furthest thing from Finn's mind as she looked at Oz's sleek torso, the bruising across her shoulder and the scar on her stomach reminders of her battles, but more importantly of her will to survive. And she loved them just as much as she loved everything else about Oz. She buried her fingers in Oz's hair and pulled her in for a kiss. "I told you." Another fiery kiss. "I trust you." Finn kissed her again and reached between them, unbuttoning her jeans and pushing them down her hips before Oz helped her kick them off her feet and tossed them to the floor. She sat up and pulled her tank top over her head and quickly removed her bra. Only her panties remained.

"Make love to me, Olivia."

Oz took her in her arms and pulled her body against her own as she pushed Finn onto her back. Finn's legs automatically curled around her hips as her tongue filled Oz's mouth. Oz's fingers trailed down Finn's side, along the length of her thigh, and then gripped her butt, and her lips and tongue trailed the length of her neck and shoulder before reaching her breasts. Oz teased the outer skin, slowly working her way toward the puckering flesh at the tip but avoiding the actual nipple, over and over again. Finn was burning, her breasts aching for more.

"Oz, you're driving me crazy."

Salvation followed as Oz's mouth covered her nipple and sucked hard, pulling as much of the soft breast into her mouth as she could, flicking her tongue across the tip of Finn's nipple maddeningly before she moved to the other breast.

Finn threaded her fingers into Oz's hair desperate to anchor herself as waves of sensation filled her body. Her heart raced and her skin burned under Oz's touch, even as goose bumps erupted in the wake of her fingers as they stroked her thighs, her sides, the soft skin of her belly, and the tender underside of her breasts. The fire built inside her, and she knew without doubt that this was everything she had ever wanted. That Oz was the woman she would spend her life loving.

She felt Oz's hand slide between their bodies and inside her panties. Her finger traced the outer lips of her center, and Finn knew that they were now drenched with her desire.

Oz groaned and pulled her mouth away from Finn's nipple. "Oh God. I need to taste you. Can I?"

"Yes."

Oz kissed her again as her fingers continued to explore between her legs. Finn moaned as Oz pulled away and kissed her way down her neck, across her chest, and down her abdomen, pulling her underwear away as she went. Finn didn't have time to feel self-conscious as she bared herself for the first time. Instead, she gripped the sheet with one hand, the other resting on Oz's head as she lowered herself between Finn's legs.

They both moaned as Oz's lips closed over her in that first intimate kiss, and Finn felt the first whispers of orgasm low in her belly. Oz's tongue swept over her in one long, delicious lick before swirling around her clit and dipping in and out of every fold of her sex. Oz let go of her hand, but she didn't have time to mourn the loss of the contact before those fingers were spreading her open and Oz's tongue played at her entrance. Her eyes opened and she looked down at Oz, the sight of her between her legs, and the sensations of her mouth feasting upon her were almost overwhelming. She could feel the fire spreading down her legs and into her chest.

"Oz, I'm so close."

Oz looked up without moving her mouth. Their eyes locked, and slowly, she slid a finger inside her. Finn couldn't have stopped the moan that escaped her lips even if she had wanted to. Oz watched her, working her finger in and out, slowly stretching the supple flesh before adding another. Finn couldn't hold her head up anymore as she clutched at Oz's shoulders and let the waves of her orgasm crash over her.

Oz slowly crawled up her body, planting soft kisses on her skin as she went until she was straddling Finn's hips and looking down at her. Finn's chest heaved as she tried to catch her breath. They kissed, soft and gentle, and Finn let her hands drift along Oz's back. Caressing the muscles on either side of her spine and running her hands into the sweat-dampened hair at the back of her neck.

"I want to touch you. Is that okay?"

Oz smiled down at her, desire shimmering in her blue eyes. "You can do anything you want, baby." She started to roll off Finn, but she held her firm.

"I like you here." She reached up and kissed her again as her hands began to explore. "Does this hurt your shoulder?"

"I'm fine." Oz's voice was rough, husky with need.

Finn couldn't help but smile, loving that she could affect Oz so much. She kissed her neck and shoulders with tiny little butterfly kisses as she removed her bra, before licking at the slightly salty skin. She smiled as Oz groaned and twitched above her. Her hands were never still, running the length of Oz's back, over her butt and down the back of her thighs before she started trailing them up the front of her legs, across her belly, and caressing her breasts. She flicked her thumbs over Oz's nipples before gently pinching them between her fingers. She had to have her mouth on them. She wanted to feel them between her lips. She started to push herself forward. Oz sat up, giving Finn all the access she needed. Finn was amazed as the flesh pebbled and tightened beneath her tongue. Each suck drew a moan from Oz, and every lick was received with a gasp. Finn reveled in each noise she drew from Oz's lips, and her confidence grew with each thrust of her hips as she searched for some contact.

She palmed her ass, gripping and squeezing as she switched to the other breast. It wasn't enough. She needed more. She needed everything. Finn trailed her hand up the inside of Oz's thigh, her arousal clearly evident well before she reached her damp underwear. She looked up at Oz's face as she touched her for the first time. Oz's eyes were closed, the look of rapture on her face made Finn want to weep at the beauty of it. She pushed the thin cotton aside and pressed her fingers on either side of Oz's clit, squeezing gently as she slid deeper into her folds, making long, slow strokes as she explored this new territory.

"Oh, baby, that's so good."

Finn's confidence grew even more, and so did her need. The scent of Oz was making her mouth water, and she wanted to know Oz as intimately as she could. She wanted to taste her. To feel the very essence of her coat her tongue and fill her very senses.

"Lie down for me."

Oz was quick to comply and Finn was fascinated by the new topography. She couldn't wait to lean over Oz's body and let her mouth cover every inch. She kissed all the way down from Oz's throat to her navel where she dipped her tongue inside before continuing down. She hooked her fingers beneath the waistband of Oz's panties and pulled them away from her skin as Oz lifted her hips. Finn bit her lip and pressed her fingers against the newly exposed flesh. Oz's golden curls were darkened by her desire, and Finn couldn't wait any more. She pressed her lips between Oz's legs and sighed as she took her first taste. *Heaven.* She wasn't nervous. She could feel Oz enjoying every touch, every kiss. She knew this was right. She knew that this was where she was meant to be.

She sucked and licked every inch of the fragrant flesh beneath her mouth. She explored and experimented as Oz bucked against her face, groaning with pleasure until her body jackknifed off the bed and she clutched at Finn's head. Her cry of release was the sweetest sound Finn had ever heard.

Finn waited until Oz's breathing had calmed, her head resting on Oz's belly, her arms hooked around her hips.

"Come up here."

Finn was only too happy to fulfill the request and crawled up Oz's body, kissing her lightly along the way.

"I love you."

"I love you too, baby."

Oz wrapped her arms around Finn and sighed contentedly as they settled against each other.

"You know that you're my one, don't you, Oz?"

Oz remembered the conversation. "One face next to yours on the pillow. One name on your lips." She nodded and kissed Finn gently, the tender passion entwining their souls. "For the rest of my life, baby."

EPILOGUE

Five weeks later

The house buzzed with activity. Loud complaints and groans came from the den as Oz and her cousins watched football. The smell coming from the kitchen where Ellie, Mrs. Richmond, and Oz's Aunt Alex were cooking made Finn's mouth water as she headed down the hall. The ringing bell stopped her and she opened the door to a well-dressed man.

"Ms. Finsbury-Sterling?"

"And you are?"

He held out his hand. "I'm Andrew Whittaker. I work for Interpol. I need your help."

Finn stared at his hand before looking him in the eye. "And what do you need my help with?"

He dropped his hand, shrugging slightly as he did so. "I'm in charge of a task force trying to apprehend Masood Mehalik." He waited, an expectant look on his face.

"Am I supposed to know who that is?"

"He's the man your father was selling biological weapons to."

Finn started to turn away. "I'm not inter—"

He caught her arm to stop her from walking away and closing the door. "I really need your help. Two scientists in the last three months have been murdered. Scientists who specialize in genetic engineering, and I have reason to believe it's because Mehalik is trying to re-create Balor."

"I'm even less interested."

"I have reason to believe that it's only a matter of time before he tries to convince you to help him."

"I would never—"

"Take your hand off her." Oz's voice was low and menacing as she clapped a hand on his shoulder. He released Finn's arm.

"Sorry, I didn't mean anything by it. Please, I just need a few minutes of your time." He pushed his fingers through his short, sandy-colored hair. "Mehalik isn't the kind of man to say no to, Ms. Finsbury-Sterling. He can be very persuasive."

"And I can be very stubborn."

He pulled a photograph out of his pocket and handed it to her. "This is what happened to the last stubborn person Mehalik met." He handed her another picture. "And this is what happened to his family."

Finn looked at the picture and swallowed back the bile that rose in her throat. Oz snatched the pictures out of her hand and tossed them back at him.

"What kind of bastard are you?"

"I want to stop this from happening to you!"

"How?"

"I want you to take over your father's company."

"Why?"

"Mehalik knows that you developed the technique that made Balor possible. He's confident you can do this. He wants to believe it, so I want you to let him. We know he's been looking for you. It's just a matter of time before he finds you. If you take over the company, he'll know how to reach you. And we need him to do so."

"Again, why?"

"We can't find him and he is determined to unleash this on the world. You know what that will do."

Finn felt her knees buckle and only Oz's hands kept her on her feet as she fought back the urge to throw up. "It's supposed to be over."

About the Author

A Stockport (near Manchester, UK) native, Andrea took her life in her hands a few years ago and crossed the great North/South divide and now lives in Norfolk with her partner, their two border collies, and two and a half cats (one isn't sure if she wants to be theirs anymore, as the lady down the street feeds her Whiskas rather than whatever is on offer at the supermarket, like they do!). Andrea spends her time running their campsite and hostel to pay the bills and scribbling down stories during the winter months.

Andrea is an avid reader and a keen musician, playing the saxophone and the guitar (just to annoy her other half—apparently!). She is also a recreational diver and takes an opportunity to head to warmer climes and discover the mysteries of life beneath the waves!

Books Available From Bold Strokes Books

Ladyfish by Andrea Bramhall. Finn's escape to the Florida Keys leads her straight into the arms of scuba diving instructor Oz as she fights for her freedom, their blossoming love…and her life! (978-1-60282-747-9)

Spanish Heart by Rachel Spangler. While on a mission to find herself in Spain, Ren Molson runs the risk of losing her heart to her tour guide, Lina Montero. (978-1-60282-748-6)

Love Match by Ali Vali. When Parker "Kong" King, the number one tennis player in the world, meets commercial pilot Captain Sydney Parish, sparks fly but not from attraction. They have the summer to see if they have a love match. (978-1-60282-749-3)

One Touch by L.T. Marie. A romance writer and a travel agent come together at their high school reunion, only to find out that the memory of that one touch never fades. (978-1-60282-750-9)

Night Shadows: Queer Horror edited by Greg Herren and J.M. Redmann. *Night Shadows* features delightfully wicked stories by some of the biggest names in queer publishing. (978-1-60282-751-6)

Secret Societies by William Holden. An outcast hustler, his unlikely "mother," his faithless lovers, and his religious persecutors—all in 1726. (978-1-60282-752-3)

The Raid by Lee Lynch. Before Stonewall, having a drink with friends or your girl could mean jail. Would these women and men still have family, a job, a place to live after…The Raid. (978-1-60282-753-0)

The You Know Who Girls by Annameekee Hesik. As they begin freshman year, Abbey Brooks and her best friend, Kate, pinky swear they'll keep away from the lesbians in Gila High, but Abbey already suspects she's one of those you-know-who girls herself and slowly learns who her true friends really are. (978-1-60282-754-7)

Wyatt: Doc Holliday's Account of an Intimate Friendship by Dale Chase. Erotica writer Dale Chase takes the remarkable friendship between Wyatt Earp, upright lawman, and Doc Holliday, southern gentlemen turned gambler and killer, to an entirely new level: hot! (978-1-60282-755-4)

Month of Sundays by Yolanda Wallace. Love doesn't always happen overnight; sometimes it takes a month of Sundays. (978-1-60282-739-4)

Jacob's War by C.P. Rowlands. ATF Special Agent Allison Jacob's task force is in the middle of an all-out war, from the streets to the boardrooms of America. Small business owner Katie Blackburn is the latest victim who accidentally breaks it wide open but may break AJ's heart at the same time. (978-1-60282-740-0)

The Pyramid Waltz by Barbara Ann Wright. Princess Katya Nar Umbriel wants a perfect romance, but her Fiendish nature and duties to the crown mean she can never tell the truth—until she meets Starbride, a woman who gets to the heart of every secret, even if it will be the death of her. (978-1-60282-741-7)

The Secret of Othello by Sam Cameron. Florida teen detectives Steven and Denny risk their lives to search for a sunken NASA satellite—but under the waves, no one can hear you scream... (978-1-60282-742-4)

Dreaming of Her by Maggie Morton. Isa has begun to dream of the most amazing woman—a woman named Lilith with a gorgeous face, an amazing body, and the ability to turn Isa on like no other. But Lilith is just a dream...isn't she? (978-1-60282-847-6)

Andy Squared by Jennifer Lavoie. Andrew never thought anyone could come between him and his twin sister, Andrea...until Ryder rode into town. (978-1-60282-743-1)

Finding Bluefield by Elan Barnehama. Set in the backdrop of Virginia and New York and spanning the years 1960–1982, Finding Bluefield chronicles the lives of Nicky Stewart, Barbara Philips, and their son, Paul, as they struggle to define themselves as a family. (978-1-60282-744-8)

The Jetsetters by David-Matthew Barnes. As rock band The Jetsetters skyrocket from obscurity to super stardom, Justin Holt, a lonely barista, and Diego Delgado, the band's guitarist, fight with everything they have to stay together, despite the chaos and fame. (978-1-60282-745-5)

Strange Bedfellows by Rob Byrnes. Partners in life and crime, Grant Lambert and Chase LaMarca, are hired to make a politician's compromising photo disappear, but what should be an easy job quickly spins out of control. (978-1-60282-746-2)

Speed Demons by Gun Brooke. When NASCAR star Evangeline Marshall returns to the race track after a close brush with death, will famous photographer Blythe Pierce document her triumph and reciprocate her love—or will they succumb to their respective demons and fail? (978-1-60282-678-6)

Summoning Shadows: A Rosso Lussuria Vampire Novel by Winter Pennington. The Rosso Lussuria vampires face enemies both old and new, and to prevail they must call on even more strange alliances, unite as a clan, and draw on every weapon within their reach—but with a clan of vampires, that's easier said than done. (978-1-60282-679-3)

Sometime Yesterday by Yvonne Heidt. When Natalie Chambers learns her Victorian house is haunted by a pair of lovers and a Dark Man, can she and her lover Van Easton solve the mystery that will set the ghosts free and banish the evil presence in the house? Or will they have to run to survive as well? (978-1-60282-680-9)

Into the Flames by Mel Bossa. In order to save one of his patients, psychiatrist Jamie Scarborough will have to confront his own monsters—including those he unknowingly helped create. (978-1-60282-681-6)

Coming Attractions: Author's Edition by Bobbi Marolt. For Helen Townsend, chasing turns to caring, and caring turns to loving, but will love take five steps back and turn to leaving? (978-1-60282-732-5)

OMGqueer, edited by Radclyffe and Katherine E. Lynch. Through stories imagined and told by youth across America, this anthology provides a snapshot of queerness at the dawn of the new millennium. (978-1-60282-682-3)

Oath of Honor by Radclyffe. A First Responders novel. First do no harm…First Physician of the United States Wes Masters discovers that being the president's doctor demands more than brains and personal sacrifice—especially when politics is the order of the day. (978-1-60282-671-7)

A Question of Ghosts by Cate Culpepper. Becca Healy hopes Dr. Joanne Call can help her learn if her mother really committed suicide—but she's not sure she can handle her mother's ghost, a decades-old mystery, and lusting after the difficult Dr. Call without some serious chocolate consumption. (978-1-60282-672-4)

The Night Off by Meghan O'Brien. When Emily Parker pays for a taboo role-playing fantasy encounter from the Xtreme Encounters escort agency, she expects to surrender control—but never imagines losing her heart to dangerous butch Nat Swayne. (978-1-60282-673-1)

Sara by Greg Herren. A mysterious and beautiful new student at Southern Heights High School stirs things up when students start dying. (978-1-60282-674-8)

Fontana by Joshua Martino. Fame, obsession, and vengeance collide in a novel that asks: What if America's greatest hero was gay? (978-1-60282-675-5)

Lemon Reef by Robin Silverman. What would you risk for the memory of your first love? When Jenna Ross learns her high school love Del Soto died on Lemon Reef, she refuses to accept the medical examiner's report of a death from natural causes and risks everything to find the truth. (978-1-60282-676-2)

The Dirty Diner: Gay Erotica on the Menu, edited by Jerry L. Wheeler. Gay erotica set in restaurants, featuring food, sex, and men—could you really ask for anything more? (978-1-60282-677-9)

Sweat: Gay Jock Erotica by Todd Gregory. Sizzling tales of smoking hot sex with the athletic studs everyone fantasizes about. (978-1-60282-669-4)